BETWEEN DOG & WOLF

RUSSIAN LIBRARY

R

The Russian Library at Columbia University Press publishes an expansive selection of Russian literature in English translation, concentrating on works
previously unavailable in English and those ripe for new translations. Works of
premodern, modern, and contemporary literature are featured, including recent
writing. The series seeks to demonstrate the breadth, surprising variety, and
global importance of the Russian literary tradition and includes not only novels
but also short stories, plays, poetry, memoirs, creative nonfiction, and works of
mixed or fluid genre.

■ □ ■

SASHA SOKOLOV

BETWEEN
DOG & WOLF

Translated and
annotated by
Alexander Boguslawski

Columbia
University
Press
New York

Columbia University Press
Publishers Since 1893
New York   Chichester, West Sussex
cup.columbia.edu
Между собакой и волком © 1980 by Sasha Sokolov
Published by arrangement with ELKOST Intl. Literary Agency
Published with the support of Read Russia, Inc., and the Institute of
    Literary Translation, Russia
Translation copyright © 2017 Alexander Boguslawski

Library of Congress Cataloging-in-Publication Data
Names: Sokolov, Sasha, 1943- author. | Boguslawski, Alexander Prus,
    translator, writer of added commentary.
Title: Between dog and wolf / Sasha Sokolov ; translated and annotated
    by Alexander Boguslawski.
Other titles: Mezhdu sobakoæi i volkom. English | Russian library
    (Columbia University Press)
Description: New York : Columbia University Press, 2017. | Series:
    Russian library | Includes bibliographical references.
Identifiers: LCCN 2016017983 (print) | LCCN 2016018735 (ebook) |
    ISBN 9780231181464 (cloth : alk. paper) | ISBN 9780231181471 (pbk.)
    | ISBN 9780231543729 (electronic)
Classification: LCC PG3549.S64 M4813 2017 (print) | LCC PG3549.S64
    (ebook) | DDC 891.73/44—dc23
LC record available at https://lccn.loc.gov/2016017983

Columbia University Press books are printed on permanent
    and durable acid-free paper.
Printed in the United States of America

Cover design: Roberto de Vicq de Cumptich
Book design: Lisa Hamm

To My Pals in Dispersion

I'm fond of friendly conversation
And of a friendly glass or two
At dusk or *entre chien et loup*—
As people say without translation.
—Aleksandr Pushkin, *Eugene Onegin*

The young man was a hunter.
—Boris Pasternak, *Doctor Zhivago*

CONTENTS

Introduction   *xi*

1 Discords Beyond the Itil   1

2 The Trapper's Tale   17

3 Notes of a Binging Hunter   27

4 Dzyndzyrela's Discords Beyond the Itil   43

5 The Trapper's Tale or Pictures from an Exhibition   61

6 Accordin to Ilya Petrikeich   71

7 Notes of a Hunter   83

8 Discords Beyond the Itil   97

9 Pictures from an Exhibition   109

10   Dzynzyrella's   121

11   Again the Notes   135

12   Discords Beyond the Itil   159

13   Pictures from an Exhibition   173

14   Accordin to Ilya Petrikeich   183

15   The Binger's Journal   201

16   The Trapper's Tale   219

17   The Last Remarks   225

18   The Note, Sent in a Separate Bottle   229

Annotations   231

INTRODUCTION

In 1976 the publishing house Ardis brought out Sasha Sokolov's first novel, *A School for Fools* (*Shkola dlia durakov*), in the original Russian, and a year later followed it with Carl Proffer's English translation. On the covers of both editions was an enthusiastic endorsement by Vladimir Nabokov: "an enchanting, tragic, and touching book." The praise by the great Russian American writer significantly contributed to the recognition of the work as a tour de force and of its author as a master of language, a unique and mature voice in not only Russian but also world literature. Numerous reviews, critical articles, and detailed studies discussed the author's dislike of plot, his use of such literary devices as stream of consciousness, lists, repetition with variations, anaphora (beginning sentences with the same word), aposiopesis (incomplete or broken-off sentences), and paronomasia (placing similar sounding words close to each other); his linguistic inventiveness and originality; and his general defiance of the Soviet literary norm—Socialist realism. These reviews, as well as numerous translations of the work into European languages, established Sokolov as a leading Russian author and, as is often the case with successful literary debuts, resulted in great curiosity and anticipation: What would the author create next, and how could he top his extraordinary achievement?

To everybody's surprise, the second novel, *Between Dog and Wolf* (*Mezhdu sobakoi i volkom*), turned out to be diametrically different from the anticipated stylistic continuation of *A School for Fools*. Sokolov started the novel before his emigration from the Soviet Union in 1975, drawing inspiration from his almost year-long work as a game warden in a hunting preserve on the Volga, during which he completed *A School for Fools*. Sokolov lived in a wooden cabin with no electricity, formerly occupied by a game warden who drowned under mysterious circumstances after shooting two dogs of one of the residents. An official investigator sent to find out what really happened could not discover the truth and the case was closed. These events became the seed of *Between Dog and Wolf*, even though, in the final version, they have been substantially altered. The first hundred pages of the manuscript dealt primarily with the whipper-in, named Yakov Ilyich Palamakhterov, but the overall construction of the novel developed later, when the author (following a comment by Nabokov to Carl Proffer), was reminded of a quatrain in Aleksandr Pushkin's *Eugene Onegin*, which he decided to use as an epigraph to echo and strengthen the novel's title: *Between Dog and Wolf*, chosen long before the epigraph's appearance. At this seminal moment, the second major character of the novel materialized—the grinder Ilya Petrikeich Zynzyrela, who would dominate the narrative in the final version. The discovery of the second character and his unique voice led Sokolov to the idea for the third major section of the work, the poems. According to interviews with the author, from then on, the work proceeded in sections: a few days spent on authorial narrative, a few days on Ilya's epistle, and, simultaneously (even when asleep), on the poems attributed to Yakov.

When the completed manuscript was submitted to the publisher, the response of Carl Proffer and his trusted Russian readers-evaluators was very different from their response to *A School for Fools*. They pondered: Who was the intended reader of the novel? Who would understand the lexical complexity of the text, which seemed impossible to read without a dictionary? Could anyone translate the work? Even after rewriting some parts and shortening the final text, Sokolov heard the same comments; fortunately, believing in the author's talent and maturity, Proffer scheduled the Russian version of the book for publication. When it finally appeared in February of 1980, it was greeted with almost complete silence. With just a few notable exceptions published later, Western critics—probably puzzled or turned off by the book's "nearly impenetrable linguistic jungle" (Elena Kravchenko, *The Prose of Sasha Sokolov: Reflections on/of the Real* [London: MHRA, 2013], 7)—failed to review the novel, while their Russian émigré colleagues produced only a small number of rather general responses, without detailed discussion of its structure, language, or importance for Russian or world literature.

In contrast, when the copies of the book were smuggled into Russia, *Between Dog and Wolf* immediately found an appreciative audience and received the Andrei Belyi prize of the underground journal *Chasy* for the best prose of 1981.

Today, scholarly discussions of the novel and analyses of its components, structure, and overall meaning appear with greater regularity. Several need to be mentioned here. There are two separate issues of *Canadian American Slavic Studies* dedicated to Sasha Sokolov, which include articles on *Between Dog and Wolf*. One (vol. 21, nos. 3–4), appeared in 1990 and was edited by Don Barton Johnson, a leading Sokolov scholar. The other (vol. 40, nos. 2–4), edited by Ludmilla Litus, came out in 2006. And in 2013 the Modern Humanities Research Association published Elena Kravchenko's *Prose of Sasha Sokolov*, a seminal study with one chapter devoted entirely to "unraveling" the complexities of *Between Dog and Wolf*. In addition, for the readers who would like to hear Sokolov's own voice and discover what he has to say about art, the artist, and the process of writing, the collection *In the House of the Hanged: Essays and vers libres* (trans. Alexander Boguslawski, University of Toronto Press, 2012) will provide many revelations and explanations.

Nevertheless, in the West, the novel still has a reputation as an esoteric work, and its very title seems to point out its status in the literary world—in the twilight zone, between dog and wolf. The expression in the title, a translation of the Latin *inter canem et lupum*, was known in its French form, *entre chien et loup*, and was probably used in Russian for the first time in *Eugene Onegin* (chapter 4, stanza 47, line 12). Originally, the idiom meant the twilight or this particular time of the day, when a shepherd is not able to distinguish between the dog guarding his herd and the wolf stalking it. An expanded reading of the idiom indicates indeterminacy, neither this nor that, a realm where nothing is certain, where everything fluctuates and changes its meaning and appearance. Thus, in relation to the novel as a whole, the title suggests that the work is a realized metaphor, and warns readers that they will have to work hard to discover what is going on—that what may appear in one chapter as a fact will be undermined by information in other parts of the novel. The work consists of eighteen chapters, interweaving prose and poetry. Novels with a combination of poetry and prose, like Pasternak's *Doctor Zhivago* or Nabokov's *Pale Fire* and *The Gift*, have an important place in the Russian literary tradition, but the number of the poems, their placement, and their relevance to the rest of the story make this novel exceptional. All the chapters are arranged in an easily recognizable pattern; in fact, the entire novel's chapter placement can be represented graphically in a simple chart:

1	2	3	4	5	6	7	8	9	10	11	12	13	14	15	16	17	18
A	B	C	A	B	A	C	A	B	A	C	A	B	A	C	B	A	C

(A) The uneducated, often dialectical, colloquial narrative
of Ilya Petrikeich Zynzyrela, addressed to the criminal
investigator Sidor Fomich Pozhilykh in connection with
Ilya's stolen crutches.

(B) The erudite, poetic, impersonal (authorial) narrative,
occasionally stylized to reflect nineteenth-century
Russian literary tradition, and related to the life of the

poet, philosopher, painter, and dog master, Yakov Ilyich Palamakhterov.

(C) The poems authored by Yakov.

Ilya's narrative is presented as *"skaz,"* a literary device brought to the attention of scholars by the Russian formalists and today generally accepted in both Russia and the West as a text focusing readers' attention on the speech patterns of the often-uneducated narrator. The readers learn a lot about the person using *skaz* because the speech patterns, the vocabulary, and the stories told focus the readers' attention on the teller. In Ilya's narrative, besides his constant struggle with and apparent enjoyment of language, his spoonerisms, malapropisms, convoluted grammar and syntax, dialectical expressions, colloquialisms, neologisms, slang, and archaisms, readers discover a vast depository of folk tales and folk customs, sayings and proverbs, popular songs and rhymes, official clichés, and quotations from the Scriptures, which he mixes up and delivers in a mindboggling firework-like display. His vocabulary is rich with synonyms; he uses, for instance, a large number of words for various kinds of boats, skates, and crutches as well as countless diminutives and augmentatives, all contributing to the opulence of his idiom. Not surprisingly, this rich linguistic layer of the novel was the most puzzling to the average (unprepared) reader of Sokolov's work.

Ilya writes a letter to the investigator, Pozhilykh, to complain that the wardens stole his crutches. His epistolary complaint can also be seen as a stream of consciousness narrative. Such narratives are characterized by rapid changes of focus, switching from one story to another, forgetting the story line, and abandoning the topic of discussion as a result of a trigger word, name, or event. In Ilya's case, such changes of focus are accompanied by the deconstruction of linear time since he narrates events from the past next to events from the present or even the future. His account gives the readers the impression that everything Beyond the Wolf is not only happening simultaneously (so the narrator can pick at will what to talk about) but will also happen again. Thus, the idea of eternal return becomes one of the key themes of Sokolov's work; it is strengthened by Yakov's poems and by the authorial narrative.

This narrative, created by the authorial persona, is very different from the uneducated, rambling narrative of Ilya. It contains poetic musings, often expressed in infinitive constructions: "To live; to know the value of deep galoshes at the time of flooding of the deep and shallow rivers. To be; to soil the dark-green leaf. To live, to be, and to see how in ditches the waybread wilts" (chapter 2). It features inserted ekphrastic vignettes (*Hunters in the Snow, Self-Portrait in Uniform, War*), an amusing account of Yakov's grandfather's visit to Moscow, rendered in a rich, stylized nineteenth-century language, strengthened in the original by the archaic spelling of adjectives and nouns, and combining descriptions of food with an obsessive use of the first name-patronymic pairs, parodying Gogol. It presents a fanciful description of the French king Louis entertaining his friends at Versailles, and a portrait of the investigator Pozhilykh, in which a poem by Pushkin leads to the poet's personal appearance in the text. Moreover, it shows many episodes from the life of young Yakov as well as his dream or vision of his death. These five sections of the novel are baroque, ornamental, and grammatically correct, with occasional neologisms appropriate to their style. From time to time readers encounter here passages of such richness and poetic beauty that Sokolov's idea of "proetry"—prose elevated to the level of poetry—literally materializes on the page. Moreover, the elimination of linear time that readers encountered in Ilya's text continues in the authorial narrative and is achieved by ingenious transitions from present to the past (for example, bibliographical details about Carus Sterne's book become a bridge to Yakov's grandfather's visit to Moscow to see his friends, and the phrase "It was getting light" takes the readers from Yakov's childhood to Versailles, to Pozhilykh, and to the discussion of the name of the settlement Malokulebyakovo—Mylokulelemovo).

Yakov's poems, the third component of the novel, are as important to the work as a whole as the narratives of Ilya and the authorial persona. First, they reveal hidden information about Yakov. Readers learn that Yakov retired or ran away to the wilderness because he was tired of hustle and bustle of the life in the city. Yakov, thus, is an exile, a character continuing the tradition of Romantic exiles (Pushkin's Aleko from *The Gypsies* and Eugene Onegin) and, undoubtedly, is also relevant to Sokolov's emigration. As a painter, philosopher, and poet, Yakov is a great choice for poetic reflections on life Beyond the Itil and on its inhabitants. Besides being grouped according to season (see below), the poems frequently deal with the idea of eternal return and circularity rather than linearity of time. Showing Yakov's education and knowledge (foreign languages, philosophy, literature and literary parody), they are written in a language that seems to blend the sophisticated vocabulary of the authorial persona and the colloquial idiom of Ilya. This should not be surprising, since Yakov spent many years drinking and hunting with the dwellers of the lands Beyond the Itil, and picked up many of their speech patterns. Writing his poems without "stress and strain," he created works that readers will appreciate as good poetry, even if the topics of the poems most often deal with events from Yakov's youth, life on the Volga, and various mishaps of the local inhabitants. Naturally, being a literary doppelgänger of Sasha Sokolov, Yakov can unabashedly acknowledge his poetic talent and express his praise for the Russian language, saying: "So I dare you to burn, you dumb-as-a-bell, my amazing, ingenious lines" (Note XXXVII) and "I salute you, my native tongue" (Note XXXII).

To return to the novel's overall structure, the separation of the last chapter, "The Note, Sent in a Separate Bottle," from the others clearly indicates that it is supposed to break the symmetry of the pattern and serve as an epilogue. The note's title, *Post scriptum*, confirms its role as the novel's coda. All the other chapters "unfold" in a mirror-like fashion, with chapter 9 at the center.

In addition to this careful chapter arrangement, which gives this postmodernist work a sense of cohesiveness and organization, Sokolov divides each poetic chapter into nine poems dealing with different seasons: autumn (chapter 3), winter (chapter 7), spring (chapter 11), and summer (chapter 15), strengthening the idea of circularity of time. The rationale for the total number of chapters (eighteen) and poems in the novel (thirty-seven) is difficult to determine, but there are several intriguing possibilities. Alexander Pushkin looms large over the entire work, from the first epigraph to literary parodies of his poems in the poetic sections of the novel, to various quotations and paraphrases in the prose fragments, and even to the poet's personal appearance in the key chapter 9. Another great poet, Boris Pasternak, is acknowledged in the second epigraph as well as in a paraphrase in one of the poems. If one takes into consideration the poets' importance to the novel, it is possible that eighteen chapters and thirty-seven poems relate to the date of Pushkin's death (1837) and to his age (thirty-seven) as well as to the age of Doctor Zhivago at his death (thirty-seven). This coincidence becomes even more plausible when one recalls the Russians' belief that geniuses often die at thirty-seven (Pushkin, Mozart, Pavel Fedotov, Velimir Khlebnikov, Leonid Gubanov) and the fact that the original version of *Between Dog and Wolf* featured more poems, later deleted from the final copy.

Since intertextuality is an important and common device of modern fiction, it is not surprising that, besides Pushkin and Pasternak, the novel is saturated with quotes from and references to Mikhail Lermontov, Ivan Turgenev, Nikolai Gogol', Ivan Krylov, Aleksandr Blok, Afanasii Fet, Nikolai Nekrasov, Il'ia Repin, Modest Mussorgskii, Vasilii Polenov, Sergei Aksakov, and Aleksei Savrasov (some scholars have also indicated possible links to Fedor Dostoevskii and Boris Pil'niak), identified in the annotations to this edition. The most important of these references are the titles of the chapters. Three chapters (3, 7, and 11) refer to Ivan Turgenev's 1852 *Notes of a Hunter* (*Zapiski okhotnika*) and, possibly, to Sergey Aksakov's *Notes* of a *Rifle-Hunter in Orenburg Province* (*Zapiski ruzheinogo okhotnika orenburgskoi guberni*), published the same year; three chapters (5, 9, and 13), to Modest Mussorgskii's celebrated 1874 *Pictures from an Exhibition* (*Kartinki s vystavki*); and one chapter (15) to last three chapters in Mikhail Lermontov's 1841 *A Hero of Our Time*, called "Pechorin's Journal" ("Zhurnal Pechorina"). In addition to the placement of the chapters, these intertextual connections provide another element solidifying the overall structure of the novel. Moreover, if readers imagine *Between Dog and Wolf* as an elaborate tapestry, woven from many-colored yarns and decorated by patterns and ornaments, they will discover further organizing principles in recurring themes, visual images, and in repetition of fragments, phrases, and even single words. The recurring themes include Ilya as the prophet Elijah; his identification as a Wolf and Yakov's identification as a Dog; Ilya's crutches; Ilya's longing after his beloved Orina; his occupation as a grinder and sharpener; and the dominant role of the river Volga (the Itil, Wolf's river), a dividing line between the living and the dead, both in Ilya's narrative and in Yakov's poems. The best example of a recurrent visual image is the ekphrastic description of Pieter Bruegel's *Hunters in the Snow*, which provides a detailed portrayal of the setting of the novel in chapter 2 and is skillfully repeated in Note XVII. It becomes a source of many reappearing images in the novel (birds, boats, skaters, a frozen river and ponds, hunters and hunting dogs, a tavern) and, in addition, provides a connection to the theme of the seasons, since Bruegel created the famous painting as a part of the series called *Months* and depicted in it activities common in December and January.

As far as phraseological repetitions are concerned, one can easily notice the recurrence of the title in chapter 12 and in many poems. Other repetitions worthy of note (some with semantic variations) include "And it was rocking on switches"; "And where are our crucians"; a discussion of what is happiness; "salt and matches"; "Dusk's everywhere . . . "; "On weekdays . . . / On the weekday . . . / On the day . . . "; "mussels"; and "orioles and woodpeckers." There are also many correspondences between prose chapters and poems: "Amztarakhan" in chapter 2 and Note XXXVII; "Brumaire(s)" in Note XII and chapter 16; "the wick(s) smoked" in Note XXIV and chapter 16; "white flies" in Note IX and chapter 9; "magpie(s) and crow(s)" in chapter 2, Note XI, and chapter 14; "thirty-fourth *versta*" in Note II and chapter 16; and "seal the windows" in chapter 9 and Note XXV. Even this small selection of recurring words and phrases shows the careful design of the novel and attests to the ingenuity and inventiveness of the author who makes observant readers aware of these repetitions, and guarantees the work's greater cohesion.

In one of his interviews, Sokolov jokingly said that he wrote *Between Dog and Wolf* to silence the critics who did not like his disregard for plot, one of the main features of *A School for Fools*. As mentioned before, the plot idea came to Sokolov when he heard the story of the game warden's mysterious drowning. The mystery was retained in the novel, making it a sort of detective story, but the characters' roles changed. While returning from a wake for Gury, who drowned during a race with a whipper-in (Yakov), Ilya kills the warden's dog after taking it for a wolf. In revenge, the wardens steal his crutches. The feud continues and Ilya shoots two more dogs, for which, as we learn in the last two chapters, Yakov and his friend Krylobylov drown Ilya. However, in the land Beyond the Wolf, nothing is certain. Readers discover that perhaps the crutches were not stolen at all but were placed in Gury's coffin as a substitute for the drowned skater's body while Ilya, drunk, was resting on the cot. This complication in the otherwise relatively simple plot corresponds to another puzzling account. Ilya gives readers two explanations for the loss of his leg: one explanation is that he was tied to the rails by Orina's lovers, and the other is that the loss was the result of an accident that occurred when he tried to jump onto a moving train. In both cases, it is up to the readers to choose the variant they prefer or find more reliable. These variants strengthen the idea of indeterminacy and should be linked to the puzzling and interchangeable names of many characters. Ilya himself is not sure where his name came from, and he spells it in many different ways. Most of the alternatives can be related to the sound made by the grinding stand or by skates on ice, but one, used by the wardens in the note about crutches, resembles Cinderella. That name turns Ilya's train accident into a strange distortion of Cinderella's loss of her slipper. Another characteristic name-shifter is Fyodor-Pyotr-Yegor, the accountant, who, challenged by the wardens, hanged himself on a stolen baluster. There is a character named Kaluga and nicknamed Kostroma (both are the names of provincial Russian towns). One will also notice that the name of the main heroine, Orina (Orya, Oryushka), and her railroad connections are echoed by Maria, also called Masha and Marina in the stories related to Yakov. If one adds to this list frequent doubling and confusion of names—two characters with the name Nicholas (Kolya, Nikolka), several characters named Yakov (Yasha) and Ivan (Vanya, Vanyechka), and the metamorphoses of the names of settlements, Mylomukomolovo, Mykomulolomovo, Malokulebyakovo, Milokurelemovo, and Malokulelemovo (besides different spellings for Bydogoshchi and Gorodnishche)—the idea that nothing in the world is what it seems is dramatically reinforced. Predictably, many readers will feel at least slightly puzzled when, at the end of the novel, they discover that both Ilya and Yakov are no longer among the living, and hence Ilya's epistle to Pozhilykh perhaps has not been written or sent to the addressee at all; in other words, the entire story has been the author's invention. That and all the other puzzling mysteries of the text bring readers to the major questions explored by Sokolov's novels: What is reality and what is fiction? What is the relationship between fiction and reality?

In a novel conceived as a realized metaphor and employing the devices of *skaz*, ekphrasis, and complex linguistic manipulations, language is the most vivid, noticeable, and essential building block at author's disposal. It allows him to immerse readers in three completely different narrative voices and establish links between them. It is not an exaggeration to call *Between Dog and Wolf* a book about language. In other words, the language/text becomes the only tangible reality. In one of his essays, "About the Other Encounter," devoted to his meeting with the writer Aleksandr Gol'dshtein, Sokolov praised Gol'dshtein for writing in the style of "proetry," which involves ironing out or even reducing to nothing the contradictions between the *what* and the *how*, and for his ability "to arrange the narrative space in such a way that the reader won't doubt even for a second that existence is precisely what is happening here and now, on the given page" (Sokolov, *In the House of the Hanged*, 76). This, of course, unconditionally applies to *Between Dog and Wolf*. Readers are drawn to the linguistic layers of the text, and the process of reading turns into the creation of meaning. As Kravchenko beautifully summarizes, "Reflected through the other space, other time, other's eyes and words, *Between Dog and Wolf* is a twilight zone in which the gap between times and spaces is transcended through language. The lost context emerges from the text, reduced to the materiality of the letter, to the surface of the page, and to the very moment of reading" (Kravchenko, *Prose of Sasha Sokolov*, 90).

All the above remarks on the structure and organization of the text should make readers aware that they are looking at a beautifully crafted and breathtaking work of art, created in the mind of a brilliant master who is in full control of his story, his characters, and the verbal material of his work. Nothing in the text happens by chance; the author orchestrates the events, reveals different points of view, surprises, and demands attention and appreciation of detail. Reading *Between Dog and Wolf* is not only rewarding and stimulating (albeit not easy); it also proves to readers that the genre of the novel is not dead, as many writers and scholars used to believe. On the contrary, today, in the hands of gifted writers, not afraid of experimentation, the novel thrives. Sokolov's masterpiece clearly displays the almost inexhaustible possibilities of modern fiction.

A FEW WORDS ABOUT TRANSLATION

Even a cursory examination of the text of *Between Dog and Wolf* reveals that the translation of Ilya's voice is the most challenging part of the project. It would not be sufficient to simply translate the text into understandable correct English. Such translation would perhaps reveal the meaning of the text but would not come close to the effect Ilya's narrative has on many Russian readers. Therefore, to render Ilya's voice, special devices had to be found to create a similar impression in English. Each idiomatic expression, whether used properly or improperly, had to have a suitable English equivalent; each pun needed to be rendered by a pun; and each characteristic misspelling had to be conveyed by a misspelling. The convoluted syntax, teeming with incomplete sentences, repetitions, shifting tenses, and irregular punctuation, had to be preserved as much as it is possible without making the text unreadable. But even then, the texts would not be fully compatible because English cannot adequately render Russian diminutives, augmentatives, or the meaning-changing prefixes and suffixes of Russian verbs so inventively employed by Sokolov. For that reason, the English translation needed to introduce additional errors and colloquialisms. This translation is saturated with colloquial but generally recognizable words like kinda, sorta, cuz, and ain't, and with double negatives. Moreover, in accordance with the rules of *skaz*, Ilya was endowed with the custom of not pronouncing the final letter "g" in all words ending in "–ing" (havin, bein, doin, nothin, somethin) and with the habit of spelling some words the way he hears them (neybor, promenaid, glasswear, hardwear, intrestin, wandrin, gard). Ilya's incorrect use of superlatives (most weakest, lastest), his linguistic originality stemming from misuse of similar-sounding words (accounter, mere future, supplethal, prodigerrant, gatecharmer), his spontaneous invention of new words (crashbaret), his reversal of the word order in certain expressions (socially beneficial / beneficially social), his use of dialecticisms, archaisms, and slang words, and his preference for vivid, expressive phrases rather than simple or neutral ones ("flew the coop" instead of "ran away," "started sawing wood" instead of "started snoring")—all this had to be rendered by finding or creating stylistically suitable English equivalents. Two characteristic examples may illustrate how translation can match the original on the level of accuracy and general tone. Describing his battle with the wolf, Ilya says *"ne otdamsia na ugryzenie"* (I will not succumb to his bite), but he uses the word *ugryzenie*, which in Russian is only used in plural, in expression *ugryzenia sovesti* (pangs of conscience). Therefore, translating the expression as "I won't succumb to his bite" would change the tone and flavor of the words. Instead, a more adequate English rendering "I won't succumb to the pangs of his fangs" was used, preserving both the humor of the original expression and Ilya's unorthodox use of the word. Similarly, when Ilya gets to the hospital after his accident, he meets another patient with one leg (possibly his long-lost son) and shares with him a pair of felt boots, *valenki*. He describes their collaboration by using a proverb, *dva sapoga para*. Literally, it means two boots make a pair, but as a proverb it is best translated as "birds of a feather flock together." However, since the word *sapog* (boot) and the number two are important in the context, the English equivalent combines and rephrases both the proverbial and the literal meaning into "Two boots of leather flock together." Equally difficult are translations of the many Russian words for a small rowboat. They must avoid all the "ethnographically" charged words like a "pirogue" or "canoe," and should include only those words that refer specifically to a boat with oars but with no sails, like a dory, a skiff, a scow, a dinghy, a craft, or a rowboat. This last word is particularly useful in rendering Ilya's spoonerism *karbas* (from *barkas*) because it can be easily converted into bowroat. As mentioned earlier, in addition to these linguistic difficulties, Ilya's narrative is saturated with intertextual references or quotations from Scriptures, songs, poems, folk tales, anecdotes, sayings, and proverbs. For Russian readers, many (but by no means all) of these quotations are easily recognizable, which often adds a humorous or unexpectedly serious element to the narrative. English readers lack this cultural background, and many quotations need to be explained in the critical apparatus accompanying the translation. However, this is not an easy task, particularly if the translator wants to be faithful to Sokolov's idea that the text should be self-explanatory and that no footnotes should interrupt the flow of the narrative. Therefore, the notes are placed at the end of the translation, and readers can find them based on key words from the text. That makes reading the English version even more challenging.

Rendering of the voice of the authorial persona, while not as taxing in terms of neologisms or unorthodox phraseology, requires careful attention to the rich vocabulary, the poetic rhythm, and the euphonic qualities of the text. Long sentences, unusual words and names requiring explanations, key ekphrastic descriptions, and nineteenth-century stylizations alternate in this narrative with lofty poetic fragments and infinitive constructions. It is easy to see that this stylistic register of the novel dramatically differs from the unsophisticated voice of Ilya the grinder and that the translation has to make this difference as clear and unmistakable as possible.

Translation of the poems presents the challenges known to all translators of poetry: preservation of the meter and rhyme without a dramatic alteration of the meaning of each poem. The major problem here is that the poems recreated in English should strive to be as good as the Russian originals; they not only should render the meaning as closely as possible but should also be beautiful, funny, poignant, tragic, ironic, and so on—that is, closely approximate the artistic quality of the Russian texts. And this, as we know from hundreds of English translations of poems by Pushkin, Lermontov, Akhmatova, Pasternak, and other famous Russian poets, quite often does not work out—something important gets irretrievably lost. It may be the euphonic quality of the original, its poetic imagery, its rhyming scheme, its meter, or all of the above. Therefore, particular care was taken to produce a series of poems that can stand on their own as poems rather than just "translations" or paltry renderings of a highly poetic original text. The translations closely render the meaning of the originals and try, whenever possible, not to add words or phrases just to produce a rhyme. When such additions are made, they do not change the overall meaning or the mood of the poem. Of course, it was sometimes necessary to slightly change the rhyming scheme (the order of feminine and masculine rhymes), but the preservation of the rhythm and meter of the poems as well as retention of their melodic, musical qualities was always a priority. However, in *Between Dog and Wolf*, even the best poetic translation presents additional problems. As mentioned earlier, Sokolov, the ultimate author of all the poems, frequently pays homage to famous Russian authors by including a veiled reference, a direct quote, or a paraphrase of their works. For many Russian readers, the homage is obvious, but for English readers it is not transparent. In such cases, again, like in the rendering of the intertextual links of Ilya's narrative, the sources can only be revealed in the critical apparatus at the end of the translation.

This translation of Sokolov's masterpiece affirms that every text, even the most complex, can be translated into another language and that it is better to translate the extraordinary literary achievements of foreign authors than leave them untranslated and thus prevent the readers from enjoying these masterpieces. However, it also acknowledges that not everything is possible in translation—some features of the original language, some cultural and historical differences, and some difficult-to-define idiosyncrasies of the author's thinking cannot be rendered exactly and precisely. Therefore, every translation turns into a long and exhausting war: during this war, the translator enjoys victories but also suffers crushing defeats. If, after completing the "campaign," the translator believes that his victories outnumbered the defeats, the endless hours spent on translation are justified. Of course, ultimately, only future readers can decide whether the translator's efforts are worthy of praise or deserve criticism.

A NOTE ON RUSSIAN NAMES

To help readers enjoy the text, all Russian names are rendered in simplified English phonetic forms: Pyotr instead of Petr, Fyodor instead of Fedor, Gury instead of Gurii, Alexander instead of Aleksandr, Ilya instead of Il'ia, and Tver Oblast rather than Tver' Oblast'. All the soft signs in the names of characters and places have been eliminated. However, in the annotations, all the personal names and quotations from Russian are transliterated according to the Library of Congress system to allow readers to easily search for the authors and their works.

ACKNOWLEDGMENTS

This translation project started many years ago, after Sokolov rejected several earlier attempts to render the work in English. My Polish translation of the work took almost ten years, but it was a great preparation and guide to dealing with the complexities of the novel. Throughout the long process of creating the English version, the author provided invaluable comments, corrections, and constant encouragement. Without his friendship and helpful suggestions, it is hard to imagine that this translation would have been completed. Moreover, in the course of working on the English text, three readers proved to be not only reliable but also indispensable to the final appearance of the work. Kathryn Davidson-Bond, my wife and my best reader, asked questions, took notes, made me keenly aware of the music in the text, and was instrumental in discussing with me my exuberant English renditions of Ilya's language; my friend, professor Paul Licata, was, as always, a diligent editor and interlocutor; and Camilo Garzon, *mi compadre*, my former student and an intellectual par excellence, who proved that good readers will appreciate the novel in English. It is equally important to acknowledge here the editors of Columbia University Press, particularly Christine Dunbar, who picked the translation to inaugurate the new series, the Russian Library, and Leslie Kriesel; their professionalism and excellence greatly contributed to the final look of this translation. To all of them, I offer my deepest gratitude and thank you.

BETWEEN
DOG & WOLF

DISCORDS BEYⱯD THE ITIL

01

The moonth's clear, no catchin up with the dates, the year's current. To Citizen Sidor Fomich Pozhilykh, with all due respect, Ilya Petrikeich Zynzyrela's *Discords Beyond the Itil*. With Your permission, I commence. Citizen Pozhilykh, I'm a man relatively peripheral to these places, but since I'm a sharpener, hence I sharpen knives-scissors, and it would be probably rather difficult to pull the wool over my eyes, even if at first glance I am a total gimp. I also happen to sharpen scythes, axes, and other hardwear, but such details would only obscure my account. That's why I don't recount the events of the years out-of-sight-and-out-of-mind, just lemme underscore that up 'til now I haven't found myself in the slammer, despite dwellin in substantial towns. Wherever they'd settle me, I didn't mind bein down and out, didn't seriously hanker after a family, and made ends meet by askin folks for help in proportion to their means and possibilities. About that I remain remorseful, havin chosen for this purpose a co-op of invaliduals named after A. Sharpenhauer. I beg Your pardon, of course, but a dedicated work den and a bill of fare are available. When it's warm, we do them knives all the time: We wander around and set out to find employment far away. In contrast, when it's freezin, we service the populace in regard to sharpenin and flattenin 'cuz from November to April, every day without holidays, loners and monsters similar to this here correspondent of Yourses clink and circle on the mirror of the waters, and when the dusk descends, You welcome them in the three-story sickler, aptly named by a whim of some passerby a crashbaret; but Thou shall not find Ilya in their midst. You'll turn blue: Why is he such a nincompoop, why doesn't he procure for himself a pair of blades, like them other folks, is he disgusted by the prospect of scratchin what's smooth with his sharps, is he snubbin a mugful of beneficially social brew? No way, I would never refuse what I'm used to and I'm not one of them sharpeners who ain't sharp. To tell the truth, I don't need a pair, but one attachable blade always hangs over the mantelpiece. It don't matter, really, that I became, unfortunately, damaged, if by nature I am flintlike: I fell in love with glidin and can't be held back, just as long as there's somethin to push off with—ding once, Mister Pozhilykh, dong once, keep swayin, keep mutterin under the shaft bow even as far as the Valday harbor—castin of bells, bakin of pretzels, peddlin of hemp— and no one can boss you around along the Itil. May I prolong? But what's precisely happenin is that lately there ain't nothin to push off with. On the fourth Thursday of December (read: on Christmas Eve), I was walkin from the other side of the river, steppin forth from one of them undertakers, probably unknown to You. We were sendin off a certain recluse who skated to his maker due to his haughty recklessness. He lived in Mylo—one could say—mukomolovo, but on the outskirts, in clusters of adder's tongue with an admixture of willow; he was a hunter, perpetually kept postal cooers, altogether quite furry-legged, but I doubt that he conducted correspondence with anyone: It's unlikely. However, he himself shuttlecocked crisp like lime bast in scorchin heat, and he was called—I don't remember what. Gury—that's what he was called, as long as we're on it. Among the amusements of that particular Gury I'd reference the followin: He was the one that adored scrapin and rollin over the slick on his sharps, which additionally resulted in us losin a client, and the undertakers, in contrast, findin one. I'll provide evidence right away. In the days of the Archer, to make it more dangerous, but more excitin, the loners of both Shallow Reach shores arrange races on the weakenin ice. It happens in the outer darkness, intentionally without heavenly lights, and the folks cut figures as well as they can and hurry-scurry playin catch and chasin each other, without seein the holes and cracks. And that's fraughtful. In matters of whirlin, everybody was always scorched by a certain Nikolay, a lad from, when everythin was said and done, the trash co-op. With the overly familiar nickname Helper, he played a sincere loser in this world, and some jokers among the envious ones meanly made fun of him, sayin that he shows off so fancifully only 'cuz he's got a knack for lurkin around dark corners; so, they said, he's used to it. What is the chronicle of his failures, if You don't mind? He, first of all, tasted the familial pandemonium, but his spouse got together with a wolf slayer and chased the Helper away from the house, second of all. Then, he knocked on the Gorodnishche shelter for the unhearin, but they showed him the door and no more: Our department's exclusively for the deaf, and you, as you can see, are also blind, so you understand yourself. For that reason the fellow shuffled to the sightless shelter: Fat chance, the limit of bunk spots has been exceeded; another thing if you had your own concertina, you'd hang around the embarcaderos and just put the proceeds into the common pot, and for that we would keep you. So Nikolay Helperov stood up in front of them in his entire shriveled height and, angrily cryin with his burnin walleyes, shouted: You overseas seedpods, if I had my own musick, would I ask you what to do, really? And at the next stage he turned up without warnin in the house of the transient homeless, and they stepped into his shoes politely, and splashed wholeheartedly. And they tempted: Live, brother, forever. And one day this dame has called on one of them; she notices the Helper in the midst of the other poor, in their circle: Who's the one so unsightly over there among you at the rink? Not to worry; it's just Nikolka here among us skatin at the rink. His circumstance is probably not too shabby, she says, if he's spinnin so lively. No, they said, it's not good, his circumstance sucks, the only joy he has left is to weave them figures. Then the dame: No, stop, you better don't let him clown around, just look at him, how unappealin. So the almshouse's tenants asked the Helper: Do us a favor, do not live, brother, forever, 'cuz there are reprimands. He did not answer nothin, as he had, besides everythin else, the reputation of a mute, and he set out far from the establishment and didn't even look back. And the co-op of collectin all kinds of trash received him warmly. They reported he didn't shine there with excessively long service, but durin a drunken incident got slightly upset and vanished somewhere, and it's rather unlikely he'll return. This is, if You don't mind, this chronicle. One wonders: Did I sharpen his unsharpened ones? And it turns out only I and nobody else from the entire collective did his sharpenin, while the remainin co-workers, squeamish, turned up their noses, even though they themselves were pachoolies not of the first freshness. I also sharpened for Gury, and for Krylobyl, and for the Wintry Man I sharpened, for the entire Itil, You understand, I sharpened. And as to Gury the Hunter, he was makin a career in race-skatin. Every chance he gets, he wants nothin else, just let him fly over the slick. Sometimes he would fly into the co-op's workshop, would fall, like a long-awaited rain durin the drought, would drop in, slightly tired, and what are we supposed to do?—we chip in a ruble each. And we start countin: Gury leaves the misty glade, from his pocket draws a blade; I will sharpen his blade fine, and you'll have to get the wine. If I—with sadness, but I'm ready. Once I wanted to tether the skate to my boot, but at that moment I noticed it longed after a rasp. Drat—the rasp got completely lost or the colleagues snagged it. Gury graciously thought for a while and said: What are you lookin for, tell? I told him. He told them: Eh, you, mechanics, return the strument, whoever snagged it, 'cuz your mate has been palmin after it for a long time. But the co-op answered: Buzz off; what the heck do we need his freakin rasp for? And also: What, do you think he will dash on the rasp to Sloboda? And You will probably start doubtin too: Does it make sense, bein based in the proximity of the crashbaret, to run seven *verstas* to Sloboda on a wild-goose chase—either on the rasp or on the crasp? Don't doubt, for, after all, the victim of the wager hurries not empty-handed; he is trundlin in a sack on his mighty hump glasswear collected in the dales and in the hills. And—perhaps You're still completely out of the loop—I hasten to give You advance notice. In the crashbaret, due to some kind of false pride, they don't accept them empties at all and trade for take-out with great scandals, by what, from the human point, they commit a commercial blunder. A very different picture can be seen in the joint at the tributary, beyond the ridge of curly, but at the first sight insignificant islands. Over there, what's yours will be accepted at a fair price, without fuss, and the stuff you had paid for you have the right to use both inside and outside. And Gury to the grinders point-blank: Well, even on the rasp. And afterward, he again to them again: For Ilya it's probably inconvenient to use the rasp, but I, obviously, could like a charm. Then and there they started eggin him on, Citizen Pozhilykh. We believe, we believe, among us you are a famous marathon whiz, you grew yourself such femurs—first quality, both thin and long; how can we stick our pitiful bonesies where they don't belong, and Ilya the Malformed even more? I won't hide it, there can be mug shots worse, but scarce. For instance, the game warden, Manul, who used to go after his fas-tidious needs to the Other Places, reported he had met there monstrosities even more atrocious. That means not everythin is lost, my dear, and as long as I manage somehow to hold the mallet and the whetstone, I will not count myself among the luckless, so don't look for despair in Ilya. I've found the rasp, whisked away the burr, and come out, loaded, on the river. I am aimin slantily, at an angle, and since the ice is thin, the entire river is under me, like opened. I reach the tributary. On it, after acceleratin 'cuz it's calm, I wheel up to Sloboda itself. I don't drag out the tittle-tattle there too much, I'm in a hurry. I perform a lawful purchase-sale, turn around, and swing back, and the dusk keeps whirlin above my foolish bean, and my Sharpenhauers light for me from afar a storm lamp, so I won't glide, against my will, by the workshops. We had a few then. You'll outrun us, wretches, as if we were standin in place, the co-op egged on, racin with you, Gury, we're passes. Yep, mechanics, yep, here, among you all, I am the only wiry runner. Just look, he told them, just look at all our hoar-frosted expanses, there's no one I wouldn't out-swoosh; where could such a lad be? We lit up, started chewin the fat, and went out to smoke in the cold. We stood on a hillock; behind us, a large wooden town— there the fellas go on a wild bender—and lower, in front of us, a river's reach, spread stock-still like on the palm of a hand. Look around, Gury informed the masters, there, on the right-hand side, we have a settlement, Malokulebyakovo. And who lives down there? Who only doesn't live in Kulebyakovo, the co-op's workmen answered evasively. For instance, a well-known miller-fatso happens to exist there, barely carried by the earth, not to mention the ice, and at the mill the miller's got a Chink, Aladdin, but we understand it won't be no honor for you to race with him. And one can also locate in Kulebyakovo a certain game warden who, as rumors have it, fell into a dry well. He's screamin, but nobody can hear him, and his wife knows where he is, but ain't interested in gettin him out 'cuz she's doin hanky-panky with a neybor, also a game warden, but more younger; betcha he had messed her head up. In one word, the game wardens are busy, not into racin. And besides them there's no one in the village. And in Ploski among more or less runners one can find the youngster Nikolay who never had his own name or, more precisely, had, but too long ago. And when that Nikolay the Helper went thru his transfiguration and flew away, this one snatched his name for himself—he did not allow, as they say, the goods to get wasted. And Gury again: And if he likes to snip some fish, it's no problem at all, and no reason for the fishermen to take offense and wish his demise. Just think—a man steals a few fishes from people and they have found themselves a reason to chew him out. True, Gury, true, the livin creatures—whether free or in snares—they're clearly nobody's, and if somebody's after all, then we know Whose, but in that case all the trappers here, it appears, are the most greatest poachers in front of Him. And in vain, in vain they bumped Nikola off one day. Here he is, by the way, takin their catch from their under-the-ice traps beyond the islands. He tied his sack, put it on his sled, and started pullin. He's shiverin, the blizzard has blasted his longsighted orbs, his *valenki* are worn out, he lost his mittens, his skates ain't sharpened, and the annoyin Wolfox shows right up. Throw me a fishie, he threatens Nikolay, throw me another, otherwise I'll send darkness on the Itil. Night scares Nikolay from Ploski more than death, so he unconditionally throws into the woods a triple of sturgeons for the Wolfox. 'Cuz, after all, if he won't make it to Gorodnishche before dark, he won't get the funds for the stuff; if he won't get the funds for the stuff, he won't drop in to the crashbaret; if he won't drop in to the crashbaret, he won't have fun with them comrades; and not to have fun with them comrades, then, really, why donkey work like that, Citizen

Pozhilykh, You be the judge. And while these activists are waitin for Nikolay with heavy clubs at the edge of the village, he approaches the suburbs with half a sack of silvery sturgeons and green slimy tenches. He declares: I salute you, the most merriest town of bast, hail to you, tall painted cockroach towers. Oh, my dear town, he says, give shelter for the upcomin night to the unlucky fisherman killed by foes, buy his goods, give him some monies to jingle in his pocket; may the old man's wrinkles become smooth; may the lonely bat spread his folded wings. And don't be a cheapskate; pour me, town, to the rim. And also, he says, introduce me, town, to some lonesome babe with high cheekbones and a tender heart. So he took off his skates and started walkin, walkin up the hill, that Nikolay from Ploski, and a hellish host of have-nots hurries to meet him, without haste: Give us and give us, they go, some of your catches for Christ's sake, otherwise it'll be even worse. Esteemed beggars, the splashers in my sack ain't mine, 'cuz everythin around us here, includin the spindles of speckled clouds, and the river, and the boats that like big-bellied widows lie strewn, abandoned, with their stomachs up, around the bathhouses, as well as our rags and we ourselves who are wearin them—all this is not mine and not yours. We know, we know, nodded the paupers, laughin like possessed, in that case give us, neverthe-less, a tail per soul; give us, furthermore, fishes that ain't yours. I see, Nikolay wails to the hapless ones on the hill, I see that it'll be, I reckon, rather hard to take you for a ride. And he hands each one a tench. Where could he go—the poor are legion and he's alone. A lonely man on the road, especially when such a blue haze hangs over the Volga, he, allow me to note, is alone in the entire world. Nikolay gives each one a tail and enters the wooden December town with the rest of his booty, and knocks with his ancient walkin stick on the gates of resonatin court-yards, and curses snarly mongrels bitin the frozen chains. And we're still standin on the riverbank; so far not many stars are shinin above us, but still. And Gury the Hunter, he announces without beatin around the bushes: To run races with Nikolay from Ploski, even if I do respect him a little, I don't consider decent; in my opinion, he's both decrepit and vain—I'll out-scrape him and embarrass.

■ □ ■

But ain't clickin, somebody suddenly said, ain't smartin over there, in Ploski, that Fyodor, on the abacus of his? That is, not necessarily Fyodor but sorta Pyotr. And, in general—Yegor. His occupation was listed as an accounter, but even he, as it was revealed afterward, was a first-rate thief: That's with whom Gury should have done his racin. Do You understand what happened? Well, when that dame appeared without warnin on the spit, they—mostly the local sitters out of the game wardens—sat there and observed the flight of geese, like al-most always, but about this sittin very few outsiders have any idea 'cuz what's happenin takes place in the bushes and in twi-lights and is hidden from those sailin on the water, and when they sit on the spit and have a few, this dame comes to them, inquirin: Say, is there among you the one I'm searchin for? Well, how should we put it, they shrug their shoulders, look for yourself, we only beg you to notice that we're all first-class and ready for everythin and anythin just to please you, the gate-charmer of our places. She started lookin for herself and later announced: I don't see among you the one I'm searchin for, but I'm noticin another one who would do for now. And she's lookin at Pyotr. Cruel shivers seized the accounter, the book-keeper flared up as if a bright flame went blazin through his veins. And he made an announcement, gettin up and shakin off hurrily-scurrily. He made an announcement, gettin up from the damp earth, where he was to transfer in the mere future: I am Yegor from Ploski; lead me wherever you wish. The dame led him, the happy one, wherever she wished, and the sitters drank, chewed their chasers, and were jealous of Pyotr. After a few days he returned to the spit, and they surrounded him and kept askin: So, Petra, did you happen to have a sweet stroll? The sitters kept askin Fyodor, to learn if he had a sweet time with the dame. And he conveyed almost nothin to them, but said this: It was so that better don't even ask. Well, but still— the wolfmen did not back off—but still, was your visit with her sweeter than a home brew? Don't ask, answered Pyotr, not even by hintin. Was the past sweeter than krambambuli for you, they asked nevertheless. What krambambuli, Fyodor, en-raged, surprised them, everythin went sweeter than Valday rot-gut. So they had a few then to Pyotr's return, and he off the cuff admits with tears that he's not considerin returnin to his heart-throb; the past is canceled, and that's why he don't need nothin, for what could he personally need after all that happened be-tween the two of them; moreover, recollections don't promise forgettin; memory, brother, don't go on debit but on credit. And that's a fact; as far as this is concerned, my dear Pozhilykh,

You can depend on me, the one who once suffered a crash at a high speed. It did not work out for you, Ilya Zynzyrella, you got deformed, warped like a sheet of plywood. We muddled by in the countryside, we huddled in a happy-go-lucky marriage in Orina's burrow, havin forgotten about problems and permits. I won't swear that our relationship rolled on smoothly, but do stress—in the beginnin it was bearable. It became unbearable, when from the switch, where she used to sort couriers, expresses, and alike, and where due to the shortage of free time hanky-panky was not really goin thru, they transferred my queen to the brick tower and made her a dispecher—to release train cars from the sortin hill. It won't do you any good that you, Ilya, purred, anticipatin her bonus for cleanliness, you sang "Joy," she lives, you kept sayin, in a tall tower, you whistled, not expectin major changes. Only afterward you latched on that, hounded by the ramjunctious boredom, she hitched herself to couplers, ran into the maintenance boors, and that if someone was not allowed into the tall tower—it was none else but you, my dear. And, havin latched on, at first you still joked: Orya, stop gettin filthy with them in unmown ditches, it's kinda not right; after all, they're just not good, this railroad brood. That's how you joked, findin inside smidgens of strength, even if every so often you could bear it no longer. Plump, curvaceous, brushin her hair with the hair pick at dawn, she kept givin me runarounds: How do you know if good or not? Meanwhile, I was lyin on my cot and emittin fumes, not willin to get up—what for, I don't have to hurry nowhere no more. She kept givin me runarounds, and there was no place to put a proof of purity on her, and the hair pick—once I looked more carefully—was not the one I presented to her on Ascension. I skinflinted, humbled myself in distant domiciles to purchase it, denied myself the necessities through the entire leaf-slayer, and then—when I looked more carefully—a different one. I started wondrin. Our attraction turned into dust; I should take off—with no sack, no bag, and no footwear. But I am not awfully mighty, I get attached; instead, I kept diggin, persuadin. What kind of a special hair pick, Oryushka, have you got? A hair pick like any other, she says thru her teeth, clutchin pins-hairpins in them. Hmm, and mine, the one I gave you, you're still takin care of it, ain't you? You bet, you bet, I took it to a museum; she shrewdly reins me in with her tongue. On the rails, she stretches the truth, I lost that hair pick, and that's all there's to it. I was cowerin like a panic-stricken animal durin the hunt, I kept proddin, fallin into doubts: Hmm, and this one, in that case, by what ruse did you get it, did someone give it to you? And the dawn, I note in passin, is breakin in the window and in the mirror, turnin into a first-class iridescent azure, and Orina's downrite bathin there, supplethal, she's splashin, exactly like in our promised pond in devil knows which summer, roughly in the month of July. Those days we haven't yet shared affections, she kept deceivin, postponin— later and later—and I kept waitin and bearin it, encouraged. And two empty cable reels floated there, swellin, like at many other reservoirs. She's thrown off all her fabrics on the bush of stag-head and steps out on the edge—shameless. Well, and then I got plugged up with the shoe cord; the threaded tape tightened like a noose. There's no way to break it, I was dealt a stubborn specimen. In short, I undid that knot with my teeth:

They were still present. And Orina was standin in her cheap pearls only, but she herself was priceless, just try to find another one like that. I did not count how many others I happened to have before her, but up to my mutilation I did not enjoy casual joys aplenty. And those joys, really—should you laugh or cry? They all make faces, all fuss around, they tease— I'll give or I won't give, afraid to be too cheap, as if I, a braggart fool, really could offer them, fancy-schmancies, anythin in exchange. And the main thing, when you finally calm them down, even then everythin somehow turns out topsy-turvy, crumpled, not complete, and quite often without real comforts. And as far as allowin themselves to give it up—never, not for the world: They stand on ceremony. In Orina's case—I suddenly saw her in all her simplicity, and fell in enrapture, of course. I could not bear it and I let her understand, by singin a stanza from one wonderful aria. You do look pretty, say, in any dress, but when you're naked you look best. It would have been better, however, if I had been less of a songbird in love, and more looked ahead; perhaps I would have noticed besides the real knot on the shoe cord the comin knot of a slightly different kind—where the freight trains are sorted, that is the choo-choo switch with various semafors and clever whatchamacallits like greasers' hooks and the greasers in person, deftly wormin themselves in without soap where they shouldn't. The first knot—thanks to the flashes of summer lightnin—I managed to untie, but the sortin one—even if all the nights there are full of fire—brought out of the blue a muddle unfatomable to any mind. But right now, I repeat, Orina stood there white and shiny, like a saber in the moonlight. To be honest, all in all it was bearable, but I remember for me personally it was unbearable; I wanted to learn as soon as possible what she was doin, and with whom, and when, that is to worm out all her ins and outs. It's not enough for you, lecherous Ilya, just to dupe and force the woman, no, you, like an irrepressible spider, suck out of her drop after drop the tincture of confessions, drawin from it the strength of pity, in order to approach and force her again. And Orina stood for a while on the edge of the pond and stepped in, and I, havin disrobed, took a dive. I dived deeply, with opened eyelids; I stared—the liquid glaze. The eye of the world was this pond with reels; a polished opal in the settin of bluish clay, clumps of willows and long slimy weeds it was. And where are our crucians?—suddenly came to my mind. I screwed up my eyes—they kept nappin in their holes, shaded by the banks, under the snags. And the snails, that is the mussels? I love them. Knockin around the world on account of my services with the lonely acordeon of mine or with a grindin foot-operated stand, wandrin in the dale of the beloved river Itil, worn out and not fond of myself, I ate countless numbers of the latter. Do they taste good? You see, I won't spare praises: Yummy. In the unheard-of area that shelters the ancientest tribe of the deaf, for whom your entire filharmonic is useless, or in a dull district, where nobody cuts, slices, or chops anythin out of rampant laziness; in the unheard-of district or in the dull area oblivious to the runnin out of the uselessly wasted light, when you played for the residents and they did not pay attention, or when you implored if they wanted to have this or that sharpened in order to get from them just enough to keep the pot boilin, but they did not bring out even the tiniest needle, you should find out from the old water yoke the way to the river and scamper, empty-bellied, to pay her a visit, as if you were goin to your mother-in-law for a formal borscht. Limp along the high roads on the only existin leg, hobble through water meadows, shaded by sparklin precious coverlet. What's that, what seems to have twinkled there so dimly, like that quiverin rot at the Bydogoshch cemetery? What flickered like silver in the pea shrubs, sorta resemblin a shimmer of your rugged aluminum mug in the rips of your never-mended bag? What glimmered there with the cold light of the flash, as if from under the fold of a merchant's coat at the market, the vessel from Crystal Goose with the priceless blue hooch sparked straight in your dried-out eyes? What is flutterin there like a sarafan's ruche, what is flappin there like mother-in-law's tongue? What and what—such an annoyin whatter, you're nothin but trouble. My buddy, this is the Wolf River, your kin. You tell her: Halloo, my sister, I'm in distress, quench my thirst with your current, feed the tramp with your mussels, gimme as many of them as you can, I enjoy their taste. Provide just them 'cuz salt and matches I always have on me; and, obviously, lay me down to sleep along the current of yours, place the softest stone under my nape. And she says: Upon examination, Ilyusha from Gorodnishchi, I don't begrudge you nothin; for instance, water—drink 'til you burst; and the same situation with the mussels—chomp and don't count. And the stone—if you want, I'll give it to you to put under your head or, if you want, on your neck, and then keep restin to your health even to the Lastest Judgment.

THE TRAPPER'S TALE

02

To live; to know the value of deep galoshes at the time of flooding of the deep and shallow rivers. To be; to soil the dark-green leaf. To live, to be, and to see how in ditches the waybread wilts. To live and to be—in step with the meandering of winter, may the hue of its micalike scaly wings change. To live and to be—may they iridesce like mother-of-pearl: any icicle, any membrane. May Maria trumpet on a shepherd's horn at the railroad, and may the latter hurry north-ward fifteen minutes of slow walk toward the sunset. A walk along the alley, positioned perpendicularly to the ramp—to the sunrise. And on the southerizon, above the city, as a result of sizable smoldering installations that mangle the skyline, may there always be a selection of barbecued and smoked clouds. To draw the distant silhouettes of the post office employees—letter carriers, gripped by anguish and the leaf fall. May your people wander around your park, and may your inclement weathers come, chilling them to the bone and causing the folds of their consignment-store coats to flap. May Maria work in the tall brick tower at the very edge of the station. May she work and may the voice of her horn, smudged by the watercolor wind, smudged like a star of someone nearsighted without glasses, command the fussy scurrying of the couplers, anxieties of the signalwomen, and the mood of the rail guardsmen. At first they were gold-toothed couplers, but later, when she was named the head of the tower, they were gradually replaced by stately engineers. May the long-distance veteran come, complaining in half whisper, with a lisp, about the shattered tender, shaky shafts, and the expanses of its long-distancedness. May the trees, donning the tattered tailcoats of the dusk, swing, wave their hands like the conductors, scarecrows, and windmen-millers. The blizzard, still confused by many with the lizard, which, even with a "b" it so resembled, although a special decree not only had determined long before their differences, but also assigned the not appropriate and not needed by the lizard "z" to the blizzard—the blizzard kept gathering speed, kept acting out, becoming relentless and merciless. In the barracks people were having fun. Ah, how my head is spinning, sang in rooms a reprehensibly empty-headed chansonnette, and her round photos, glued to the records, spun around, stuck on gramophone figs. To draw from memory the bottom of the ravine, overgrown with ferns, and the dam holding the reservoir of drinking waters; to draw the entire reservoir, crammed with the props of all possible regattas in the season of watermelons and drizzling precipitations, shaped like little circles and sticks, and the sailor-reader, who, at the whim of the artist, may sit on the stone slope of the dam, having raised up the collar of his pea jacket, smoke his pipe, and read a navy-colored book—about the sea. Have a drink and a chaser. And she herself drank and had a chaser. They called her Maria. The engineer drank, had a chaser, called her Marina, and chewed over the same rail and road gloom, treading water from Orekhovo to Zuevo. The bearings kept cracking, the axle boxes kept heating up, the manometer readings were announced, and before every bridge, before every tunnel, unfailingly, the damper was closed and the siphon was opened. To draw a passenger station: a dilapidated pavilion with a cone-shaped false turret and a beer stand with a stream of dark coats and green hats; to draw the remnants of a monastery wall, the viaduct with a section of the highway, and the pond at the foot of a high embankment. At the neighbors' raved an Italian concertina, and a habanera, a polka, or a quadrille pounded the crumbling joists. May the hubbub steamily tumble out through the opened window vents and as pastel-hued rags—washed-out and full of holes— may it hang on clotheslines and after a while, blown off by the wind, disperse over the park as flocks of jackdaws and crows, alight on the branches, swarm, ethereal and aloof, and later, with the husks of silence, with its clots, fall down on the alleys. May the gusts of the ground wind brush its remnants into the ravine, into the dark blue haze of the river torrent. I love you, my old park, confessed the artist, flipped upside down, completely worn out and listless, under the stairs, in the truncated storeroom of the carton master who, in his spare time, collected candy wrappers. To draw the heavy, nebulous, slovenly face of Maria and frequently, instead of the expected portrait, may the inexperienced draftsman create the image of her mask, as it were; and the mask wanted to wake up, to come to life, but its tormenting lethargic debility turned out to be stronger than its feeble wishes—it did not wake up. But he saw, he saw—on her meaty lips and droopy-lead lids flickered the flashes of mystery. It will be revealed after midnight, when through sleep you will hear how, outside, the rain engineer will start raving in a whisper and the entire earth, Masha, drunk, poisoned by the tincture of autumn, will dolorously submit to him, accepting his pushy minuscule seed. Later, may her anthropomorphous shadow wander across the wall, searching for the rattler of matches and for engineer's cigarettes. Kazbek or Kazbich? In any case, even if he had a herd of a thousand mares, he would have given it all away for one Azamat. But if the girl who went out with that ship's boy to that meadow, where the sailors take their merry girlfriends to play on swings, if she agreed to go there also with you, she would probably fly and squeal in a high voice with you too. You stood in the darkness of the forest, unseen. It was neither evening nor day, and at the reservoir the sails were still present and the trainers on motorboats kept croaking commands for rowers into bullhorns. She squealed like lapwings in the field, when you walk across in semidarkness, having set the traps for foxes and cherishing in advance the real rifle, promised by the engineer. Or when the ship's boy has led her by hand to the abandoned slips, and the lapwings have been flying about, and the slips are filthy, and the rain and time cannot catch up with washing them off, and now and then a dead rat, a stiff toad, or a lifeless shrike. May Maria howl, running out on the dam, calling "Come home," while the light-carrier wind—may it blow in the darkness and extinguish for good the windows of the barracks, eye after eye, one after another. May the waves get bolder. The other ship's boy, a veritable chimney from the early youthful years, groaning with the saddle like an old man, buzzing with the dynamo and flashing with the headlamp, may cough by on two wheels in the direction of the expiration of the furlough. Maria was sewing. What was Masha sewing? Masha was mending the engineer's coat. The engineer was happy. He sat on the couch and read the train schedule. Or the timetable. The blizzard was approaching. In the thickets of tubular fragile plants, with the open fractures smelling like the first frosts, in the thickets next to the muddy stream, croakers prophesied the universal flood. There, in the ravine, once—*her* notebook: a half-washed-out name. It contained sufferings in the Russian language. In particular, it reported that Papa bought skates for Nikolay, that a squirrel gnaws nuts, that granddaughter is young and grandmother vice versa, that sister is playing piano and brother bala—but instead of balalaika, to the middle of the notebook stretched a solid, uninterrupted balabala, a bolero of the pimply barrack life, overheard and written down by the true love of the youngster with an anemic forehead of an artist neither called nor recognized who, years later, answering the reproaches of a special commission that up until now he has not presented to its attention a reasonable account of the hunting roundup, more precisely, of the circumstances accompanying the return of the hunters from the roundup, being, in essence, the necessary attributes of the return—since are the circumstances not determining and stipulating the entire development and appearance of the phenomenon, is it not alive thanks to them, and what is the phenomenon without accompanying circumstances— answering the reproaches of the commission, he may reply: I do not perceive sufficient reasons, for the sake of which my impressions about such trivialities would be able to substantially help in the inspection's work; therefore I would truly prefer to keep them exclusively to myself. However, if You so insist—please. We are returning at dusk. You, I suppose, are already acquainted with each other or, more precisely, with this wonderful time of the day and are irrevocably enchanted by it, like I am, and thus reveal remarkable taste, exceptional feel for the color, and an inclination for melancholic contemplation. There are, as a rule, several of us—huntsmen and up to a dozen dogs in the pack. It is December. In order not to attract the gawkers and not to lower the quality of the picture by my awkward, still-city-like gait, I am trying to stay at the end of the procession; therefore, I see neither the faces nor the muzzles; only someone's profile flashes momentarily. Gray hats of the hunters—You are probably familiar with this heavy and firm but also fuzzy felt of our provincial factories, to which snow sticks in lumps with such a remarkable tenacity, whether it falls on the headgear or the headgear falls into a snowdrift—the gray hats of the hunters are pulled low, over their ears, as the saying goes, and that is why one can not see their napes, either. One of us, in addition to the usual equipment—a dagger, a game bag, and a spear—is burdened by our shared trophy: The fox had been slain already at dawn. By the way, take a good look at our mongrels and abortzois. Horrendously long, ugly, curved monkey-like and resembling Filippov pretzels, do their tails leave at least a flicker of hope for pure blood? It is no secret—pitiful is the exterior of my hounds: skin and bones, and completely matted coats. By the way, there is among them one bloated, wobbly, with a hideously short snout—a spook matching the piglet that some simple folk roast over the bonfire in front of the tavern entrance, where, having assured us they would catch up soon, some huntsmen dropped in to wait out a very strong gust of headwind. Is there any need to mention that right now we are on the summit of a large hill, condemned, like the entire site, to the fresh Christmas snow, and our figures contrast quite well with this background? After leaving the tavern on the left, we have almost passed it and begin to descend into the valley. In front of us stretches a perennially familiar panorama. This is the dale of the river, and a town in this dale next to this river, and ponds, and barns in the distance, and the sky above everything listed. This is our country; we live here, and while some of us live in town, the others live in the village, beyond the emerald river. We easily distinguish the dike and the mill, the church and the horse carts on the roads, the library, the hospice, and the bathhouse. We see the steep roof of the invalids' home, the grinding establishment, the shelter for the deaf, and the market. And a mass of skaters on the ice of the river and the ponds. Their voices and skates sound resonant, their faces are flushed. Here—brownish clumps of leafless trees, resembling the fur of unknown animals; there—washerwomen, rinsing the linen in an ice hole. In addition, boats frozen into ice, and levees, and birds—oh, a mass of birds both on the branches and simply in the celery-smelling space—firebirds, faded, discolored, or having completely replaced their whimsical garb with the modest feathers of magpies and crows. What a marvelous country, out of this world, a visitor halts in admiration. The simplicity and modesty of the walnut frame only enhances the enchanting beauty of the landscape and the excellence of the color glazing.

Of course, our sketch does not pretend to describe and evaluate all the other pictures exhibited at the vernissage: We will only stop for a moment next to some of them. *Self-Portrait in Uniform*. The canvas is to such a degree distinctive that one simply has to be amazed. It has been said that having finished the work, its author was literally shaken by the depth of his self-perception; success caught the artist completely unawares. Having unsociably locked himself in his atelier, located at that time in the orangery, he, after getting somnambulistically lost among photinias with tiny blooms and mannequins indifferent to everything, and repeating ceaselessly "I do not believe it, I do not believe it," stubbornly refuses to believe that it is not him there, in the corner, leaning over the easel, but only his image, even if it is extraordinarily similar to the original. And when his relatives, assisted by the gardener and the cutter, having broken the door, finally convinced the master in his own originality—he burst into tears. The color reproduction of *Self-Portrait in Uniform* will adorn the frontispiece of our monograph about this remarkable man; its publication is eagerly anticipated day in and day out. And how significant is the fact that the appearance of one of the subtlest, most refined realists of the recent past coincided with such a remarkable date as the five-hundredth anniversary of the pin. The artist himself thought that the mentioned coincidence was far from accidental and emphasized this on every appropriate occasion, seeing in it either the gesture of Providence or the digit of Mnemosyne. Say, in one of his poems, the painter, with his characteristic candor, announces: Well, gentlemen, in the year from the invention of the pin 541, on the last Friday of November, approximately at six o'clock, at a considerable distance from any capitals, in the middle of Russia, and at the same time on the shore of a deep and wide river, someone is drunkenly beating the tambourine. The dusk has already forced the eyes to open wide, obscured the vistas, and abolished all traces of light. The silhouette of the musician is about to dissolve. For that reason, groaning and tripping over the folds of the Amztarakhan robe that gives an impression of being completely frayed, suffering from the chill emanating from the mossy stones of the cellar, shuddering from disgust at the sight of multiple millipedes, and begging the hiccups to move over to the submissive passion-bearers Fedot and Yakov, let us roll out into God's world the barrel of the narrative—and let us finally knock out the bung. That is how, gazing through a small window during a relatively late hour of one of the pitiful days of another inclement year and trying to gather his thoughts, the hero of this story philosophized. *Vita sine libertate nihil*, he philosophized, *vivere est militare*. He was not fresh and not young.

NOTES ₒ A BINGING HUNTER

03

NOTE I

IMPRESSION

Look around! Countless insects are flying
And still follow honey trails as before,
But too many subtle signs are implying
That the summer won't be back anymore.

Not by chance, on mornings of amber,
More translucent than the skin of the moon,
Gypsy moth, after hot-weather slumber,
Flies to find a new wife very soon.

At the market—hurly-burly, slashed prices.
Bergamot pears? We have them. So sweet!
And if you are a bird, a few slices
Of potato beetle's larvae you'll eat.

Childhood is sadness itself. There, in the wastes,
Grandkids search for grandpa's tobacco,

Cabbage whites and field browns they chase
And they sing an old dance tune from Cracow:

When, alas, our grandma will die,
We will lay her to rest, dust to dust,
So she'll turn into a white butterfly
When a hundred or a thousand years pass.

Nothing's changed in the yard's verdant thicket,
Only asters, not poppies, bloom now.
More haphazard are the chirps of the cricket.
And the hammock? No one's weighing it down.

Shrubs and bushes give us an impression
That they flaunt the hue of their bugs,
While a cohort of young craftsmen in session
Red Cahors in the cooper's yard chugs.

NOTE II

PREPARATION OF CARTRIDGES

1

I strolled the other day
In the forest of pine.
The sand of its trails,
Its needle and its leaf,
Including arrowleaf—

Everything was dry.
And I was mad that I
Was foolish to put on
These wetwalkers of mine
And don a slicker too.

So now, more mindful, I,
Getting ready to go,
Retired both the waders and the raincoat.
Then sunshine rain caught me on my way—
I ran and tried to hide;
When I came home, I shook all over.

My lonesome babe kept scolding: Serves you right,
I warned you—legs are throbbing—but you
Preferred to listen to the wagging dog's tail—
You banned the coat, discarded the gummies.
Oh, daydreamer, she went on, oh, hothead.

2

You have a magic box!
In it you keep all things
Needed for hunting with a rifle.
So with no further words
Open it; from inside
Take out some carton tubes,
And also a few caps
Invented by the late Monsieur Gévelot.

And in these carton tubes
Thrust these Gévelot caps
And sprinkle powder there.
Go, fellow!

Using a thick sack cut into small lots,
Or worn felt boots, or flannel pajamas,
Insert a plug; follow with some shot;
And then another plug securely jam in.

Sir French is sitting headless on a chair.
My dear field marshal, it seems you're not well.
The gentleman became slightly wrinkled.
Who dared to do this? Maybe Jomini
Swung his sharp saber from beyond La Manche?

Sir French is sitting stately on the chair,
The sizes of the shot are six and five,
But since the barrel is caliber twenty,
The shells' caliber is also twenty-two.

My powder's smoky like grandpa's tobacco,
And flashes of old age astonished my forehead,
The clock tick-tocks, imagining one thing,
Imagining the other, imagining something.

My lonesome babe's asleep, chock-full of kissel.
Well, may she dream of my love for her.

And I—of hunting.

NOTE III

THE TIME BETWEEN

The time between wolf and hound
Is good for a chat soul to soul.
Though the lunch isn't lavish at all,
You'll be able to talk round and round
With both, the wolf and the hound.

It's good that near the pond,
Sitting on a branch of oak tree,
The Hoopoe pipes with great glee
And repeats on and on:
How good I feel by the pond.

A handcar mournfully brays
From the *versta* thirty-and-four.
The vistas can't be bare any more.
The store is closed for a day.
Boredom. The handcar still brays.

A jug dripped a drop on the plate,
The cricket knows its place well.
But really, can anyone tell
Whether it's early or late?
It dripped again on the plate.

You'll be able to talk round and round,
Of course, if the topic is right.
If it's not, have a good night:
Evening drags, as if spellbound,
After the wolf and the hound.

NOTE IV

THE GRINDER

(A CONVERSATION WITH A CRITIC)

Don't sleep on the ground—you'll get weary,
You'll be barely moving at all!
Scat, my carper, stop nagging, you're dreary!
I am dreaming that a valiant flag-bearer
Gave me weapons that used to be fairer,
And they need to be sharpened—they're dull.

Do I love such weather, so pleasing,
When the clouds are suddenly gone,
And the masses can notice much easier
The appearance, let's not say: of a cuckoo,
But correctly, let's say: of the Hoopoe
Who is cranking his grinding flint stone?

You bet. But what, one may ponder,
The sound of the Hoopoe's loud grind

Resembles at this moment of wonder?
It sounds like someone is crunching
The old chicken bone you were munching,
But then left it, unfinished, behind.

Enlightenment's reins briefly dropping,
In a turban and caftan, *hakeem*,
The folk *akyn*, all in motion,
Across a steep gully is hopping,
Comparing, full of emotions,
The grinding to the sound of a stream.

What a dank, clammy autumn! It's taxing.
But the Hoopoe is bothered not
By the fact he doesn't have access
To dull scythes, or sickles, or axes,
But because nobody asks him:
Please, put on my scarf and my coat.

At the moment, the grinder figure,
A dullard, a dolt, round the bend,
Upset that he's not a gravedigger,
A builder, a tinker, a baker,
A light carrier or a toy maker,
Sings something about motherland.

That's life: By the invalids' home,
Which, in winter, has a rink at its gate,

The Hoopoe approaches the lame,
Or rather, one-legged gnome,
Blind and mute, hunchbacked, and tame,
And keeps honing his lone figure skate.

Just look—and pass by, heed this lesson:
Someone's grief is not a true grief.
Even more, 'cause no one can lessen
Pains of those whom fate so distresses
That the scorching sun can't impress them,
Hence, no deluge can bring them relief.

Darkness falls. Irked by fate's treason,
Like a hungry Gorgon would do,
The leaf fall's whispering season
Stalks the verb-herd servile and sleazy,
But—sees no rhyme and no reason,
And the actual herd—is gone too.

NOTE V

OCTOBER

Is it really October? Such a balmy air
That if not for the rustling of leaf fall,
One could simply forget about everything
And for hours stare into farnowheres.

And smell sagebrush.

But one has to live, to act, to go on,
Worry about the presence of kindling,
One has to sew new squirrel slip-ons,
Stockpile mushrooms and go hunting.

Inasmuch as winter is certain.

Carelessly showing the white of face,
Here I am; I'd like to listen to the Hoopoe.
Go on, rattle, cuckoo, my dear hooting whoop,
Tiny toy, trifle, trinket, true treasure.

Who knows where and for what reason
Someone with a drum roams the copses;
Spindlewort, fusoria, fusanum,
Scarletberry, snakeberry, solanum.

With a glow of roll-ups,
Fragments of vulgar phrases,
A part of speech known by the name of cough,
And with the moaning of rowlocks
Resembling the mallard's call,
Approaches a gaggle of ragged freeshooters.

It's beginning.

NOTE VI

PAS D'ESPAIGNE

(RECOLLECTION OF THE CITY)

Mozart's music was merrily sounding
One day in the old city park,
A lady was blissfully longing,
But for whom, she was still in the dark.
Among the musicians, excited,
A visiting cornet spun around,
And for tête-à-tête he invited
The lady to a quaint *restaurant.*
Pas d'Espaigne is a wonderful dance,
Because it's so easy to learn:
Two steps back, then two to advance,
Turn around, and repeat all again.
In the evening, when all dancers vanished,
He became her friend and her crush.
He appeared to her to be Spanish,
And, all of a sudden, she blushed.
Next day, at the quay, she was musing:
Should she ask for a farewell encore?
In the old city park Mozart's music
From that morning sounded no more.

NOTE VII

POSTAL CHORES IN THE MONTH OF NOVEMBER

The leaves and the birds—they all went flying.
The first—off trees, the other—southbound.
Soon, on warm mittens we'll be relying
So our hands can be safe and sound.

Yet ere the frosts and blizzards commence,
To orphan winter prelude in light gray,
Nigh is the time of Saint Vitus's dance,
Devoted brother of the bag and jail.

In this connection, letters—piles of them,
And telegrams—ready for this day,
Have to be sent. Just two words: I am.
To all addresses. And without delay.

Have to be sent, while telegraph wires
Can still be seen and we're still not late.
I am—before people light their fires,
Before the cities finally lock their gates.

Have to be sent. Where's the ink for my *stilo*?
Perhaps the twilight sucked it up dry?

I am! And to the Chinese, to Manila:
Bin ich?—asking for their advice—Am I?

Have to be sent, with a short note—urgent,
By a swift gryphon or by the pale mare,
Or, using the term of the postal agent,
Pounded like cutlets, leaving none to spare.

That's what I chose and, whacked by asthma,
Went to the cellar, for a swig down there.
And when I crawled out, pleasantly plastered,
A *vespertilio* flashed in the air.

NOTE VIII

INSOMNIA

There's no sleep in either eye
(The chemist's right, alas—years fly),
But who would need it anyway,
With a velveteen ribbon around its crown,
And with a bit of a tilt?
At the first sight—just a sieve.

I see it all as if it were now:
Darkness entered my pines,
Caressed this and that,
And then, out of the blue

A hat with a tilt floated up;
Such a dashing chapeau.

Thin fog stole out from the stream,
A racer slithered into the sward to sleep.
An oriole kept sewing evening into night.
I figured: That's who needed a sieve!
Only, I thought, why with a tilt?
And a crane stood in the reeds.

I wiped my monocle and put it on—
My goodness, it's only a canotier . . .
The mallards burst out from the sedge—frrr!
Thinking about it, just how many years
Flowed ever since into the sieve with a tilt?
Alas, the chemist is quite right, oh my.

NOTE IX

AS IF ONE SALTED . . .

Some mornings, when your boredom rages,
It seems you're waiting for some tip.
Either you skim through Pushkin's pages
Or Pushchin's volume dully flip.

The hunt no longer seems arresting.
Your whipper-in does not take down

The horn and harness idly resting.
And hunting grounds in sadness drown.

And you're so glum, as one may gather,
That faithful ale can't make life right.
Should you clean your chibouk or rather
Challenge your neighbor to a fight?

Or your old robe that's tight and scratches
Should you demand to cut today,
So for the new one you'll have patches?
Or should you simply run away?

Instead, to calm depression's fervor,
You take a stroll *pour l'appetite*.
And later, with your household servants
You play *cerceau* just *à petit*.

Or risking a snob's reputation,
You proudly board your charabanc
With English Club's bright decorations,
And ride stiff like a wooden chunk.

It's fall, may readers be reminded,
Therefore, the last leaf will alight,
When your gaze, truly absentminded,
Will bless it on its final flight.

Dusk, like a wolf from forest's stubble,
Yawns, when the lights go on, at last.
But you forget about your troubles
And urge the coachman, shouting: Fast!

Because white flies begin to flutter
High in the air, for all to see.
You rush home, open window shutters:
Oh, nanny, look—what can it be?

As if one salted over yonder
Bathhouses, barns, and every hut . . .
Ah, snow has fallen! What a wonder!
And winter started just like that.

DZYNDZYRELA'S DISCORDS BEYOND THE ITIL

04

It was Pyotr, one smart aleck from Sloboda, who took somethin to town—either to sell or to buy; it's impossible to make out from such a distance: I went far away lookin for seasonal work and my storm lamp doesn't purrcolate much in the alien darkness, while my years ain't a match for bird's sight. Pyotr is quite fine, but Pavel, his nephew, is worried, he's sendin him a triangular letter. Their furry-legged postal cooer arrives at the lodge, sees how Pyotr with the other huntin gards mercilessly abuses the wine, tosses them knucklebones, starts makin noise with songs. The cooer pecks Pyotr on his temple and keeps sayin: You, Pyotr, drink your fill, but understand the drill. Pyotr takes the letter, opens it, and somethin is written there. My dear uncle Pete—that's what is written there—I am no longer hopin you'll bring back any yeast, but I keep hopin that durin your mercantile absence from our places you did not live like a heartless windbag, but that you boldly dreamed about the alphabet. In tears, Pyotr begs his comrades in the crashbaret: Help me with advice 'cuz I'm dyin here. Pavel sent me to Gorodnishche; who knows whether to sell or to buy, I just know he's mad I'm slower than molasses in

January, and right now I've got neither the merchandise nor the money, and even less the yeast vital to him. He's naggin me from the other shore: Do whatever you want, he says, but abstain from an empty-handed return. Well, perhaps it will be possible to reciprocally extract the hooch-brewin yeast from someone, but where can one get the letter *zhe*; it has stumped us, enlighteners. With the letter *ge*, shares Pyotr, we came up without a problem; it resembles the gallows, it does, 'cuz on the gallows you can pronounce only that letter: *ge, ge,* and *ge.* The letter *de* is like a dacha, *be* almost like *ve*, and *ve* almost like *be*, but *zhe*—that one's mysterious. At that moment, worn out by everyday hardships and by lashin incessant downpours, I also report to the crashbaret in person—a prophet who stole from Christians two hours of light in the month of July—I drop in to celebrate the conclusion of my unsuccessful to the hilt and to the core business. I met a certain blind man in an unsightly place, and he volunteered to accompany me to the water for repose. And I trudged after him, trustin him in everythin, but the darkness engulfed us and for that reason he did not notice a huntin pit and tumbled in. I also fell in, followin the leader, 'cuz my belt was tied to his with a strong rope so we wouldn't get separated. Halloo, we did not get separated, we moaned with banged heads and with dislocations, halloo, we did not get separated, we kept jokin, continuin our journey with difficulty. But we were jokin untimely, comrades in misfortune. 'Cuz, when it turned light, I discovered that my grindin stand suffered durin the fall more than we did. The main wheel had cracked in many places and in that region it was impossible to find a competent wheel fixer or a cooper to undertake the real repair. Therefore, havin suffered enough from sharpenin on the damaged construction, exosted, I was re-turnin to the winter quarters ahead of schedule. I was ploddin with empty pockets and nothin clinked in them. And as long as I was ploddin, figurin out with what I was gonna pay in the eatery, the main wheel was breakin more and more; it was the Hay-rot season. Beside myself, I drop in and greet the tramps present there. And meanwhile, the rim finally split in two and fell apart. I looked: The pieces were lyin at my feet. Cursin my unenviable lot, angry, I roughed up the apparatus to take out from circulation the crosspiece with the bushin, which, with-out the rim, looked strangely orphaned. I took it out, threw it on the floor, and spat. And the crosspiece fell precisely be-tween them, between them two rim fragments, while they were lyin sorta resemblin two thin crescents, with backs to each other and with faces—here and there: one young, the other Krylobyl, on the wane. And then Krylobyl, the wise war-den, about whom songs were already made in those days, when we, dear Pozhilykh of mine, weren't even close to bein present, he, who was registered here from the very beginnin of begin-nins, always wore garments lined with fish fur, and brewed hooch and rotgut from times immemorial, he squinted, moon-faced, and turned to Pyotr. 'Nuf grievin about your grief, Lukich: Ain't the thing thrown on the floor by one beggar a treasure for another one? Look more carefully: Ain't the thing you're searchin for lyin in the dust of this sickler, thrown there neglectfully by Ilya? Pyotr reproaches the warden, puttin him to shame: You like to play games with my weak mind, what the hell for do I and Pavel need the worthless wheel of the grindin mechanism, and it is still unknown whether the owner will let us take it, perhaps he himself needs it? Krylobyl teaches the one bein taught in the crashbaret on the hill: I don't wanna teach you to pick up someone's things; you yourself know how to do it; I am teachin you somethin else. You are speakin in riddles, Pyotr said to Krylobyl, you're teachin in riddles, to Krylobyl said Pyotr, oh, in riddles. And they had a drink. And the others, with the exception of this here correspondent of Yourses, also had a swig, while the latter just licked his lips. Well, said Krylobyl, sniffin his sleeve as a chaser, what kind of sound can be heard at the Wolf River, when one of our grinders starts workin on his grindin stand, ain't it *zhe-zhe-zhe*? Exactly. That's why I am askin, Krylobyl continued talkin to Pyotr: The wheel from the grindin stand, which is lyin in the dust of this sickler turned upside down, ain't it sorta-kinda the sought letter? The public looked and gasped—ha, the spittin image. Verily, verily you're teachin, Pavel and I will have a *zhe*, Pyotr rejoiced, only it's a pity that money, he rejoiced, I don't have, otherwise I would treat you accordin to your needs. Don't rack your brains too much, Krylobyl calms him down, don't despair, go and borrow from someone. But from whom can I borrow, despairs Pyotr, if here everybody gets hold of money by borrowin. And did you try to ask Manul, Manul beckoned to him. And this Manul, permit me to recommend, up to a certain time did not use money, even though he enjoyed himself, 'cuz he was treated for free, on the house, splittin for this purpose a certain madam with a not so bad fysik, who was a server here, in the establishment, and indulged the warden in everythin from A to Z, and for that reason he was able to put away his pension for rainy days. And when they came, when Manul's paramour, light bay from head to toe, sailed away on the inspector's cutter and left for her abandonee a written note, "Don't look for me, please," then Manul set out to have a talk with the inspector in the Other Places, and came back only three years ago. Nothin happened to him—he started enjoyin himself again, but now at real cost and, like all of us, makin purchases with what we call cash, which, however, so far he has, while in our anaconda purses there is a fundamental confusion. Pyotr sits down next to Manul the warden and looks at him from the bottom of his heart. After a while, the latter asks Pyotr: Why are you starin at me, haven't you ever seen me before, and don't you have nothin else to stare at? Exetera. Well, you see, I wanna try, Pyotr apologizes, to borrow some means from you. So go ahead, try, Manul instructs, otherwise what's the use starin in vain? Hearin this, Pyotr replies to Manul with simplicity: Warden-warden, be my friend, lend me some. I can never be your friend, pal; after all, I am a warden and you're just an upstreamer, but money, don't be cross, I will give you—I'm not a cheapskate. And gives him big money. The public lived it up well on Manul's savins, Sidor Fomich, and they also nodded to me to join them. 'Cuz, after all, whose wheel cracked, if one thinks about it? Ain't no misfortune without good fortune, and so Dzynzyrela suddenly got lucky.

■ □ ■

And the river answers my request: I will give you a stone to put either under your head or on your neck—take it, be my guest, but in the latter case don't blame me, you won't eat them mussels to your health, alas, but they will eat you with pleasure. I respond: Hold on, I'll postpone my despair for a while, gimme the mussels now at dusk. Take off your new fashionable pantofle, she says, roll up your *galife* as high as it'll possibly go, step into me up to your knees, and wander slowly, pinchin the bottom with your foot; I guarantee you'll discover what you need in a jiffy. I follow the river's advice and step into it, flowin, and eventually stuff my shoulder bag to the gills. I set up in some hollow a bonfire—I keep fryin, boilin, bakin, and simultaneously dryin my unsofiscated rags, which, God be praised, I still own. They get bigger every passin year; I am witherin, wiltin, and at the same time I'm losin my mind. A certain lonesome babe—I repent, I repent, I attached myself to her without wakin up the sacred feelins, just to have a harbor, a warm bench, or a couch to throw my bones on, as in the workshop the drafts blow from all the cracks, the bed is dank, scares-nightmares crawl out from all the corners—so this lonesome babe, washin my substantial apparels, kept esplainin that my flesh is dryin out 'cuz I have no strength to forget Orina. You are stuck on her, said my friend, you are stuck, and as a result, my life's bitter. And when you're sleepin, sometimes you grab me, you shove your puppy in all my places, but you call her—and I'm jealous. You're achin for the tart with your entire feeble, booze-infused guts and your brains half and half with your snot drip out from you and spread on your work clothes, and the winds are dryin them. That's right, Sidor Fomich, You will touch when we personally meet, You will touch the fabric of my mantilla—see, like a scab. I pity you, the woman grieved about me, nomadic is your lot, you are a bunch of grass, dry and scattered; it would be better if He took you to Himself quickly, so you wouldn't suffer no more hardships in this world, wouldn't blabber nonsense, wouldn't abuse them ironwares in vain, wouldn't make sparks at night, wouldn't hide them dawns from the useful citizens, wouldn't long no more for the cheater. Otherwise, your bean will finally dry up like the vobla and you will become completely stupid, like the dolt at the mill who has lost all his wits as if someone hit him with a heavy sack. That's how she grieved, adjustin my old rags, and her jeremiad resounded far and wide. And I was thinkin to myself, sittin in the nappin shed: Abandon hopes for my quick departure, I will loom here-there a little more, I will be an eyesore for some folks a bit longer, I will breathe down the neck of some folks, I will still lift my walleye unto the sky. Mumbo-jumbo, You will probably think, what kind of a shed are you talkin about? What can I say? A shed like any other, only for nappin. There are containers, all kinds of things, spices, food, and about half a dozen of mousetraps manufactured by the Sankt-Petersburg spring co-op. Hard to believe: Is it possible that the need for them clapsnaps reached even the main capital? There are also brooms, and bathhouse twigs, a stockpile of candles, everythin's in order, everythin's shipshape. But besides this you notice somethin particular: There is a mattress filled with all kinds of stuff. You break your back the entire day, circulate from house to house or from workshop to workshop, drop in for an hour to the crashbaret, then you glide under the wing of your fiendish witch, and she starts grumblin: Go split some logs, go chop the wood, otherwise, lazybones, in due course you'll fly out from these digs. So you're forced to hop and gallop to the log pile, hit and split wood with the hatchet. And the only light in your window—spring, April, when you can finally vanish into thin air—will shine beyond the Itil until the first mornin frosts. And for now, kiddo, there's no place to go, and the blizzard, fella, wolfs you down. So I chopped, hacked—and from that moment until supper Ilya's involved in a smoke break in the shed and a nap on the cherished junk. *Gutenacht* to me, but if the nap doesn't happen? I toss and turn and, in order not to lie there uselessly, I patch them gaps in education. The books I own are few but wonderful, old. There's among them one about a mouse. It's not big, I agree, but, after all, the mistress ain't large either. Once upon a time, it claims, there lived an old man and an old woman. Fine, I agree. And they had, supposedly, Fenist the bird. Again, I'm not arguin, it's a natural thing; the folk around here are quite poor, but despite that, one or two speckled specimens occasionally settle down in the attics of some individual owners. But not long, as a rule, not long, unfortunately, is the life of them little souls. Somewhere, most likely, it is long, but not here, Beyond the Wolf. For reference: I don't know about you, instigators, but we, grinders and wardens, consider Beyond the Wolf those places that lie across the Wolf River, regardless from which side you look. I'll esplain on an example. The lonesome babe sends Ilya for some late morels—she's started cravin, You see, somethin salty. I had begged the dinghy from the co-op and set off to the Mangy Pines. And You remain in the city, even though, undoubtfully, I invited You, too: Keep me company, I said. But then, it's not clear if You have a basket. But even if You don't—no problem, ask some folks to let You carry one for a while, You're an experienced impersonator, refusal would be surprisin. However, in order not to cast a shadow on the fence, so to speak, and complicate the enterprise, I—when You start askin— I will wait in a hidey-hole. I am worried that if they realize that You're sailin for mushrooms with me, then in Gorodnishche's eyes You'll get, unexpectedly, smeared with dirt. I will wait, I will, I'll pinch some sorrel on the pasture, I'll pull out some wild horseradish for later. Don't reproach me for curiosity, but do You, on Your part, consume this lovely root? Don't be shy, just lemme know. Your word is law. Before You had a chance to blink—I already pulled out enough for You, too. And somethin else: Rubber boots, have You managed to procure rubber boots for Yourself? I don't have them, but don't compare Yourself to me, I am not the best example, from Easter until the Intercession I strut around barefooted—I'm used to it, my sole is abrasive, eternal: My heel's like sandpaper, but even it gets penetrated by mornin dews. However, I don't complain, someone much more famous than we had suffered, recommendin we do the same. In contrast, on the Intercession, when the frosts harden all the mud—right away I put my *valenok* on and no fiend is a match for me. And when the waters freeze—go ahead, tie a blade with a rope and vamoose. Therefore, anythin else maybe, but a boot, figurelatively speakin, doesn't pinch us. Perhaps You will prick up Your ears in my address: That there's no boot in the grinder's possession—there's no special wonder either, but by whose generosity did he get hold of the *valenok*? I'll make a confession: I snagged the footwear one day.

■ □ ■

Cold, mold, hunger everywhere, ground drafts, typhus—
whatever you want—but with *valenki* there's a defective. True,
in the ward, let's give it its due, there was a pair—but one for all,
so the patients could take turns and manage their promenaids.
Usually with a certain colleague we managed for two. Fortune
smiled on us, you may say; he's missin this one and I the opposite, so we sniffed each other out like two mutts. Two boots of
leather flock together; everybody around recognized us with
respect. To change the dressin, to get a supply of pills from a
nurse, to deploy ourselves in the corner with the auntie from
the female ward—everywhere we scurry side by side. Where,
as in the song, goes the right hoof, there the left claw follows;
however, over there it resembles more the first, and over here it
takes more after the second. Irreplaceable for each other we
were also durin the abovementioned promenaids. 'Cuz, really,
is it possible to manage a lot individually in the nippy outside—complete gloom. Some barely walkin almost-goner will
stroll for five minutes, admire the orphan lindens, remember
his father's orchard—and he's had enough. He'll track back,
frownin, take off the *valenki* and throw them away: Who'd like
to slide them checkers with me, he asks, sorta makin a smile
with his mouth, while melancholy's eatin him up. Look, be so
kind, into my stern eyes, look, perhaps, for the last time—that's
his philosophy. And my and my colleague's is opposite. We divide this snow-dusted pair with our hands tremblin from joy,
each of us puts on what's his, and we're hoppin into the open
air. It is wonderful outside—our native land. Kinda mother,
but strikingly sly, deceitful. In the beginnin, overall, it appears
to be—land like land, only poor, with nothin in it. But after

you've made yourself at home, looked more carefully—there's everythin in it, except *valenki*. We hobble, resolutely, to pediatric haunts—come and see: here you've got a frozen hill, and a snow fortress, like Pyotr Alexeich had in Botfortovo, and the hospital cats, fat, well-nourished on our hospital fare, with their cheeks, as the sayin goes, visible from the back. There is also the hospital coal sled—we used it, too. After sleddin, gettin filthy, and fillin our boot tops with snow, we start a snowball fight with the recuperatin young'uns. They hurt, they laugh, and thru the pane their doctor shakes his fist in vain, when he sees it. At first the kids kept their distance from us, especially from me. And why not; even I, before becomin familiar with myself, was afraid to stare in mirrors—such a mug is no joke, not to mention that the leg of my pajamas flutters empty. But gradually the tykes became tame, even got attached to us, I'd say. Sometimes, we only hear: Grampa Lyusha—that's what they called me—Grampa Lyusha, tell us a story, give us a piggyback ride, and don't hide your stump, show us. That is, they drove us bonkers. At the same time, to Alfeyev, Yakov Ilyich, they stuck like leaves from bathhouse twigs. And he was a poet, a versifier, he put together delightful couplets for them; You and I are nothin in comparison with him, my Sidor, Isidor. I would quote these compositions of his, but I'm afraid You won't approve; they are picturesque, that is, decent not for everybody. For instance, the poem about the homeless dog. Once a bitch her cooter against the fence knocked, and now she is achin—her cooter got blocked. And after that I am quite embarrassed, Fomich. Just imagine: But three friendly stud dogs helped her with the pain, they did what was needed—

she's happy again. Just think! And other pieces similar to that. How much fun our nippers had! Well, we did some work, had fun with the tots—and the night is fallin. It's time for us, consequently, to get to the theater. In the thicket stood, secluded, under the number one, a hunchbacked house. Not really a house but a former chapel with an amputated cross, and some whitish plants, perhaps willows, were bendin over it, like anatomists. And a sign with old-fashioned letters announced: Anatomical Theater. A familiar orderly carried out his duties there. Right away we go to see him in the cellar: Are you keepin watch? Come on, show us your artists. The orderly opens the vaults wide: Have a look, I don't mind, so far I don't charge for shows. He knew them by histories of their illnesses, with all the details, by heart—who took poison, who burned from cancer, who got crushed, and who went simply out of stupidity. I remember, he had in storage for about two weeks a gal of non-advanced age. On the skinny side, redheaded, collarbones and ankels, with curly hair everywhere. Her relatives could not be found; it would be time to bury her—but there's a problem, there's no one to do it. She was nice, very nice, and though dead, but not sad; she was smilin—as if it was not about her— and the decay did not touch her body at all, unlike it does to many others. I dare to hope that the serafims were gardin her better. She passed away from hot shakes, she entrusted herself, unlucky, to some young guy, but was not able to forget him soon enough—and goodbye. Orya, I am grief-stricken, Orya, is there anyone for whom you did not come true, couldn't you have sheltered Ilya at least? He, the beast, would have saved you, the beauty, from all adversities, and you'd manage

together somehow. 'Cuz what is unhappiness and what is happiness, if you think about it? Unhappiness is when there is no
happiness, and happiness, Orya, is when there's no unhappiness. But 'nuf grievin. So, dear orderly, splash for us, please,
some governmental pure grain, give the invaliduals a small
servin from the big health services. We are suppin and talkin.
To our hospitable host—a question: How can you stand it to
work in such a Tartar, ain't it depressin, ain't it disgustin?
There's disrespect, sounds the answer; pathology is a cruel
thing, the postmortem medics have no pity on our body, they
keep guttin, God forbid you croak, they won't miss a spot. And
the young female student doctors do the same—such smar-
ty-panties, they grab whatever they can. But move your own
brain, where could I hop off from the given position, where
else would I be able to decant free firewater for all of you lost
souls? And he himself in turn gets desperately concerned about
us: What on earth made you the way you are, if it's not a secret?
I tell him—so and so, this and that way. And Alfeyev, Yakov
Ilyich—started spreadin war rumors. He reports that not too
long ago there began, supposedly, the most fiercest campaign,
and he was shaved, as ill luck would have it, to fight on these
fronts. To the positions, he recalls, a girl saw the soldier off. She
saw him off, but there's shootin, there—the brave commander
orders: Forward march—he's cussin—and if you don't, I'll
shoot you. No way out—he had to march, and so, obviously,
his leg got torn away and thrown behind the fascines. He
screamed, he admits, like one bein slaughtered. A poet, a lo-
quacious rhymester was Yakov Ilyich: Okeydokey, soldier's
walkin, okeydokey, to the war. Or somethin more or less

civilian, related to transport: When my dear wife, he says, to the conductor was promoted, with the controller an affair she plotted; I don't know whether I should even care, but I already don't pay for my fare. Usually our conversations in the mortuary kept flowin like a stream, but even they flowed by and away, they poured down like the sand in an hourglass. Everythin passes, but the worthy things first of all. Hello, discharge—you descended, broke loose. Namely, one resplendent mornin, the general hospital evacuator, doctor, visits the dinin hall. Even not just a doctor but a hulk of a doc, a fatso. We are havin lunch: dinner, that is. It's brought to our attention that tomorrow mornin Sidorov and Petrov with all their possessions are hobblin to disinfection, and afterward with affidavits of inability to work are limpin without delay home. We're in trouble, I and Yakov. 'Cuz just for the sake of a good yarn I mentioned here Sidorov and Petrov. Upon verification, it turned out that no Petrov and even less Sidorov were figures on this flayer's removal list. Alfeyev and Your humble Ilya were figures there. Mayday, Yakov Ilyich, I whispered, we're bein condemned to discharge. And he is requestin an additional servin. And our chef-cook, she asks angrily: What, didn't you stuff yourself enough? Alfeyev answers meekly: When I was a nut case, a medic woman advised me: When some unpleasant thing happens, munch as much as you can of somethin—and everythin will vanish in a trice. What kind of unpleasant thing, the fat cook curses the poet, you are stretchin me over the rack. Well, such, Alfeyev replies calmly, such, that the chicken we had for the second course turned out to be old, and it all got stuck in my teeth. I started wondrin again, not for the first time.

From where, reveal the secret hidin nothin, from what kind of a highway such irrepressible enthusiasts had come about; after all, no such speckled bird has yet hatched from the world egg that this health center is fated to chew. Our doctors of science used to fatten us up with porridge, and Alfeyev claims that it got stuck. And not long, not long, I repeat, these small creatures live, since they should never peck on wasps. But even the cooer did not peck Petrukha on his temple as hard as they are peckin on wasps. And these are infected, sick, and it so happens that the feathered race goes through a plague. In my nappin book it's written: The speckled one tasted the golden wasps and laid for the old folks an egg, not an ordinary one but golden. It would seem nothin better could be even expected—take it and fry. But not everythin turns to Allah's glory beyond the Itil. The old woman tried to break it, tried to break the egg—but not quite. Her husband, a feeble seedpod, had no luck either. At that moment a relatively small gray mouse was runnin by, attendin to her simple needs, and she saw the culinary difficulties. She gained speed, waved her tail, and brushed the egg off on the floor. The egg fell and—bang—cracked. I realize, I realize, You are befuddled again: Why have you, disfigured Ilya, told me this mouth-to-mouth fable, what impelled-compelled you? I am also apologetic, if that's the case, for dumbfoundin You with my bewilderin story. But why, I'd like to know, for what reason did they create the above parable at all, what is, I am askin, the point of this once-upon-a-time tale? That a mouse is stronger than a man? Doubtful, somethin like that does not happen even Beyond the Wolf, and ain't the feeble old people livin right there? Or what? That, perhaps, all of us should protect mice, that they can be useful if one needs to break somethin in the household? About this we hold strictly personal opinion. The same way as we exterminated from times immemorial, we gard the tradition now. Are they frog princesses? Do they promise with a human voice a broken trough? Please, don't chastise me, Fomich, but I don't understand suggestions of this kind. A completely different case is a cabbage, a goat, and a wolf—that I understand, at least that is a riddle. But not now—now the discharge is tormentin me. And the witchcook gives Yakov Ilyich a second helpin. We each chow down a half and start thinkin. Outside, a sheer blizzard twists the tangled hair of the bushes in the front yard and we, urchins, find ourselves short of *valenki*. In addition to the situcraption here, we don't hold in our hands any profession whatsoever. Where should we, figurelatively speakin, go to learn? You'll get out, get discharged—and the snowstorm will sweep you up like a street sweeper with his filthy sweepin broom. Friggin-frigged-frig, we started thinkin. And Yakov declares: Whatever it takes, but our beloved *valenki* we should remove from the ward, we got attached to them—even more so 'cuz they have galoshes. What do you mean?—I asked. I mean a side-warmer far away, when a Gypsy slyboots takes his sheepskin to the consignment store, when there's mud-slush—and we're on skis. I've grasped my comrade's reasonin at once and propose before official discharge, without any reparations, to take to our heels. And documents? What do you need these documents for, you won't get full by eatin papers, especially if they're fake. At least I have real ones, he says, but not my own, at the front I served as another Yakov, I blew away my exemption to him in backgammon.

For the sake of appearance, we've paged through the journal *Pig-Breedin and Youth* and we're sorta gettin ready for a stroll. The floor attendant squinted his eyes and understood: You're splittin? So we're kissin the communal *valenki* goodbye? Fine, take them, we'll still keep shirts on our backs, with one pair we won't get nowhere all the same. We bowed low, took our leave, and descended to the pit: Hey, orderly, orderly, give us some chlamyses, after all, how are we gonna reach our destination only in pajamas? And Ivan shakes out from his depot heap upon heap of garments: Dig in. How many kindhearted souls are scattered around our damp cellars! May you prosper, Uncle Vanechka, our male nurse, we are deeply in debt to your generosity. He esplained: Relatives bring new toilettes for the artists, and out of fear quite often don't ask for the worn ones. I selected then for myself a blue admiral's gala *galife*, I selected then a clerk's top hat with a tilt and a brick-colored Jewish *lapserdak* of cheviot wool. I believe I made a right choice; all three fabrics are durable, up until now they are my only outfit. What Alfeyev chose—I don't recall right now, and abhor makin things up. Perhaps he took the fashionable striped pants of antique moiré and a plaid jacket of thick zhorzhet. We got dressed, we got robed—So long, benefactor—and we bolted in a duet away from all these bandages, findin out beforehand information about the needed station: of the railroad, that is. Hop, don't stop, hop, don't stop, granny sowed the peas for crop; we gave it all we got, pullin our peaked caps down over our eyes like daredevils. But the storm's turbulence, You understand, also gave it all it got, roughin us up.

05

THE TRAPPER'S TALE OR
PICTURES FROM AN EXHIBITION

Yakov Ilyich Palamakhterov (by the way, here is his
Self-Portrait in Uniform; and yet, does it make sense
to duplicate such impressive canvases without having any perceptible talent for this and understanding beforehand that the visitor will only briefly look at the copy as at the
most boring detail here; therefore, a little later, getting more
and more lost and confusing reality with fantasy, he may declare once and for all: Yes, everything was exactly like that;
and, evaluating it from the side or in a mirror, he may remain
completely satisfied with his, no, not his, wait a moment, the
hero's, of course, the hero's actions and features; to duplicate
self-portraits in uniforms—I beg your pardon!) and so, Yakov
Ilyich Palamakhterov tried not to attract attention. In vain. It
would be difficult to imagine a man who, thanks to his lack of
talent for mimicry, would less resemble the Brazilian hunting
spider or humpbacked Patagonian crickets—cf. Carus Sterne,
Evolution of the World, Werden und Vergehen, translated from
the German, vol. 3, World Association Publishers, Moscow, 22
Bolshaya Nikitskaya, printed by I. N. Kushnerov and Company,
Pimenov Street, entrance from the courtyard; the courtyard is not

paved; mud is all over. From the carriage that had arrived, two printers in aprons, soiled with God only knows what, push paper rolls directly into the puddle. The splashes created by the fallen rolls greatly amuse the workers. Having been splattered, one after another the bales keep rolling along the courtyard, getting wrapped into a finger-thick layer of loamy slush. Noticing the mischief and ruination from the third-story window, above the arch, St. Petersburg typesetter Nikodim Yermolaich Palamakhterov, great-grandfather of Yakov Ilyich, dispatched specially to Moscow on business of the book publishing company Enlightenment, located on the Nevsky, opens the window and curses the lads at the top of his lungs. In front of us stands a dandyish, slightly too elegant subject who was able to change his travel clothes into the apparel appropriate for a visitor (he is wearing a fashionable wool combo and a fashionable, but not excessively so, cravat) and who dropped in this morning to see his old acquaintance and colleague, employed here at Kushnerov's, and who is not in his office now—he went out, but will be right back, will just give the order to start in two colors, will collect the proofs and ask for the samovar to be brought in; good point, after all, *mein Hertz*, one can not keep gulping only Entre-Deux-Mers. Having heard above their heads the thunderous words of the visiting Zeus, the printers, whom we left below, attempt to drop all the paper cargo in a different place, which they consider dry, soiling themselves and the rolls even more than before; at the same time the movements of the printers are extremely chaotic and force one to think about the newly discovered apparatus of Monsieur Lumière, who acquired the patent last year and—according to rumors—already received a pretty centime for his invention, named by someone's brilliant mind a cinematograph. Attracted by the noise, the constable, a good friend of the typesetter from Moscow, and, in a way, also of the one from the capital, enters the courtyard from the street. Displaying his yellow aiguillettes, rattling with his spurs, and huffing under his mustache, he ascends the back stairs, unfortunately, quite greasy; in boots, wider than tall, but a fantastic cardplayer, skirt-chaser, not a complete fool in matters of drinking, with a saber—and altogether a great chap. Bah, Ksenofont Ardalyonych—seeing him filling the door, our visitor exclaims a greeting—it has been ages! Much, much water flowed by, Nikodim Yermolaich, Ksenofont Ardalyonych replies, advancing with his hands stretched out for an embrace. What brings You here? And since Nikodim Yermolaich sits down on one, hence Ksenofont Ardalyonych sits down on the other stylish Viennese mahogany chair, which, purchased by the company for nine and a half rubles in assignations, mercilessly cracks during this cruel ordeal, and the continuing inseparability of its parts for a moment appears to the zealous enlightener quite problematic. However, the alarm turns out to be false and the maker-up, relieved, releases a stupendous cloud of smoke that gives Ksenofont Ardalyonych a reason to show interest in what club his friend is registered right now, and also in the type of the tobacco smoked by Nikodim Yermolaich: Do You prefer Havanas? It turns out that for the last three years Nikodim Yermolaich has had an honor to be a member of the Jockey Club, and it is a rare week that he is not at the hippodrome. And as far as the tobacco is concerned—Yes, You guessed, the same, manufactured in Bremen.

Super-pleasant, not only the extraordinary lightness but also *ambré*, and whatever You would wish for. And look how convenient, everything's already precut. Most obliged, but we're still puffing the Asmolov smokes like before. Ah, excuse my straightforwardness, You disregard them in vain, after all, You know, Ptolomey Dorofeich himself gives them praise. Really? You must be kidding! Why would I be kidding, my dearest Ksenofont Ardalyonych? I and Ptolomey Dorofeich are like You and I now—namely, he is a liberal of the most unusual disposition, even though, supposedly, a Mason and, as they say, not the last figurant in the lodge. What? To lie, Ksenofont Ardalyonych, I do not have reasons—I sell it for as much as I bought it, and as far as the Havanas, do not even bother doubting, I personally offered him a light more than once. How come, do You attend his *jour fixes*? I am not an amateur of unreasonable modesty, the man from Petersburg answered with this spontaneous dignity that nowadays cannot be found not only in unimportant but also in very important individuals, I do not hold it as my principle. Not only *jour fixes*, he continued, aim higher; I am an insider even at his benefits. From there they went more briskly. Beyond the windows, the signs of the major prospects sped by; on the Palace Square, splashing with the slush the portly policeman from toes to head, the charabanc of chatter turned and, having flashed with its spokes, shot out onto the Nevsky—it sped by the salons and restaurants, by mirrored shop windows and façades worth millions. They chatted about the new Buhre clock and about African Boers, they agreed that the former ticks too loudly and the latter, even though boorish bandits, are quite bold—and do not judge so you will not be judged. At the same time they recalled the trial and judgment of the robbers of the Swiss bank and the recent major robbery of the Colorado train, and Ksenofont Ardalyonych did not fail to stick a pin into the Americans: Eh, what bashi-bazouks, he complained. As soon as they started talking about bashi-bazouks proper who, during the last campaign, seized about a hundred of our blunderbusses, bazookas, and other muzzle-loaders, and in a barbaric way harquebussed the captured cuirassiers and cavalier guards; as soon as they touched upon the sad topic of the dozen unfortunate quartermasters and orderlies from the uhlan and artillery ranks that were taken hostage and later drowned on the captured French felucca sailing under an Italian flag and blown up near Balaklava by a Turkish torpedo; as soon as they had mentioned all this, when, burdened by a stack of galley proofs, the resident head maker-up finally entered the office. On the man who came in, besides the unclean lace-ups from Ehrlich, the untidy appearance of which only affirms the business acumen of their owner, the reader discovers pinstripe pants and a frock coat. Nikodim Yermolaich, why are You—he barks out straight from the threshold and with a slight reproach, after only exchanging bows with the constable—why are You screaming like a Jericho trumpet; it can be heard as far as the typesetting hall. Have mercy, Ignaty Varfolomeich—the enlightener excuses himself—but should they be allowed to bathe in puddles such first-rate paper? Be so kind, take a look. All three—Ksenofont Ardalyonych, Nikodim Yermolaich, and Ignaty Varfolomeich—approach the window. Yessiree, *bellevue*, what else is there to say—the guardian of order concludes, having glanced at what is going on in

the courtyard—and yet, paving would do no harm. But how—
the typographer complains—who would give us money for
such trifles, under the present circumstances? Well, allow me
to express my curiosity, dear sir, what displeases You in our
circumstances; moreover, what are You publishing here—
pointing to the proofs, the police official continues his interro-
gation—proclamations? Give me a break, brother—the dis-
heartened maker-up comes up with a rebuke, handing his
interlocutor one of the printed sheets. Having scanned several
lines, the uniform of the heavenly color falls into unfeigned
agitation: Wow, just listen, gentlemen, what kind of appetizing
disguise has been observed in a certain Brazilian hunting spider, living on oranges! Brazilian? Nikodim Yermolaich asks
with curiosity so genuine that one would think he spent his
entire life on this subject. Its cephalothorax, Ksenofont Ardalyonych quotes, turned transparent white, like paraffin,
while its porcelain-white abdomen sprouts seven fingerlike,
orange-colored growths, representing stamens of the orange
blossom. Hidden under this magical attire, the constable continues reading, the spider successfully performs its deadly
deeds. Just think, my friends, what a rascal! Shocking, the
guest from the Neva anxiously agrees, I am at a loss for
words. And also note, Ksenofont Ardalyonych widens the ex-
cursus, that among the humpbacked crickets we find several
species that to an illusion resemble the curved-back thorns
growing on the branches of *Leguminosae* inhabited by them.
And the bird's eye? The host's question is so unexpected and
seems so contradictory to the general tone of the conversation
that Ksenofont Ardalyonych and Nikodim Yermolaich are

startled, as if someone suddenly fired a montechristo. Do You know, Ignaty Varfolomeich orated in the meantime, are You aware, esteemed gentlemen, what the bird's eye is? I know better what a bread pie is, ruffled up like a sparrow, the visiting polygraphist rushes forward with a pun. Well, should we not assume, the constable dares to enter the conversation, that the bird's eye, speaking, of course, roughly, is nothing else but the eye, permit me to say, of a bird, even if quite small. Fiddlesticks, Ignaty Varfolomeich, a bilious and highly egotistic person altogether, condescendingly replies; the name of the bird's eye, the typesetter triumphantly announces, is given to the kind of birch burl, which is so rare, and for this reason also expensive, that the doors made of it in the train cars of His Imperial Majesty are priced at one hundred seventy rubles each. Ksenofont Ardalyonych and Nikodim Yermolaich were literally thrown off their positions. They got confused to such a degree that for a moment became Ksenofont Yermolaich and Nikodim Ardalyonych: The mentioned number mightily mesmerizes the opponents of Ignaty Varfolomeich. And God only knows how long their confusion would have lasted if the porter Avdey, a sleepy peasant with a pitch-black beard reaching up to his dull and birdlike tiny eyes and with a similarly dull metal badge, did not come to say to the master that they should not be angry—the samovar completely broke and that is why there will be no tea, but, say, if needed, there is plenty of fresh beer, brought on a pledge from the cabbie, one should only procure a deed of purchase, and if in addition to beer they had wished to have some singing girls, they should send a courier to the Yar right away. Eh, brother, You are, methinks, not a total oaf, the policeman addresses the sentinel—and soon the table cannot be recognized. The prints and typesets are gone. In their place stand three mugs with beer, being filled, in keeping with their depletion, from a medium-size barrel that, with obvious importance, towers above the modest, but not lacking in refinement, selection of dishes: oysters; some anchovies; about a pound and a half of unpressed caviar; sturgeon's spine—not tzimmes but also not to be called bad; and about three dozen lobsters. The Gypsies are late. Waiting for them, the companions arranged a game of lotto, and none else but Ksenofont Ardalyonych shouts out the numbers. Seventy-seven, he shouts out. A match made in heaven, rhymes Palamakhterov, even though he has no match. Forty-two! We have that too, the man from Petersburg assures, although again his numbers do not correspond. Deception of Nikodim Yermolaich is as petty as it is obvious, and as outsiders we are quite embarrassed for him; but the pretending of Yakov Ilyich stands out black on white. Possessing from his birth the enchanting gift of artistic contemplation, but being both shy and frail, now and then he tried not to attract attention to the fact that he was the one whom he, naturally, simply was not able not to be, since he possessed what he possessed. For that reason, probably, Yakov Ilyich's attempts turned into complete blunders and consequently led not to the desirable but to undesirable results, again and again drawing to the gifted youngster uninterrupted, although not always favorable attention of the crowd. Do you remember how once, long ago, he let his mind wander, and a gust of the April chiller did not wait with ripping off the skullcap from his proudly carried head? It is really not important that the street, as ill luck would have it, teeming with concerned well-wishers, kept admonishing the hero, warning: Pick it up, you will catch a cold! Ostentatiously ignoring the shouts, taking care not to look back, and arrogantly not stopping but turning the pedals forward and—cynically and flippantly chirring with the spokes, the chain, and the cog of free wheel—backward, attempting to present everything as if he had nothing to do with it, he continued riding, the way he definitely wanted it to be seen through the eyes of the side spectator, with melancholic detachment. But, you know, a certain superfluous stooping that unexpectedly appeared for an instant in the entire subtle look of the courier (exactly like his great-grandfather, his grandfather used to say), diminished, even nullified his efforts to make his bodily movements carefree, froze them, made them childishly angular and exposed the daydreaming errand boy, with his feeble straight-haired head, to the curses of the mob: Scatterbrain, dimwit—the street carped and hooted. And if it were, let us suppose, not simply a slouching, chirring courier but a real humpbacked cricket from Patagonia, then, with such a mediocre ability not to attract attention, it would have been immediately pecked apart. But, fortunately, it was precisely a courier—a messenger-thinker, a painter-runner, an artist-carrier, and the nagging feeling that everything in our inexplicable *here* takes place and exists only supposedly did not leave him that evening even for a moment. That is how, either absentmindedly looking through the window or paging in the diffused light of a smoldering lamp through Carus Sterne—once respectable and solid, but now thinned, reduced by smoking and bodily urges, and yet even now adequately representing the sole volume of this modest home library—Yakov Ilyich Palamakhterov, the incorruptible witness and whipper-in of his practical and unforgiving time, philosophized and speculated.

ACCORDIN TO ILYA PETRIKEICH

06

With what does the station's waitin room wallop us tactlessly on the nose? Don't consider it a complaint, but in its mass the public stinks like a wet and homeless dog. Our armpits started hurtin from ice-covered roads, migraine blurred our eyes. Due to fatigue, we visit a railroad drinkin hole—we're takin medicine. I asked Alfeyev, where are you goin now? He considers: Mother Russia is huge, playful, and she barks like a she-wolf in the fog, and we, like flies, hop on the top of her, and she bites us out one after another as we hop, and it's impossible to figure out where it would be best to jump off, halloo, ever. True, Yasha, halloo, in our radiant country we're all like a bone stuck in its throat, we're all debtors, we're all at fault. And my real mother, he said, perhaps died, and I'm lackin a permanent father 'cuz of alcoholism; I only heard he was called Ilya. Yasha, my dear, perhaps I am he, perhaps there happened some kids in a hurry, after all, life is also huge. I allow that, answered Ilyich, but if it's so, why did you completely abandon my mother, did not help the woman get her son on his feet, did not give him a vocational education; after all that, you are a rat for me and not dad.

And he got offended. Yakov Ilyich, I cheered him up, stop bein cross, perhaps I am no father of yours at all, calm down a bit, do not get too excited, do not. Excuse me, he says, I blew my top, perhaps you ain't my father. But it's possible, I am hangin on contrariwise, it's possible that precisely your father, who knows? Therefore, let me be not simply a father but a possible-father, I will be a possible-father to you. Be so, uttered Alfeyev, why should I care? In that case, I take the lad on his word, you could lend me, such an inexact dad of yours, money for a ticket without a reserved seat: Gimme an advance, I need to get to the Tower Junction, to a certain Joy Whatshername. Don't refuse the request, help the old man, ain't you his flesh and blood, perhaps? Yakov Ilyich sheds crocodile tears at the train station: Daddy, Ilyusha, prodigerant, you're gettin ready to see our mother, even if she's no longer among the livin, perhaps. I got confused: Why her exactly? 'Cuz, he says, she also worked at the station. And what about her last name, first name, and initials in general? Well, I don't give a darn about them initials, he screamed, whatever they might be, why are you goin on like a stranger of little faith? And he bought me a ticket to the Tower Junction. For farewell we hugged, smooched—so take care, we won't see each other, the huge she-wolf is spread far and wide. And he gave me substantial notes; I received them, crumpled them, stashed them in my *valenok*—and adieu. I am ridin on the train, broodin: You're a miserable wretch, Yakov Ilyich, an orphan, your father is a swindler, a rapscallion, he did not help your mother at all, and the latter was of easy virtue, and there is, very likely, hardly a spot to put a proof of purity on her, even if she ain't the one Whatshername. Those from the Tower

Junction, they are all nothin but fine broads—whether this one or the twelfth, but, anyway, I am goin to this one, 'cuz the twelfth I don't freakin need. That's what I was thinkin about my relatives, languishin in the pitiful car with no reserved seats, amidst all the others afflicted, like me, by poverty. And it was rockin on switches. Roll up your eyelids like a pant leg, bare your stump, too—so it is more spectacular—and scoot to the car with reserved seats: Your instrument's with you. Immediately start a melody and announce over the knockin and dancin of the wheels that you know no peace, and don't have any joy either—you suffered a misfortune. And after that esplain what happened. But don't be concerned about nourishment, don't beg for Christ's sake, don't moan and don't groan, and, speakin heart-to-heart, carry high the lofty name of the folk invalidual, since even the most horriblest of us is better than fowls of the air. And those who get emotional—they will loosen their purse strings on their own. So you begin the concert. I will stretch a spool of thread to the green lea's end, or I'll pound a telegram to my dearest friend. Here it is, the much-beloved Russian song; it flows and splashes all over the premises—and the journey is long. And from where, You'll inquire, do you, Ilya, have an acordeon, have you sold some manure, Your Lameness? No, I haven't sold any manure and such an extraordinary dough, to buy the music, I haven't ever held in my hands out of principle. But our real world does not befall us without such generous souls as our orderly. They brought to Uncle Vanya at the theater an artist from the outskirts, a victim of dangerous razors, in a tilted cap and with a gold tooth. And he was, apparently, such a passionate musician that even his *kirza* boots were like an acordeon. At the same time his three-row instrument was brought along with him. The male nurse credited the account on behalf of the poor, but, he used to say, the bandura appears to be of no use: Whenever I try to play, right away it becomes clear I don't know how: either my hands are shakin or my voice breaks up. But I, I kept promisin, I know how, just let me. They handed it over. How I pulled the bellows, how I worked out a fingerin on them pimples! Now play somethin ours, the orderly implores, yank away! Once the boozin started, I whipped chastushkas at a full swing. Crematorium they were tryin, homeless vagrant they were fryin (the management's so shrewd), they look in—and he is teasin: Close the door, my butt is freezin. Whoever was present there in the cellar broke into a crazy dance, and look, even Yakov Ilyich on his one and only makes a freak of himself. Uncle Vanya also bends his knees and I hear, as if in a heavenly swoon: I see, I see, you can, here's the hurdy-gurdy for you from my white shoulder.

■ □ ■

And in trains they simply could not stop praisin me. One courier even called me to his compartment: Let me pour you a drink. Ain't You disgusted hobnobbin with me? Phew, he laughs, I used to gobble from the common bowl with worse than you. And he pours. Why are You temptin me, citizen, what if I don't hold back? Be so kind, go ahead. And he's completely bare, like a cantaloupe. I gulped. And he goes: At a train station there sat a soldier, a rake and dandy, brother-in-arms, just a lieutenant by rankin order, but a field marshal of female charms. I am a brainy bayan player, I made up a melody for him on the fly, in two-fourths. A certain madam entered the station, and she was serious, graceful, and neat; lieutenant quickly stood at attention and dropped his breeches straight at her feet. And a chorus. And I, too, said my travelin companion, was a lieutenant, like in the song. I wore cartridge belts and a mustache, but due to my manners and my rank, I was registered as a deputy. But not of some railroad female charms, no, in my license I was registered as a deputy inspector of all cast-iron roads. And he pours me, just imagine, Armenian delight. You must have lost Your mind, to waste three stars on a person with no passport. And he only sparkles with his buttons. And for that reason, he admits, the railroad destiny is dear to me, I got used to it, I'm ashamed to say, I love, excuse me, scrambled eggs and tearin at full speed in an express rushin on. And where do you think I am goin right now? Don't be angry, I answered, I have no clue about Your travel plans, so far I am not buyin Your tickets. So far others are buyin tickets for Ilya. Do you think that I planned to visit for a while my brother in Kazan?— the lieutenant kept questionin. Who knows what You do, I personally would gladly go to visit my brother out of the blue, and then enjoy yourself as much as you like, eat-drink-sleep. If you get bored, you can call to a get-together the neyborly Musia or you can wander with a dragnet for a while. You wander like that, You know, up to your waist in water, and the slimy clay keeps squeezin like leeches between your toes, it even curls. I get your drift, the inspector nods; frankly, my own brother is a drunk. What can I say, deputy, a brother—a brother is there, but he doesn't send me lately any invitations, and what's goin on with him, I have no clue: Did he get married, is he sick, or is he clinkin with his irons somewhere? No need to guess, he answered, obviously with them. But, to be honest, lieutenant, I don't recall that he scribbled to me particularly often; no, not often did he scribble to me, even to express it better—he never wrote to me at all. In irons you won't do much writin, the lieutenant kept noddin, in the environs of Kandalaksha. Yes, and, You see, it's unlikely that I would put my head on a choppin block for You to prove that this brother exists anywhere at all; I suspect that he's not present in my inventory, regrettably—neither in Kazan and Ryazan, nor in Syzran. Well, then, he says, allow me, I will pour you for that again. And both of us took a swig. And the train speeds on with widely open orbs, cuts the young night like a sharp speed skate, shines into a distance somewhere with a pair of manul's eyes. In the scraps of the same night dozes, quietly snoozin, snuggled like a needle in a haystack, the transit passenger after surgery, like I, and to him the train seems to have a completely unearthly destination. Woe is me, old chap, the inspector sighed, in Syzran my relatives don't live right now, in contrast, in Millerovo, please—in Millerovo there's a full *assorti*; incidently, my godsister passed away there not long ago. And he introduces himself: Yemelyan Zhizhirella. Holy crap, I declared. And immediately embraced him, fatso, and he me, a humble stick. And we drained one for *Bruderschaft.* So why didn't you write to me, I reproached, you could've at least dropped me a postcard; and you dare to call yourself a onewomber. Don't get mad so quickly, he esplained, I had no time to write letters in the environs of Kandalaksha, in the slammer, better tell me, why do you forget your relatives:

For example, durin the wake in Millerovo I don't recall seein you at all, hadn't you received the news? As far as receivin is concerned, I did receive it, by hand delivery. Right away, I grab my cap, catch the droshky—and to the station. I run up to a formidable one with a saber: What's where here? He points out. And the saber has a little wheel at the bottom, to drag it more smoothly. Miss, be so kind, a ticket with a reserved seat to Millerovo. A saber like that is stronger than a bullet, 'cuz sooner or later the lead will get flattened, but from the steel you won't wiggle out at any price, from this here steel. At the platform— high culture: spittoons and a kiosk. Eighteen minutes. And uncertainty seized me. When I arrive—there will be no end to gossip, they'll imagine, most likely, who knows what. They have no clue, my skinflint kinsfolk, that not everybody is necessarily a cheapskate. Ilya does not need what's someone else's, he doesn't even have what's his own, but try and esplain. You can choke on your wake, I won't go. I am standin. Here the conductor sounds the boardin, there the wagon usher curses, and over there an old lady knocks like a moth against a window glass: Dimka, her grandson, be so kind to notice, is departin to visit his uncle in Uglich. Watch out, my urchin, don't go walkin in the heat without mittens. You yourself, skinny worm, keep both eyes open, otherwise someone may prematurely shake off your dust. Well, old man, I address the chief, are we doin the departure? And why are You intrested?—he pulled his railroad cap on his brow. I answer that for me it doesn't really matter, that I would like to ask about somethin else, and the departure itself doesn't bother me from any side, that—who cares about departure, go on, depart. About what else?—he teases. Have

You ever been present at trottin competitions? It's not the right word—present, I loitered there, I used to lose big sums on wagers. So You must remember how the hippodrome was burnin and the sparks were flyin, right? How could I not remember, they kept flyin, at first there were even plans to cancel the heat. There were plans, but the deal fizzled off—and the horses started traversin. From the very start, I remember, Polykleitus, the black three-year-old from Polytechnician and Kleptomania, jumped forward, but the mare Sour Cream reached the second turn first, and Polykleitus dropped to the third, and who was ridin him at the moment—my memory broke the loop. Well, if it broke then it broke, said the railman, but we better finish now with them horses, 'cuz to interrupt the departure, bein elderly, does not become You. You're puttin on much air, old man, why don't You, instead of ringin the bell, quickly deal us a hand? Right then, the saber rolls in: What's up? Well, this—the departee proposes to deal a hand. Well, delay won't make it rusty, it's not a little wheel, we only need to procure unmarked cards. Just wait with the cards, he's simply tryin to interrupt the departure. Have mercy, the gard flew into a rage; this is simply espionage of some kind. Don't chastise, it won't happen again, You understand, Your bell brought past thoughts to my mind, one was hangin at the races before the fire—like two peas in a pod. It clinked and clanked—and started rollin irrepressibly. In those twisted years, I had with me, even though personally I don't believe it today, a commendable suitcase of crocodile leather. By the way, why twisted? Years like years, not more twisted than the others. A suitcase of crocodile leather, I repeat, with locks, in those years like years, I, Dzyndzyrella, dare to claim, did have. I grab it—and take to my heels. And it's lashin—hard to describe. As we know, both the train and the rain were goin—one to Millerovo, the other all day. Dear bro, Yemelyan declares, how great it is to ride at full speed together to visit you in Kazan; after all, we haven't seen each other for so long. Wait a minute, I'm gettin anxious, and did you send me a postalgram? Why do you ask, straight from the road. So now I am runnin along the embarcadero, I catch up with the train car, but to jump in, due to the lack of conviction, I'm afraid. Polishin floors in all possible places in those years like years, I carried in my suitcase waxes, rags, rubbed felt, and brushes of pig bristle. My train usher with signal flags in cases screams his lungs out from the gangway: Let go, or You'll suddenly plunge and make a fool of Yourself, like many others did. Linen mistress, don't mock the passenger misfortune, go plunge Yourself. And to Yemelyan I said that, halloo—his dispatch will not catch up with me and that most likely he's hurryin to Kazan in vain—I will not run out. While to You, Sidor Fomich, I am writin approximately what follows. One day some folk come to the ferryman, and he's sleepin soundly like a baby. Yes, this I understand, this is a riddle, 'cuz it's a riddle and not simply a peasant true story. Only I don't understand to which ferryman: We have two ferrymen on the Itil. That one makes money on that side, this one—on the contrary—on this one. The first, Yeryoma nicknamed Cad; the second, in contrast, Foma, and without any nickname. He's called respectfully by his last name, so why make a fuss, don't you think? Doom—that's the last name of our boatman. And let's suppose they come exactly to him: There's work. He woke up—what kind of work? Why

are you full of yourself for no reason, they say, as if besides fer-
ryin you had a clue about some other trade? I won't allow anyone to lecture me, noted Foma, you better lay out the fact. And
the deputy flew into a rage, stomps his feet, as if I was guilty;
even I, the orphan, never met myself in Kazan, to tell the truth.
Well, so where am I rushin now, the inspector shouts, tell me.
Deputy, I draw a blank about your intricate itineraries, but if
you have in your hands your travel document, don't consider
this disrespectful and look at it—it's stated there. To be endlessly in trouble is Ilya Dzhynzhirela's lot. Plunge Yourself, my
train usher heard my words. I said it to him rashly—and
plunged myself. What a mess, pal, I plunged, fell like a sack
under the wheels, and my bare footsie got sliced off like with a
sickle. I see—someone familiar with a blade flies down from
the heavenly rafters to help. Six-winged serafim, gardian, swing
your *yatagan* once, chop off the whole me from these here
places: I'm hurtin a lot, clumsy me. And the chief arrived in
time to scold. For You it's nothin, he got envious, You've secured a sanatorium for Yourself, but people will get a repri-
mand on Your account. Don't curse, after all, weather's wet, so
one slips. A thought: Apparently the expedition failed, crashed,
the last rites are waitin for Ilya. And I'm in trouble again,
when, smug, I advise the lieutenant to look at his ticket. You're
a boob, he cuts me off, a deputy due to his title is not obliged to
buy tickets, and even when he buys sometimes, he buys a special one to any destination, and whether you look at that ticket
or not, everythin's a fog, and whether its presenter is goin here
or there, nobody understands, only the ticket with the reserved
seat flutters in the wind and a coupon for obtainin bedsheets

rustles. Yep, you sure didn't luck out, my countryman, but apparently not always and not everywhere deputies have advantages. It turns out that non-deputies sometimes know better where their road leads. Take me for example—to Orina, gimme her here and now, I'm holdin my course to her.

NOTES OF A HUNTER

NOTE X

OVER THE FIRST POWDERED SNOW

The recipes of Bordeaux Gypsy women
Who are pressing deux côtes and châteaux
While the street-organs' waltzes are streaming
The distilling plant does not know.
But inspectors know and adore—
For that reason, they never feel blue—
The sacred strength of Cahors,
With their thick maroon bottom goo.
Of this drink, first rejected, then stolen,
In embroidered bags of their own,
Many jugs and bottles they're hauling
Right over the first powdered snow.
They bring many tasty provisions:
Canned goods and sausage, and cheese.
My inspectors, my rustlers, envision
That these endless feasts never cease!

But there brightly sparked as before—
'Cause the utter darkness moved far—
In the whitened grave of the shores
Negru de Purcari red tar.
Though the curious hunter is saying:
Where do pheasants get fat around here?
Through the scraps of the dogs' furious baying
Sesame!—that's all we can hear.
Co-imbiber! The last gulp, my dear bloke,
Stash in your flabby cheek and hold there.
It's time. Whir in barrels' half chokes,
And in chokes, you whirlwind, whir-whir.

NOTE XI

CASTING A SPELL

May the Magpie be sick, may the Crow be sick too,
May the Dog be healthy and glad.
A cripple was walking around the world blue
And his crutches were splattered with blood.

His crutches walked over the snow's bluish crust
And the clouds were revealing God's face.
And while sand-covered Libya was choking in dust
The Netherlands held the ice-skating race.

The Wolf was taught by the mage hereabout,
So leaving his lair in the woods,
Just after the sunset, the Wolf would crawl out
And heal the Dog as he could.

May the Magpie be sick, may the Crow be sick too,
But thanks to Wolf's love, in its name,
From the black river Crow to the river Nerl blue
May the sick dogs be healthy and game.

And in their shabby coats, in the blue world, outbound,
Not concerned if it is night or day,
Valiant hunters, making magpie-like chirping sounds,
Chased the ermines from the copses away.

Village folks, but alert and rarely forgive.
May Magpie the Thief still be sick.
They've spied out the place where this fellow lives
And lifted, the rascals, his sticks.

They drank them away and that would be all,
But when winter unleashed ice and snow,
Between self and Wolf, when sleep takes its toll,
The Dog to the Wolf used to go.

The Magpie is sick and the Crow is sick too,
The blizzard for the cloud ride can't wait.
Village folks, mainly loners with nothing to do,
Glide on skates with hands on their waists.

And from the flat Brugge to the mountainous Liopp,
Or to Bydogoshchi from as far as Bobrov,
Factory hunters, loudly shouting, "Hey, hop!"
Drink, enshaded by the snow-covered groves.

At last, our cripple a new shotgun obtained
And found other crutches somehow.
Though his empty pant leg may still feel the pain
He's a factory hunter right now.

NOTE XII

PHILOSOPHICAL

Confusion—it's an inevitable fault
Of clueless philosophers, passions, ages . . .
What kind of luck made me such a dolt
That I could not make sense of them all
Or rather could, but less and less, in stages?

When ways of knowledge came to be too dreary,
And city life, unsettling, hard to follow,
First, I became a hunter—ordinary,
But later turned into a binger—merry,
With gaze both enlightened and quite hollow.

I like all months, December up to March,
Plus April, May and June, July and August,

And Virgo always warms my lonely heart,
And Brumaires, whose rosy garb, so smart,
Brings to my mind the famous bird named Argus.

Now chilly winter in my garden stands
Like emptiness forgotten in a glass.
The glass, forgotten, on the table stands.
The table, forgotten, in the garden stands,
Forgotten on the winter's white tray-grass.

Dear maestro, on the stovepipe wail
Something Christmasy—and make it andante.
Cold, with icicles on its lip, today,
Winter stands here, like a thing per se,
Noticing, really, neither Kant nor canto.

NOTE XIII

VALDAY DREAM

Just before the stars unfold
From the smoke I'm crying.
The wolf's tail—be cold, be cold,
The dog's—warmed by fire.
By the hearth, deep in his lair,
Cat snores, as he dozes.
And his boot, in disrepair,
Sticking nail exposes.

And he dreams, this Valday Cat,
Purring-Puss, while snoozing:
On the bridge sit wolves all set,
Therefore, he is musing:
If I were a dog, I'd love
The Wolf who's so lonely,
And if I were a wolf I'd howl
After the Dog only.
From a window I'll look out
Or glance from another—
A snow-dusted pine stands proud
In the glade snow-smothered.
Witches chat of times of old
By the graveyard's pyre.
Holy tail—be cold, be cold,
Devil's—warmed by fire.
And completely bluish-gray
Is mica-covered Volga.
The Dog's riding in a sleigh,
Prodding the Wolf onward.

NOTE XIV

FISHING UNDER ICE

Neither the sturgeon fish live in this river
Nor the Chauliodus fish in a shoal.
So why do I, like an anglerfish, shiver,
With my mouth open by the ice hole?

Fellow, limp home and better be gone!
The time for playing has passed.
And the curtain of tattered dawn
Onto Europe concealed *wasisdas*.

Listen, you Binger, scram or you'll lose!—
I held myself in a firm rein.
Better swallow some rotgut, infused
Half and half with the tears of grain.

Whom is God guiding down over here,
With a lamp, on ice skates, half bent?
Well, Aladdin Bartrutdinov is near,
By Allah the Tatar is sent.

Eh you, humpback, you are no angel,
Go to hell, you blasted slime!
What's your lamp for, you alien stranger,
During this somnolent time?

Yakshi, you fish bait, did you catch your fill?
Hunchbacked pony, skedaddle, rock!
You are a disease, you make the soul ill,
Bartrutdinov's been a hundred years *yok*.

He fell through the ice while skating at dusk,
And only surfaced after a year.
In his pocket dominoes as well as a flask,
And chewed off by fish lips and ears.

I forgot the date he came back afloat.
Pyotr and Pavel found him at large.
They finished the flask, then played whack the goat,
And informed the folks in charge.

He took off. Ah, what a deceiver.
And he used to be a loner first class.
Neither the chimaera fish live in this river,
Nor the fish, for instance, hump bass.

NOTE XV

ARCHIVAL

Oh, I will feel so stuffy
Filling the dusty shelves
Of the archival stacks.
Eh, I'll be bored to death.
One day and out of breath
An archivist will come.
He'll start to excavate me,
My doodles he'll decipher,
And dig up in old files
A ticket to Kunstkammer,
A petal from some summer,
And 'mid the other notes,
This one he'll find, indeed,

And 'bout himself he'll read.
Ha ha, he'll laugh, ha ha,
All through the archive. Rude,
Unpleasant, and irate,
A hunter out of date
And yet astute and shrewd.
And how excited he'll be
With what he had found out.
And he will be, just be,
While I'll be gone, away,
Each week and every day.
But how eternal I'll be—
No present and no past,
Away from taking chances,
In crowded circumstances,
And suffocating dust.

NOTE XVI

A VERSE ABOUT A BEAUTIFUL LONESOME BABE

Over the coffeepot the steam waves
Like a capitulation flag from a trench.
Brew me some coffee, my lovely wench,
Because this draft is worthy of raves.

Keep waving, broadcast the news from Brazil,
This aroma is praised all around,
With chicory it can always be found,
Even when from Brazil there is nil.

By fate we're so often rebuked
That chicory we love like the Erzia,
But aren't we somebody's ersatz
And isn't our goose fully cooked?

For that reason, though I know in my soul
That all beauties are easy to flatter,
I declare that it does not matter
Who is mending my coat and my shawl.

Notwithstanding that no one can sew
Out of sweet talk fur coats, I'll opine:
Oh, my lonesome babe, you're so fine,
And your mug's not to drink from, you know.

So I sharpen my penknife, I do:
Since the day of your angel is near,
Having nothing to give you, my dear,
A boar's hide I will scrape just for you.

Brew me now, at the threshold of dusk,
In midevening, at pre-winter's boding,
Pseudo-coffee that a quasimodic
False matchmaker had kindly loaned us.

NOTE XVII

TO THE UNKNOWN PAINTER

Buddy! Like a Serb can't make
A Croatian *chisma* fit,
And our own memorial wake
Or the cabbage soup's high price
Often bore us quite a bit,
The same way this harsh advice
Painters like you really need.
Either you mixed up the features
And impressions of the past
Or the Gorodnishche's picture
Without glasses you recast.
Hence the hunters you arranged
In old-fashioned cowls and clothes
Seem to me no less than strange,
Even more, in panty hose.
And the deal would not have ended
With success, as we would like,
If the hunt we had attended
Not with guns but with a pike.
On which, well seen from this angle,
Right behind the hunter's back,
Hangs the image of a tangled
Wolf-dog, waving like a flag.
On the things' established order
You applied a fancy veil:

Hunting bags with gold embroidered
Are at odds with our trails.
And from crashbaret three lookers
Seem too pretty and too neat,
When, unhurried, they are cooking
A plump piglet on the spit.
And this dolce vita, master,
Shaded by the roofs askew,
Which you tried so hard to muster
With your brush, palette, and luster,
It is gone, wrapped in weeds' cluster.
But crows are the same—so shoo!
Nonetheless—what a great picture,
Look around you once or twice,
And admire those bewitching
Brews of sky, and snow, and ice.
In the time of twilight pealing,
The ice skaters' puppy squealing
Can be heard from far beyond—
On the river and the ponds.
If I were a merchant mogul
Your oil painting I would buy,
Hang it o'er my cot to ogle,
And, forgetting all, I'd lie.
But because I am a tippler,
I will buy me some green wine
And I'll see the same, but triple
When the drink starts working fine.
Here's my fatherland: Though glorious,

It cares not for poor folks' strife,
But how lovely's the notorious
Vanity of our life.

NOTE XVIII

TRANSFIGURATION OF
NIKOLAY HELPEROV
(A JUNKMAN'S STORY)

There's a reason for the vagrants to attest:
Sweet agarics on the Volga are the best.
But some people just surprise us, when they muse:
Vodka is the worst of poisons, of no use.
By this judgment, pardon us, we're not impressed,
We, the junk folk, life without it cannot see.
True, sometimes we *imbibamus* in excess,
But in turn how much transfigured we may be.
Once from house to house we wandered-tramped,
Asking people: Help your guests, for goodness sake,
Bring outside your garbage pile, clean your dump:
Metal, glass, and even bones we gladly take.
Dusk has fallen. And of course—a snowing fest.
Freaking bitch, don't you growl and don't you bark!
We set out to see the tailor, get some rest,
Helper Kolya schlepped with us, and it was dark.
Kolya Helperov, I meant to say, who was old,
Broken up, a guy with badly twisted legs.

We are pilgrims—he's one far above us all,
We are cripples—he's one far above the rest.
Our Kolya-Nikolay owns simply nil,
Only crutches. And it snows, it really snows.
Weather sucks. The bells clamor on the hill,
And to find a place for slumber fly the daws.
They fly straight across the river, scalawags,
To the town of thieves and beggars for a nap.
While we're lugging on a hand sleigh garbage bags—
Three archangels of recycling the old scrap.
Ah, the time of dog and wolf I love so much:
It's like kindness mixed with sadness, isn't it?
I will also have a smoke; hold the match!
So, we're schlepping to the tailor, I repeat.
Sewing clothing for the shelter of the blind,
Our tailor's sitting there by candlelight.
Open up, dear fellow creature, be so kind,
Welcome us—exhausted merchants—for the night.
We were sitting by the window, feeling fine,
Night was turning gray like pants too often washed.
I forget now, where we finally got the wine,
But remember—we got very soundly sloshed.
In the morning, we see: Kolya learned to fly!
Crutches—like a pair of wings he bore.
He had turned into a falcon, poor old guy.
Drank too much. And he simply was no more.

DISCORDS BEYOND THE ITIL

08

I have scooped up, keep on readin, the hooch of human passions, tasted the rot of dreadful, deceitful broads, and the poison almost choked me. The dusk lasted and the darkness continued, and at dawn opened, like a wound, the unquenchable drought for the clean, for the crystal-clear water. I used whatever I had for a belt and stepped, figurelatively speakin, into the deep, squirmin. What is happiness and what is unhappiness, my dear Pozhilykh? Don't pass, the answer ain't complicated: Happiness is when it is. But I don't complain; everythin will get milled over. We'll finish clinkin with our unsharpened skates, hurtin from oaken clubs, frolickin and dancin, and one day in the mornin we'll cast off to Bydogozhd. So many toasts will be drunk in our honor, so many tears will be spilled, so many collars will be ripped by our pals from each other's coats on the ninth day. Earlier, we were seein others off, sailin noisily in sloops, and now others will revel followin us in dories, while we will peacefully lie in the front one with our sole akimbo. Foma Doom himself on the occasion of such an event rekindled his past—grabbed the oars. He is rowin, for sure, but at the same time on the sly searches with his bare foot the pockets of my gala apparel. You're tryin in vain, my dear, they cleaned up all the creases before you, not even one bit of tobacco is left. No, don't take me wrong, I'm not complainin—there will be flour. I wandered a lot, worked and exosted myself, yet even more I twiddled my thumbs. I toughened and matured, got smooth and burnished, like a well-worn yoke. I turned into last year's old loaf, a callus and gristle, and wasn't I a fancy bun just last evenin? I'll turn around, fold my earflaps up, and look at myself hurryin in burlap along the speckled way—there I feel high, close to the Lordie, there I feel glorious. I'll feast my eyes. Who am I, they ask sometimes, and for whom? I'm a matchmaker and brother for someone, for someone a godfather, and occasionally a son-in-law, I guess, no more, no less. But sometimes—I am nobody for nobody, only for myself, and even then not entirely. Now a slicker and roisterer, I tumble into the burdock—tomorrow a marsh hawk, I'm hootin like an owl in the pine grove. But when I sleep myself sober I'm a prophet again. That's nothin, really, compared to the moment when once in a blue moon, I walk along the speckled path to do my sharpenin: I turned into a Sharpener, a craftsman of the unfamiliar suns. There, on the right side, burn the Fiery Stozhary—here, on the left, rises Krylobyl, the club-footed hunter. Behind me are the Nurses, in front—Orina-Foolina and her progeny Orion. I wandered a lot around the world's fringes and defined many constellations. There is a constellation of Lonesome Babe, only I cannot figure out which one; there are Lieutenants, Buoy Keepers, and Inspectors. There is a Bingin Hunter, a lively carouser in this world, a fine fellow—notorious for his unquenchable thirst and extraordinary boldness as far as and includin the Kimry model sluices. He's writin somethin, flippin the pages: Will You allow me to cite a few thoughts? Ain't it wrong, he claims, to pour this year's wine into an old barrel? It will tear apart all its seams, it will warp the thing, and, what's even worse, it will spill out. Good, good advice, nothin to argue about. The only thing—it doesn't concern us, he's not talkin about our destitute Beyond the Wolf, since how could we get hold of so much wine to fill at once the entire barrel—makes no difference whether new or secondhand—for what kind, allow me to express my doubts, of You know what? Much more useful is the other lesson there. It's senseless, he teaches, to place new patches on the ripped junk—unsightly. And in addition, why would You tear apart what is whole? Well, this—this is about us, this we understand. But, honestly, even that really is of no use; after all, is there any-thin new among these tatters of ours? And there was one more incident. A sower was, supposedly, sowin. It's not clear where—on the Fallows, on Lazarus Field, or by Granny's Cross. And this also happened: One beggar woman met the Wintry Man in the woods and from fright Kondraty caught her. Gradually, they found her. The raven pecked her eyes out, worms ate the mushrooms in her basket, and the pines stand around as they stood before, until they'll burn. So they placed on that clearin a memorial cross. And the sower threw one grain next to the road, dropped the second on rocky ground, the third into the thorns, and only the fourth he managed to plant more or less successfully. All told, a gyrfalcon grasped one grain, a kite the second, and a quail the third. And what did You think? Whether they want to or not, they need to take care of nourishment. However, the fourth grain managed to make it and produced, out of the blue, an immeasurable crop—a hundred grains. I read for a while the hunter's book and realized: Everythin will get milled over. Don't worry, the constellation Pozhilykh can be seen among us too. Lookin from below, You are positioned two elbows above the Wintry Man's star. You resemble a handful of fireflies. And he glows in the darkness like a large shiner, even though, upon verification, he's a squirt. The given warden as a person is of ordinary age, but as himself, he's visible, noticeable. Smallpox slightly changed his portrait, then—the hunt marked him with shot, the frost and wine burned his nose, and a rabid fox bit off his ear: We can understand that granny. I see—now the Wintry Man is drivin his spouse to perish; he could not take it anymore. My Sharpenhauers with Gury the gameslayer on the outskirts started smokin, they're talkin, and Ilya Dzynzyrella in a far-off work location told the elder sister: I desire your mussels, gimme as many as you can, salt and matches are present. Dusk's everywhere; evenin's everywhere; Itil's all over. But there, where the Wintry Man is squeakin with his carriage—fall descended from heavens, at my colleagues' place, in Gorodnishche—a snowstorm began, and on my Wolf River—orioles and woodpeckers. I do what the elder sister orders and step up to my knees into the wave. I stuff my shoulder bag to the gills and set a small fire. I can hear—the masters are buzzin in December at the foot of the hill. They are talkin mainly about Pyotr; the grinders ain't sure what's goin on with him. He, Yegor, returned then to the sitters on the spit and told them that after that dame there is nothin to break the clouds in his existens; he may as well hang himself. They started cheerin him up: You'll always have time to hang yourself, better let's chat. Well, if you wanna chat, let's chat, Pyotr, adamant, agreed right away. Do you know the village Overbrowears? Yes, I do, a sawmill is workin there, supposedly. Right, so let's wager a bet that you won't lift from there even one baluster, and even if you lift it, you'll be too sissy to choke on it, you won't have the guts, it's doubtful, let's say, you won't gag on it, you'll pass, you'll chicken out, etc. That's what the sitters told Pyotr on the spit, that's what they, the sitters, kept sayin to Fyodor, and Ilya is gettin ready for supper, he's fryin the mussels on the coals. The breeze has calmed down, the ripples on the water and on my soul have settled completely, and the nightingale in adder's tongue is spinnin cock-and-bull stories. Well, they're talkin about the sawmill and I about the factory. I heard a voice: Keep in mind that in the comin future they will establish a factory at the mouth of the stream Slush, and not of any kind, just so, but to make buttons. When they establish it, when it gets goin, and when it begins makin buttons, everybody will start walkin buttoned to the hilt. And they will need mother-of-pearl aplenty—just keep draggin it in. So they will open next to the factory a point, not of honin skates to a point but a collection point, and they'll start collectin mussels from the populace of the entire land 'cuz quite a lot of mother-of-pearl is hidin in them. And to the one who deposits more useful stuff than the others, the factory will present a dory. I'm tellin You as it is, I heard the voice: Don't be lazy, collect the treasures. I wandered a lot and ate many suppers, and how many mussels I laid bare, no one can count. I hid a mass of the empty folds, cleverly fashioned in the manner of beggars' palms, the priceless folds, dull at the bottom. I was hidin them openly, spreadin them on the ground 'cuz the thing lyin in plain sight is lyin there hidden better than anythin. Therefore, You, after learnin the secret, stay away, don't You debit my pearls, else You shall find You know what. Well, if You wanna turn them around in Your hands, go on, turn, I will not forbid You, but after You've turned them, put them back where You found them, otherwise it'll end up that *Carl stole from Clara a coral tiara.* I request this to be announced like an order, so they comply; after all, they're all chimney pots first-class. And they got into a habit of convertin them all into ashtrays. Enough, a certain day, You know, will come. The moment I notice that the barges with woodcutters float by to saw timber, I grab a sack as capacious and as intact as possible and scurry at a brisk clip around the beevaks of the bygone feasts. I collect them, deliver to the address, and the boat is mine. Not too shabby a dory, everybody will comment, Ilya had procured for himself, not just so-so. And what did You think, I will say, You assumed that I am a blockhead, a numskull? You hoped that the grinder has mush in his stockpot? No, enviers, no, freeloaders, I only look like a dude without all his marbles, only pretend to snuggle with manure. A bright future will begin for me with my personal dinghy. That's when we, passionate mushroom pickers, will get into a habit of goin after forest berries there, Beyond the Wolf. And even though I am invitin You cordially, there's tension about transportation. Nevertheless, I believe, someday we will get even to the other side; let's just work out a short delay. I repeat, get Yourself—hook or crook—some gummies, 'cuz to have the ankels stung by the nettles in the hollows is just a nuisance, but there are also vipers hidin in gullies. Yes, and grab a raincoat in case of unexpected rain. Be well, my gangly friend in a mackintosh and a cap, climb in, the stern has been longin after You. I already spread there some mint, lungwort, and hemlock so it would smell nice, to get rid of the unwanted odor. And we finally cast off, banterin. And more precisely, at the last moment You started whinin, refused to go—and I set out alone. I set out to gallivant in my first-rate hazel groves, bequeeted to me one fall by a certain old-timer. He bequeeted them, showed me, and before spring chose to join the dead. But the hazel groves are really tiptop, in each cluster there are more nuts than a homeless goat has, not to offend her, dingleberries under her tail. True, to my shame, afterward I had not visited this real estate of mine even once. What a tale, why would I not go there anymore in the co-op's dory? 'Cuz we had drunk the co-op's vessel away usin the co-op's method about twenty-five times. It's as simple as steamin turnips, but it allows us to launch all kinds of provisions or foodstuffs more than once. Every now and then, there is no money: No problem, it's their business, but there is a cat. Obviously, not ours, the grinders'; we don't need it; so far, mice don't munch on iron; the miller, You see, has a cat. And one of our loafers pretends to be a wandrin cripple and goes to the miller on the hill: What village do You have here? Don't take it amiss, he says, it's Malokulebyakovo. And I thought that it would be Mylomukomolovo. No, Mykomulolomovo is an old song, we were called Mykomulolomovo long ago. Hmm, and where is Milokurelemovo in this case? Malokulelemovo, quoth he, is in a completely different location, mallow we never kulelemed. And while they talk all this nonsense, our slickers with a sack keep their watch for the cat behind the barn. The miller calls on a foggy dawn his Siberian angora, wanders, thunderous, along the Itil, but the cat's far away. Get it together, dunderhead, the culprits will release it into good hands. And right away a new shift rolls up its sleeves. I believe the co-workers won't lemme down and will remove the mouser from the buyer in the same way. A similar brouhaha could be observed with the dory. I can't say now from whom we had pilfered it first, the event is too distant, and it's not really important. I'll only note that later we floated it many times and regularly and also always without fail to those who understood the deal. At the end, however, we failed, brought shame on ourselves; we passed it to one quite irresponsible. Havin finished the transaction, after the sunset, we appear like thieves under the cover of the night around the riverside dock, where, accordin to the forcast information, that fellow was plannin to keep our scow. We look—there's no flat-bottom boat, only a pile of splinters lies nearby. It becomes clear: Right when we were bargainin with the poor wretch, someone cleaned up his bathhouse. They took the basket, the scrubber, a sliver of soap, and the beaker. And in addition they pulled out the net from the stream 'cuz that bathhouse was near the stream. The wardens did it, no doubt about it. And when the buyer arrived home in his new purchase and discovered the loss, he started shakin all over. Why are you laughin?—asked some Cheremis folks that sat not far from there, beltin the grape—What's so funny? How can I not laugh, answered this Vasya—'cuz it was he. How can I not laugh, he answered; I saw among the damages of fate the single singular ray of light—the trap net full of holes—and I dreamed of becomin a fisherman, I wanted to buy a dory. And observe: Either the dory is *uke* and the net *e-e*, or the dory *e-e* and the net *uke*, got stolen. No, Micheas the Morasthite taught wrong that everyone setteth a net for his brother; here we have a different picture: You, brother, set a net and your bro absconds with it. And so Vasily findeth an ax and heweth our craft due to its uselessness, rejoicin in his heart. And this way we became boatless in our nunset years, we utterly lost our craft usin our co-op's method. So how can I, he says, not be laughin?

■ □ ■

And yet, Fomich, let's assume that You and I managed to get a rowboat. We prepared, got hold of the gummies, the basket, and the raincoat, and what is typical—I set off and You abstained. I started worryin: Did You catch the flu, are You sick? No, the health fits the norm, simply some work-related problems showed up—I'm in a hurry to get familiar with Your letter, so my mushrooms, unfortunately, will have to wait. Truth's on Your side, a bird in the hand is better than two in the bush, get familiar, generously raise my hopes. I pushed off with the usual—and like a harmless water strider started measurin the wide-open space with my jerks. The rowlocks are cryin exactly like lapwings, they're not oiled at all. Did You notice what weather we're havin? Pure delight, superior to the previous. It would be great to grab from You on this occasion a couple of smokes, and put the first between my teeth, the second behind my ear for later. Impossible beauty. The old pine forest is red; the woods are like a fox with burn marks; the Itil flows like a pearly honey, you can eat it with a spoon. And the water is translucent, like in the moonlight, and millions-gazillions of empties lie on the bottom, and you can read with ease any label stuck on them, as if thru the counter's glass. I could dive, gather the disowned vessels—and right away to Sloboda. Eh? Calm down, these are all silly dreams, it's enormously deep, and, in general, we're not divers. In contrast, for leeches it's accessible—they keep suckin. And where are the crucians, that is, the ruffs? I looked carefully—they were snoozin in the holes, in the shadow of the banks, under the tree roots, and Orina was swimmin above me, spreadin her thighs completely like a frog. She was swimmin on the surface like in a mirror, as if temptin, and her long hair was draggin like algae along her sides and spine, and her breasts—to be honest— were movin like a pair of large tenches among other fishes. From my distant nearby I could without any pangs of conscience get impressions from the woman, and I was inspectin her all, as long as I had enough air, and when I did not, I would come up, take a few breaths, and back. With her saucy figure she was teasin geese in Ilya on purpose, but I held my temper in check, not givin amnesty to my nerves, and proudly kept my patience—keep teasin, keep teasin, we, the orphans, don't need to get used to it, we can bear it. But keep in mind: When my cravins get too strong due to long prayers, I will force you, snub nose, in every possible way and then, a kinless worm, I will shamelessly warm up the stick of my flesh, I will ride you good and proper. And as for the mussels, they were also there, scattered all over. Some were just lyin simply scattered, reflectin the light, and the others were creepin along accurately, who knows where, and were leavin on the pliable, loose ground such tracks as if the crawlin Gorynych had made them, very thin. Matches and salt, You are hintin, did I have with me? Not entirely: Among the other special items, they were located in my clothes, and they, in turn, in scabiosas, in thick bushes. Before my maimin, and even later—up to that lonesome babe that stitched all my cylinders dead shot, so I wouldn't aimlessly poke with my hands in my pockets—preservin the customs of my ancestors, I kept all my possessions there. Nowadays, I pack my stuff partially in my bag and partially into an empty tied-up pant leg—comfort. They say that unhappiness leads to happiness, but mine surely didn't. That's it. What I had predicted for Orina in my mind, did happen. I visit her on the same date in July, You understand, on the twentieth accordin to the Old Style, it's Ilya's name day and her day off for overtime. No sense to sit inside— let's go and have some fun. Time—close to five. Its weak, gentle air was gettin cooler, but the frogs, what the heck, started croakin like insane, they sensed my mood. I had with me fourteen rubles in change; I collected them at the station in the mornin. Out of that, just under the platform I found about a ruble—our passenger is still a loser. And all in all, it's wonderful under the platform, cozy—you smoke, cough, and nobody gives a spit where you are and, perhaps, who. In contrast, thru the cracks between the boards you can be curious and observe everythin perfectly: For instance, some ladies for some reason don't wear undies at all. Well, so Orina took an advance a day earlier—have yourself a blast. There was, existed, in those tricky years like years, a joint—not a joint, a shop—not a shop, and properly speakin, a snack bar. It was located a stone's throw from the barracks, more than close; it was gapin with its window frames at the road.

We got supplies and found a quiet spot behind the dike, among the acacias, in the midst of lady's smocks. For Orya, accordin to not our custom, I spread down my jacket, and myself—simply like that. We had a bite: dried Azov sea roach, third quality— even now it stands in front of my eyes. We sang, chanted, and then I quoted her from memory a few racy adventures. And it was gettin overcast, the storm was approachin from the res- ervoir, and I started regrettin my ploy, 'cuz the croakers made us sick and tired—completely sick and tired with their loud chorus. I considered turnin the clouds back, but laziness over- whelmed me, I got sauced up and feeble. God be with it, I am thinkin, let the hidden water in the clouds thunder, perhaps it'll pass by. But no, it started pourin. It caught us on the meadow, by the swings. Everythin turned gloomy, started shakin, drip- pin. Let's run, she hurries. And drags me to the shore. An over- turned abandoned scow was lyin there on the pebbles upside down and a short slingshot supported its rim, makin it possible to get under. The matches got wet, but a flint stone and steel did not refuse—I set the punk on fire in a flash. Dry crumbly splinters and used mouthpieces from *papirosy*, and all kinds of flammable trifles I found in excess, so the fire started right away. The light wonderfully illuminated Orina, and it also lit Ilya up, and our shadows started crawlin along the coarse boat sides. Bugbear's walkin, full of life, carries seven slippers: for himself, for his wife, and a slipper for each nipper, I remember tellin her. The gusher scratches and scrapes the planks, but we are dry, we are talkin and restin on the old junk. You revealed to me your life stories, my friend says to me, so if you want— I will also tell you a few things.

PICTURES FROM AN EXHIBITION

09

A friend of the family, a courier clerk, whose ancestors, Sicilian negotiators, once arrived in Russia for
a shipment of tarantassi and, on their way back, got
stuck forever in the impassable mud somewhere between
Konotop and Syzran, and whose portrait shines by its absence
in the exposition, shows interest in our hero. When the latter,
in the words of the first, reaches the required level of respectability, the public servant advises the young man to follow in
his footsteps and through his protection makes it possible for
him to enroll in the courier institute. The fate of the artist had
been decided. His face, possessing features of refined sensual-
ity, attracted attention by its clear expression of character. Particularly during parades and reviews. Particularly equine ones.
In those moments, he would become twice as energetic and
proud. In contrast, the physiognomies of the remaining riders
were mediocre; the ears of many, seemingly in order to catch
the clatter of the hooves better, were hopelessly sticking out.
From the windows of the classroom every hour—a river cess-
pool, and often the enthusiastic youngster dares to sail on it in
a monstrous trough. How obtrusively paper and slime drag

after the blades of oars! Yanko is not afraid of the wind or waves; when he grows up, he will appear in the twilight of his life as a master cook in the cooking joint slippery from grease. Methodical stirring with a ladle and whirling of foul-smelling slop will suddenly vividly resemble the pictures from the carefree past, from the period of lonely boat races with himself—feverish and frail—when in the morning, the mugs of the neighboring buildings, yawning in the dirty-yellow hospital dankness of the outskirts' fogs, make you feel faint and when that—true, pockmarked, and rotten-toothed—girl behind the plywood partition, setting out to her defectological universities, snivels about her school-writing accessories that scattered all over the floor, and sings without a tune and without end: Rain, dear rain, please be done, I will go to Arestan—eleven years old, harelipped, conceived in a drunken stupor—and you, at the dawn of your deprived youth, are waking up, covered with peels and petals of whitewash dropping from the ceiling, you're waking up, trying to understand: Is it you or someone else waking up right there, and not knowing: Is it he or someone else, for instance—precisely you, but also a neglected weakling who is waking up here, doomed to miseries of the anemic day, while mother rustles with a newspaper, swooshes with her coat, scratches with the key, and goes out to become an accountant in the haberdashery named after the politician Razin: Stepan Timofeevich, where the heck did you put the ledger? And meanwhile, a poorly cut, yet solidly sewn dashing military instructor in suspenders, having beforehand dressed the chair in an impeccably ironed French coat, walked among the courier machines typical for the years of the campaign. He was arriving bright-faced, ruddy like all guardsmen, with a couple of fear-less, seemingly filled with terror, ashen bulging eyes. *Portrait of a Military Instructor*. He walked with narrow, laden steps, and, dropping morsels of Morse code, announced that the first use of a tank in battle took place during the Indian summer of 1916 on the Bzura. *War*. The air is gray, listless, and serene. Rain fell a day before; the sleepy front-line plants are slowly stripping. And when the gunfire calms down, one can hear how the stiff and heavy leaves of the oak tree in the grove fall, nose-diving, and the crows chatter in the same grove on the hill, marked on topographical maps as number two hundred seventeen. Be-sides that, one can hear that in the sawmill someone is sawing with a saw and someone is screeching on a concertina. And in the trenches and ditches of the enemy, beyond the tangled, ter-ribly corroded barbed wires, beyond the small pile of motley, multinational, bare-toothed, and barefooted corpses, the Aus-trian flutes, in counterpoint with the Magyar drums, whistle the annoying "Kaiser's Hunting March," utterly alien to the Russian heart. In one word, toward winter the view from the classroom's window becomes too repetitive. And it is apparent that the more you study it, the more static it gets. And does not every *Homo sapiens* that is hurrying somewhere resemble Achilles? Nobody is able to catch up with one's tortoise, reach something close by, whatever it could be. A survey of the late fall. Occupation—a passerby. Place of work—the street. The length of employment in the given field—eternity. The situa-tion is not better with the other moving objects—they are not moving, making everything questionable. The migration of flocks lasts unacceptably long. They soar above the ribbed, dark maroon roofs, barely waving their wings. There is a wind orchestra in the park, but on the benches—many free seats. Naturally, the sound is flowing as if the gramophone completely lost its breath. Let it be so. The same about movement of every kind; more precisely—non-movement, about the static character of the entire *Winter's Eve in the City*: Let it be so. Literature lessons were going on. The shoes of the teacher, on which, like a pair of used-up lonely accordions, descended the socks, were unusually worn out, they were wrecked. It seemed you were looking at the footwear of an inveterate walker, an enthusiastic pilgrim, a wandering cripple, and perhaps even the very Ahasuerus—the celebrated shoemaker without a shoe shop, the one who gained world fame by his impulsiveness, and who admitted his mistake but still got what he deserved. And yet, as for the static character of the winter's eve in the city: Let it be so. But unexpectedly on the screen of the window unfolded the black-and-white silent movie of *The First Snowfall* and if the street until now has not offered to the downcast eyes any energetic subjects, be so kind and find them, display them, imagine them for yourself, and project them on the screen without delay. Here are for you newspaper boys in once-fashionable plaid kepi, shouting out sensational headlines. Much obliged, but you are not taking into account that sensations have been officially banned, these boys have retired, and the newspapers are sold only in kiosks. In that case, show the former boys that now turned into a living embodiment of untreatable illnesses, and as far as sensations— because of the lack of the present ones—collect yesterday's. Here they are, the little devils, rushing down the bridge along the cast-iron Imperial railings with eagles, trying to peddle to the encountered Achilleses the so-called fresh issues. By the way, rushing is a strong word; however, in comparison with the Achilleses, they are almost rushing. And notice that some of them are traveling on invalids' carts, and one had already been dressed for the last journey: The oaken burden had been placed on runners, and the co-workers of the deceased are dragging it over the fresh powder. How do you find their faces? They are worn out. Did time have no mercy on them? Absolutely not. Well, and their souls? Alas, their souls are maimed beyond recognition, simply not worth a broken farthing. The march of gloomy subjects with the fangs yellow from acorn coffee in their wrinkled mouths, carrying under their arms bundles of sheets yellowed by spite and false accusations, convulsing like Saint Vitus and maliciously grimacing, was making the mercantile move along the route of the A-tram. The so-called white flies were swarming above the peddlers, blinding them, tickling their blackhead-covered, overripe noses, and sticking to their shoulders like dandruff. The distributors kept tripping on the bumpy ground, falling, struggling, spilling their cargo, and, to collect it, crawling on all fours with a guilty look. After all, they were very heavy, these dirt-cheap bundles. But perhaps they were not newspapers at all, perhaps the retirees carried for sale histories of their illnesses—such heavy ones—of such serious ones? No, no, these were exactly newspapers—histories of the illnesses of history—such heavy ones—of such serious ones, and the histories of their own illnesses the paper boys carried inside; they were themselves histories of these diseases. Poor codgers, for a long time they were unable to conquer the barely noticeable hump in the pavement—black ice! Almost reaching the summit, the co-workers, one after another, slid down holding their historical load, and some of them managed to keep staying on their feet, while the others did not. After sliding down to the bottom, they undertook the new ascent and slid again—Sisyphus after Sisyphus: What fun! And now provide the sound. Fine, catch it! First, whizzing and moaning, asthmatic cough, shuffling of footwear, clearing of throats, sobbing, etc. After that, someone who lost something yells: So where is my something? In response—silence, everybody is too busy, everybody is captivated by the process of movement; it is a procession. The procedure of dragging the improvised catafalque—the sounds of the dragging. A shout: Fresh news! A scream: *Russian Gazette!* Then all at once, but different things: *The Voice! New Times! Stock Exchange Circular! St. Petersburg Leaflet!* Panting with pneumatic braking mechanisms, the streetcar catches up with and passes the press-sellers, and the bustling mumble of the twelve pairs of wheels, even though its sounds are muted by the snow flurries, deafens this dissonant roar. Finally, the last car showed the veterans its oval-shaped cockroach butt, with a protruding and swinging sausage of the turnbuckle, with the letter A, walking in agronomist's arshin-wide steps, and with moping human mugs behind the dull round windows of the car's vestibule. The clock above the gate of the park of cultural recreation was attesting to the most boring stretch of the day—the spades trumped one o'clock and made a lead to two. Night visited Japan, and karatekas of Hokkaido, having shouted enough "Ha," wallowed on their tatami. In China, dogs' heads were being cut off. Turkey

smelled of coffee and tobacco. In Albania, despite the earth-
quake, by the house of the patriot Kastrioti, a mob of dark-
complexioned gawkers rejoiced. Romania was curing its hang-
over with Rymnikskoye wine, legs were becoming light and
went dancing by themselves, and nobody knew whether it is
Tuesday or Thursday. The unemployed Italy merrily rode under the olive trees on stolen velocycles, and the lira, as always,
was not worth a spit. Lighthouses and sirens of Gibraltar heartened seafarers riding out a storm, and here, in Russia, in the
former merry village Botfortovo, the retired newspaper tom-
boys attempted to get rid of retired news. Meeting of the Em-
perors in Holstein! Bashi-bazouks slaughtered fifteen thousand in Bulgaria! All is calm on Shipka! Trans-Siberian railroad
finished! Tsai Hsun condemned to hara-kiri! Evacuation in
Manchuria! Incident in Casablanca! Go out—willy-nilly, with
a heavy soul, tumbleweed rolls freely and jumps like a ball, dic-
tated Ahasuerus. The pens worked diligently. Parcae and
Moirae condemned the students to courier life, and in front of
them were all the riches of the world. It was getting light. In
Lapland the cows had not been milked yet, in Nazareth the
muezzin had not cried out yet, but in the hunting cottage of the
French king, revelers were still drinking Chartreuse. Having
finished prattling about the courtesans and balls, they stumbled out with their goblets on the balcony and, grabbing the
horn from each other's hands, bellowed to the stars a complaint of the young bull killed at the Catalan corrida. Afterward, they shot into the air: The shots were heard as far as Versailles. The borzois there were nervous and barked from time
to time; the guards kept shuddering and waking up. Fräuleins

in peignoirs and with night lamps in their hands gossiped in the galleries: Oh, *mon Dieu*, when will he finally settle down—*monarque*, but behaves like Pierrot. Friends, the one mentioned announces, standing close to the balustrade, surrounded by the cortege and the dog pack, I propose a toast to this daredevil who will empty in one gulp the barrel of my musket, filled with Burgundy. The weapon is brought out. Its butt is richly inlaid. The host puts it in the hands of one of the participants: Give it a try, *mon cher*. A failure befalls the Graf; he is unable to drink even a half. The barrel is refilled and, to the accompaniment of the hunters' laughter, given to the next of them. He also suffers a fiasco. The musket is moving in a circle and the circle, finally, closes—only the first among equals has not yet tested his skill. Frenchmen, he says, your benevolent Ludovic is hastening to your rescue. Right now he will empty the vessel, although in a manner completely different than yours—just watch. The monarch plugs the barrel with a cork and pours some Dutch powder on the flashpan. Deathly pallor covers the faces of those present. Your—they scream in terror, moving to the sides; the king shoots (the musket explodes) and falls down; everybody anxiously runs to the outstretched body—Highness! Ludovic is silent, his wonderful visage, painted hundreds of times by European masters, is disfigured and the snow-white masquerade costume—completely bespattered. Ah, my little boy, whispers the queen who woke up for a moment in her boudoir from the distant gunshot that reminded her of a pop of a carnival popgun, my sweet mischief-maker. The white curls of the beautiful hair of Her Majesty are spread over her high-piled pillows; she is having a sad dream: A brazen boar with the physiognomy of the hunchbacked whipper-in, whom she despises, rapturously caresses her in the shadow of the camellias next to the baths. Having accomplished the evil deed, the lascivious game vanishes in the thicket. Shame and disgust seize the queen. She has a feeling that some of the wardens that were hiding in the gazebo and were the clandestine witnesses of the indecent scene, would want to make fun of her most august disgrace. It was getting light. The investigator for special cases, Pozhilykh, a specialist without any kind of special identifying marks, wore a convertible coat-tent and a field bag across his shoulder. In the bag—standard document blanks, a tightly rolled-up saber sheath, a pocket flashlight, a measuring tape, a magnifying glass, a fountain pen, a detailed map of the area, and an eyeglass holder, in which, beneath the lining, lies a photograph of the female worker of the local public library that holds in its collection about a hundred grayish volumes. *Pozhilykh's Sunday*. Supper, vermouth, clouds of smoke. Tobacco is moist and has a combined aftertaste of cologne and kerosene—a result of carelessness of those responsible for packaging, storing, and shipping. Eyes are drawn to scrambled eggs with sausage, *laberdan*, and a can of very salty Caspian sardines. One can distinguish the month of the catch and the day of salting, one can also read the Turkic signature of the controller. Among furniture, besides chairs and a table, there is a settee, narrow and uncomfortable in every respect. And a simple sideboard—made of walnut. On the shelves—a few plates and saucers and a few slightly moldy pieces of bread. One can also notice there a container with office glue—to seal the windows. Cut the paper strips from the newspaper margins, and glue them on before the first frosts. The view from one of the inspector's windows reveals a wooden shed, full of cracks; the view from the other—the same shed. In summer, when the window frames are wide open, there is a smell of honeysuckle and elder, the aroma of chopped wood, and the sounds of a shaded side street—a fly, a moped, a tarantas, and the steps of a resident. Being a representative of the office of the prosecutor, Pozhilykh lies down around ten. He reads in bed a journal published in the capital, not shirking verses and poems, and frequently reciting from memory what sank in, what he remembers. Particularly—*As I Drove Up to Izhory*. Moreover, he imagines Izhory as a large wooden town on a hill in the middle of a spacious parched pasture. Across the field, orange-tinted like a pumpkin, under the pleasant sky of a not very warm midday, rolls the dormeuse with crude shock absorbers made from forged iron. The passenger, dark-skinned and lively, with carelessly combed curly sideburns, leans out and, gently holding his top hat with his hand, engages in recollections: I remembered our story, glances of your dark blue eyes. Izhory is getting closer and the golden cupolas keep gleaming. In case of a trip beyond the boundaries of the district, especially if in the pearly dampness of the mist, brightly glowing, soars a trace of a strange deceit, or it is just cold, he puts on a wind-shielding padded jacket and a felt cloak of solid construction. Having spent the night, he gives an order to harness the horses, and right away. Clinking is heard, it is getting light. Eh, I will give you a ride over the bumps, the driver with eyes resembling the rabbit's, in a fox-skin coat, rapaciously baring teeth in his wolf's muzzle, winks from the driver's bench. And it is true—the road is not blacktopped. On the right, one and a half or maybe even more *verstas* away—there is a river. Beyond the river—a village with many bathhouses and boats on the shore. The church is fully reflected. Reflected are also the crows, swarming around the belfry like black pieces of fabric cut by a tailor and lifted up by the zephyr. The given village, if one were to trust the maps, has a long and senseless name. One can hear in it the whirring movement of a mill's grinding wheel; it seems to wave from afar the quadriga of its wings, not aware of their other, lofty purpose. One can also hear the sounds of loading; tapping with their boots and grunting on the entire middle of August, some laborers are carrying whitish five-pood bundles and order the one standing on the wagon: Here, grab them! He truly scrambles. In addition, in the given name glimmers the speech impairment of the miller's helper, a dimwit and spindle-legs, who, answering your question—What village is this?—says nothing, only keeps sucking a lollipop on a stick and, as if nothing happened, turns into ice your visiting soul with the stare practiced around Izhory. For a musical ear, our name reverberates with the entire symphony; after all, one can also discover in it the voice of the miller himself who, having heard the above-mentioned conversation, hurries to provide assistance—if we can only say such a thing about a person who barely walks, being burdened by the overabundance of health—hurries to assist the one with the speech impairment. But the miller himself also seems to have stuffed his mouth with something—most likely with some millstones, because the grains of his words are pouring on the traveler with the flour of noise. And it does not help that in a moment the hallowed name will flash in the fog: To determine clearly—is it Malokule-byakovo or Mylokulelemovo—there is not enough perspicacity.

10

DZYNZYRELLA'S

Well, she says, as a rule, I live all the time in the barracks here. We have a cozy park, with swings, the residents are also quite friendly, and there is a ravine—walk to your heart's content. Earlier a certain granny, the old ragpicker, shared quarters with me. She smelled of old stuff worser than you do, and I was only gettin into prime, my hands, fittin my years, smelled of milk, my hair was wavy, curly. And I wanted to walk; I'll go out and walk all day. On the glades it is pleasant—magpies, rooks. When they fly up—half of the sky is gone. And don't leave nothin shiny—they'll steal it. Sometimes I would shout: Shoo from my money! I used to pick large dandelions, collect clover for food; after all, fate did not spoil me with sweets. And once a trapper captured a fox cub, what a joy! And he predicted: When it grows up it'll be a fox. But not long the fox cub stayed with us—it got lost. I searched in the woods—there's no fox, what pity, what sadness. Later we went with Granny to search for wasted coal on the railroad embankment. We have to fire our stove, the fall is comin. The gray slag from locomotives, Orina tells me, as if I never searched for it myself, the gray slag from locomotives they throw out, and in the gray there is black, what didn't burn away; you noticed it—pick it up and that's it. And we found the fox on the rails, sliced up. Apparently some strangers caught it and tied it with twine to its doom. Woe is the fox, it perished, sharp teeth, very long tail. And Granny: Don't wail now, this ain't ours, ours was smaller; let's better pull the skin off. No, Granny, don't pretend, it's ours, it grew up in summer. And the trapper later asks about the fox. But I hid the truth. The trapper was our neybor, but I wasn't goin out with him. At first, I was goin alone, with nobody. But, after all, age takes its toll and a young sailor turned my head: Jokin aside, what's there to fear, he says. What do you think, he finally got what he wanted. At the very beginnin, quietly—he kept touchin, snugglin. His mouth was so sweet. I am laughin: What, did you munch some fruit drops? And the sailor: I always use them—you know, we need to get rid of the tobacco odor, otherwise our commander will give us hell, we're not allowed to smoke, we're underage. When we return to our craft from a furlow, he arranges inspections: Well, cadets, breathe, he demands, right away. Other fellows buy mints in the boat's apothecary, but in my opinion fruit drops are more useful, although so far my teeth are not too good, I grew up in evacuation, around Chistopol, so they're all completely rotten, but then from mints a blister bursts just like that on your tongue, and fruit drops you chew your entire way back—and no worries. You can also chew tea or coffee beans, only the packaged tea in your pocket will spill out for sure and when the commander starts turnin your pockets inside out, he'll decide it's tobacco, and you won't prove that it's tea, and if you do prove it—that's another minus: After all, tea can also be smoked and it can be turned into a strong brew, so with tea you'll get burned in both cases, and with coffee too. No, honestly, fruit drops are more reliable than everythin else, no snags, and to hell with these cavities, if you think about it, the main thing is, the nerves are worth more. And will you gimme some? If you agree, he said, the entire tin is yours. And I wasn't spoiled by sweets. So he led me, obviously, ashore, and dragged me under the boat here, but I am still not trustin him too much. Then he lit a cigarette and is gettin ready to burn the skin on my stomach. So what was I to do, I would have not done it with him otherwise. He was puny though, Ilyusha, punier than you. Probably Chistopol was showin, but we haven't slept a wink all the same. We got out when it was already grayish, and when we started I could still see through the entry gap his trainin gunboat in the middle: We are at the roadstead, he bragged. The boat looked all dark gray, and the gun—in the sack. And it was windy—waves, splatter. At home Granny met me and started reamin me out, she splattered the fruit drops all over the floor. Well, so after that I haven't said no to the youngster no more. One day he shows up—he's wearin a pea jacket: You see, what lousy weather, finito. So you won't visit after this? No, I'll drop in when spring comes, he says, why would I traipse over snowdrifts senselessly, and Granny, he hints, will not allow us to do it in the room, and under the dinghy it's almost unthinkable, packed with snow, so all the very best to you until later. And a certain man lived then in the neyborin barrack, did handicrafts, had a room under the stairs, and smelled of leather and wax. There's more in store—Granny gives me the fox's hide: Here, take it over there, perhaps this chap will stitch you soft loafers for free. Why not, I can stitch them, he said, but for free, for *mersi*, so far, nothin's done here. When he started takin measurements of my foot, he locked the door right away, put the hook in—and you know what. Drop in for fittins, he instructed, and I started comin often to them fittins. He had stitched nice mocs in January; for strength he applied the vamps, for looks he edged them with the fox's tail—not bad. It was comfy to walk in them along the piles of blown snow to visit him, softer than soft. And toward the spring—I'm already in the family way. And you cannot keep the cat in the bag forever—right?—so in the barracks they started all kind of gossip. Granny lamented: Every hour somethin worse, she said, our Orina liked to walk and became a streetwalker, just wait what will happen next, she kept worryin. And along the fresh grass, the sailor boy—ahoy—calls again under the scow; he hauled there a bunch of old junk from the ship. And it so happened that in the mornin I am with the handyman, and at sunset I hurry to the river shore. And I got so used to it, so into it, that if one or two days go by without the usual—then I'm in trouble, I squirm, languish inwardly, as if a piece of ice was burnin inside me. You're turnin into a pro, the sailor suggested. Do you mind if on the weekend I bring a pal with me? And two of them arranged their visits, but even together they could not keep up with me. But then, suddenly, they got a big leave from the gunboat—the order was given—and they presented me with four. I started protestin, I won't manage with all, and I did not like the way the new ones talked; if you listened, they seemed awfully crude about everythin. And then they purposely pretended that there will be only two of them at a time, like usual, and their friends will wait close by. But when he and his pal in one pair have finished gratin me, then they whistle on the other two wooers. I understood my predicament—decided to get rid of them, but again only threw my words to the wind. That's how they tricked me and in addition got me all bruised up. We've got ourselves a swell discharge, one of them es-plained later, otherwise you wander like a homeless pup, don't know where to go; after all, we ain't locals, acquaintances—zilch, and we've got to kill time, we're young, after all. Well, we can drop in to the barber to make ourselves spic-and-span, or to the Armenian to get our shoes buffed squeaky-clean, to change the laces, or to the movies, or to the skatin rink in the worst case. But the skatin rink ain't open all year, and the mov-ies they show all year ain't funny, and if you wanna smoke, smoke in your sleeve or they'll escort you out. And even at the skatin rink you can't run fast that much, his pal nodded, you get a furlow, go to the park, rent them blades, get them sharp-ened, go here-there, have some *mors* in the buffet, then sprint once down the main alley—and right away you're drenched, you can wring your outfit dry, 'cuz it does not befit us to leave our pea jackets on the hooks: They'll damage them, fray them, tread on the fleet's honor. So from that time on they made it their custom to do it in turns. One of them is in, and the rest stay outside. And they noticed some youngster spyin on them from the bushes. They've caught him, dragged him in, they're mockin. I asked: Let me be with him alone. They went out, for them it makes no difference, they started bakin potatoes. At first my trapper was shy, such a touch-me-not, but when I fon-dled him more carefully, he got tamed. I dozed off, and when I

woke up—he vanished. The sailors came back, offered me potatoes, three axes, and in October I gave birth—before due
date. Everythin's not like with normal people, Granny kept
complainin. And many things happened around. The sailors
went missin, the shoemaker also faded away, Granny disappeared somewhere, and my son is gone, but I am still here, I
live here permanently, as a rule. The geese in Ilya started rufflin
their feathers, Fomich. 'Cuz, after all, what kind of a sucker,
flashed thru my mind, I appear to her and to myself, what kind
of stupid games were we playin, why did we have to drag and
stretch everythin for months, why did I want to show her my
respectability-humility? I thought like that and I thought in
jerks, a water strider. My jerky path thru life tore off by itself,
like an old rag. As if my everlastin attire got ripped by dogs, and
partially it did, indeed. I considered this parable seriously and
with the deeply saddened soul realized that this granny, great-
granny, foresaw everythin to the core, not for naught she was a
celebrated ragpicker. Yep, Orina, you were known as a walker
and turned into a typical strumpet. Don't be cross, I am tired of
bein prim and proper, so I will force you, teaser, right now,
here, on the gunboat junk, not waitin for other occasions. I am
eternally infirm, but I wasn't always. And I came closer. I will
howl about it, as it is written, like the jackals and weep like a
wolverine. Ilya was so tempted that he became a clown, he got
derailed on account of a skirt; he turned into a cat in heat; his
reputation got tarnished. If I only knew where you're gonna
plop down, I would spread some straw there and would au-
thoritatively burn with lightnin all the shameful tatters, I would
turn them to ash on behalf of the celestial powers, even though,

lately, I haven't seen any special allocations from that agency at all. But, in the end, one's livin not by manna alone, there will always be enough mussels for us, there will. So I am fryin them slowly; it's almost supper. Dusk's all around; evenin's all about; Itil's all over. But there, where the Wintry Man drives his spouse in the carriage to meet the Grim Reaper, a dry leaf coils in flight into a roll-up; around Gorodnishche, where they talk about Yegor—that is, about Fyodor—it's pure December, and on our Wolf River, though it's hard to believe, orioles and woodpeckers. Steamy and hot are the mussels in their Gehenna, they screech; I feel sorry for them. Nevertheless, I swallow, eat one after another, scrapin from mother-of-pearl what's edible. The Wintry Man is also sad to get rid of his wife, but he doesn't change his mind either. I pity you, he laments, after all, I am drivin you to drown you. Well, you don't have to, she, the old rascal, gives him advice, just look back how many years we served together. But that's exactly it, the Wintry Man complains, so many years that I cannot stand you one day more, you're dreary. But I'm askin, he continues, put yourself in my position and don't hold a big grudge against your oaf. No worries, she absolves his sin, to each his own, don't miss your chance, only you too, my friend, don't judge me too harshly: Most likely, I will bother you now and then. Do not, she says, wait for me necessarily every night, and yet, now and then I'll drop in to scare you. The masters about Pyotr: What's with Fyodor? And none of them knows nothin properly; they all forgot everythin outrite, negligent dummies. Only I, standin for some reason among them in December, kept everythin in memory. And so, the sitters worked the accounter up about hangin—no, you ain't brave, even though you're Yegory. He got offended at the guzzlers, 'cuz they questioned his darin— and shortly afterward left the spit, to prove, in the same blue haze, that he won't allow such numbers. And he pilfered what he needed where he needed, and hanged without hysterics on the waxed twine wound eight times, havin thrown that renowned baluster across from one pine to the other at a proper height. And the gardians of the hunt find him in such an independent position and summon a medic from Gorodnishche: We request, you understand, your help. He dragged himself in, they showed him—go on, heal. The medic says to them: Personally, I am attestin asfyxiation. And we thought that our clime's givin him fits; well, but as far as bein, will he be? I don't promise what I can't promise, the quack told them. Medical profession knows better, they say, it turns out he kicked the bucket, poor lonely wretch, he croaked. True, that dame sheltered him at the very end, but even that ain't worth much— like from Friday to Thursday, like a carrot and a stick. It would be amusin to find out who will be next with her now, with whom will she have fun and whom, they kept guessin, she'll make an orphan. That's what the wardens of Shallow Reach were guessin at the outskirts of the village Overbrowears, and she has already, one should think, secretly chosen whom exactly. It got clear later, durin the wake after Fyodor, where due to the relatively close approach of muscle-buildin winter they did not shun to invite me too. We lugged him to Vygodoshchi, deliberated for a while, and decided to take the wake outside, to the area shared by all, to the islands of Tavern Dawn, about which the departed always spoke with such admiration. There's perhaps no place on the entire Wolf River more fittin than these scraps of land. At the first sight, just an ordinary spot, damp and muddy; well, a birch tree flickers here or there, or a mountain ash. But you'll spend a borin week there, do some fishin and lie in the sward with a band of river brigands, lookin at billowin clouds and you'll utter with sobs, quietly-softly: Lord, how good it is to be here with You. Would you believe the way the water flows—as if it were molasses, flows—as if it were standin; the dome of the firmament unnoticeably sneaks the entire night toward mornin, and the Heavenly Kingdom itself is like that: Either it comes—or it doesn't. But if you look closer—the Itil is rushin, rushin with its entire liquid body. It would be wonderful, word of honor, to give up the ghost on those free patches. I'm dreamin about departin durin the forest harvest, sweetenin my lips with a handful of wild strawberries and sinkin into the Life Everlastin with them. Really, Lord, I am hangin here for no reason, and in general—what did I lose here, what didn't I see, whom did I come to visit? Or haven't I turned the coarse grindin wheel? No, I don't need nothin, I haven't lost nothin, and I belong here like a saddle on a pig. Where are you, time of my death, why do you dillydally in the distance, gimme a sign. But you return to the dry land and right away, as a result of all this fussbustle, you forget your reasonin, you suffer and do donkey work unlike Pyotr and them other valiant cripples that preferred a reliable rope to drudgery. Yeah, we ain't risk-takin, darin creatures; not high, upon verification, is our soarin.

■ □ ■

Krylobyl, the dragon-seer, durin the wake stood up at dawn, completely illuminated by the fire, all covered with grass blades and creepy-crawlies, and proclaimed in a loud voice, so the sleepers around the other fires, includin the wandrin ones, on his and other islands, would wake up: Reclinin brethren, we are now escortin into nonexistence such a couth of the local hunts, as Fyodor, Yegor, Pyotr. We all knew him, that's why we are sad, for that reason we're ceaselessly drinkin without closin our eyes. So let's commemorate the deceased like real people, let's announce to each other what kind of splendiferous dweller he turned out to be. It got noisier than before that Monday around the islands; the invited and uninvited started rememberin the good deeds of the strangled, and began thirstin for another round. In the blackout on Tuesday my turn came, and I report that, I won't hide it, the one responsible for our sad celebrations was a praiseworthy client and that I did grind his racin or damascene blades regularly and sharply, in accord with the bill of fare. On Wensday a certain gray-winged mail carrier takes the floor. Fyodor, he admits, was my soul mate, so I always delivered his mail within reasonable deadlines, haven't opened his letters out of pure curiosity, and if I did open, I sealed them back properly. And on Thursday the undertaker found plenty to talk about. Our departed, he assures, was an irreplaceable upstreamer, but I am also nobody's fool—I knocked down for him a restin place first-class. Mischief-makers they are, these undertakers, dreadful. Here's an example. Have You ever tried to dig in the ground with a shovel in freezin season? It turns out too mechanical, hard as a rock. So the Bygodoshch folks at first wore themselves out, exosted themselves with frozen diggin.

And they got bored by such a waste of time, they stopped diggin in the cold, they dig in summer and fall, for future use. That is, they'll approximate how many folks in the vicinity will depart in season and they make that many pits—they ain't too lazy to add a few just in case, and later they simply need to even it up here and there, and it's done. And considerin that from the middle of the fourth quarter to the middle of the second they charge accordin to the frozen price list, it becomes obvious and enviable—winter will be fantabulous for them. And Kaluga nicknamed Kostroma happened to turn up among us, with a mug double-chinned and sturdy, so sturdy that there was no neck. He did not respect the village hustle, sat on an island, in a barrel, all shaggy, and had no special likin for the authorities whatsoever. On Sunday he floats in on a raft to our backwater and states: Pyotr should not have gone with that broad. Intrestin, what you'd have done, they argued with the wolfman, it's not you who is choosin her but other way around. Doesn't matter, he answered, he shouldn't have gone; if he didn't, he wouldn't have gone cuckoo 'cuz of her and wouldn't share the bottle with the sitters, and if he didn't share, he would be celebratin with all of us. Watch out, Krylobyl fortold Kaluga, or the cup may come to you. The same day at sunset Kostroma wakes up with an odd feelin: Who was beckonin me from the sedge right now? Nobody beckoned you right now. No, somebody beckoned, I need to go and see. He dived into the sharp sedge and vanished, and when he turned up at the third dawn, they surrounded him and kept askin: Well? He told them: She. Was it sweet? Don't ask. He's grimacin, as if he was havin a seizure. Watch out, Krylobyl warned him, so it doesn't get bitter.

On Wensday, Kaluga ate belladonna berries; dyin, he warned: Be on gard; from childhood I stared at it and was cautious, but today I saw a bush and put caution aside: The berry is ripe, large, and so is my misery—we had fun, she told me, and now forget it. Therefore, go ahead, touch, these hooves of mine are already like ice. And he became thoughtful. Just look, what bad luck, complaints are spreadin all over the islands, the bream in the rivers is on the spawn, tears the nets, and here—either a wake or a funeral. I'll digress. Have You guessed who that dame is, Fomich? Once I was snoozin in my nappin shed—I had a dream about eggs: Someone will appear, so you better know. I woke up and hobbled outside to pray. A turquoise star fell from the sky, the Volga cooled down, my friends and pals thinned out, the fences are all covered in hoarfrost, and I myself am no more than just a name on her tablets. Both laughable and rather short I am, a nitwit. The night is like a debtor's jail: Who knows when they'll drag you out. But You—whoever You are—don't abandon me. That's how I prayed. And then right away the voice: A certain person will visit your places and everythin here will turn topsy-turvy. I went, warned; they don't believe me. What kind of stuff are you talkin about, what else can turn topsy-turvy here? As you wish. And one day that Karaban, a man of non-advanced age, visited our familiar crash-baret. At the threshold he stumbled, and his small transparent container in the shape of a flask smashed into smithereens. 'Nuf guzzlin, he snapped in distress. It became quiet like in the deaf and mutes' shelter. They brought him a treat. He swigged it. I was restin, he relates, under the elms, near the site of the bathhouse fire, by the pant-washin deck. The night was like any other, only greenish, 'cuz of the star, and the moon was like any other, only ginger. And down the ginger-moon road, like along the decks, from Gybodoshchi to Gorodnishche here, over the river reach, approaches, in no hurry, a puzzlin unknown woman. At first I decided—some auntie thought she would take a bath, she forgot that our splashhouse had burned long ago. But then I looked closely and it was none else but the Life Everlastin. She's lookin kind, modest, she's wearin no clothes whatsoever, but you can sense she knows what she's worth, and she's gorgeous—to tears. She sat down next to me, and we exchanged caresses, not straight on but as if someone had forbidden us—lightly as a feather. We fooled around for a while—and she went away, the speak-of-the-devil. All in all, it's clear—she visited us, she did, concluded Karaban. We had a swig then, and a chaser. We're not guzzlin, he says, but takin medicine, and not just any which way, but like pristipomas.

AGAIN THE NOTES

NOTE XIX

PORTRAIT OF A FAMILIAR WARDEN

March is crunchy and crispy,
Icicles clink and clank,
Melting spots seem to whisper
And their breath makes you drunk.

Into dusky gray haven
By the hoarfrost enhanced,
You step out, still unshaven,
In your jacket and pants.

You have boots that are loose,
But that isn't the point,
One can make simple shoes
From them and put them on.

It's not hard altogether,
And it's easy to prove:
One just needs the spare leather
Cut from boots and remove.

You're a rambler-rag hoarder,
You are lame, but all right,
Your strange land's on the border
Just between day and night.

A yoke walks by the fence,
And a lone bucket swings.
Even this makes more sense
Than do all other things.

You're a passionate trickster,
Though your pranks are age-old,
But don't cry, there's a fixter
Of all snags in the world.

You're a warden, a guardian,
With five fingers per hand:
Snow is marked in the garden,
There are prints in the sand.

Like in old fairy stories,
Among mighty pine trees
Curly and without worries
You live almost for free.

Your whole life's but a puff,
Or a brief wound-up breeze,
And your lonesome babe's laugh
Who's so willing to please.

You live in warden's hovel;
There's an oil lamp, a pail,
An accordion, a shovel,
And a gun on a nail.

On the newspapers' stack
A bold headline is found:
Sterlets in Sterlitamak
And tomato—abound.

You're a roisterer seasoned,
If you drink—then a *shtof.*
And for that single reason
Your own dog you call Wolf.

To the dear riverbank
Run on your tippy-toes.
You are full, you are drunk,
And snuff covers your nose.

You are tripping and falling
And, like a frolicking crew,
Down the slope you are rolling.
Oh my dear, look at you!

NOTE XX

A BALLAD ABOUT THE FIRE CHIEF
FROM GORODNISHCHE

Again in your dreams you onions desire,
The slush and the splatter make winter roads glum,
As soon as the drizzle digests all this mire
To do fire drills the interns will come.
They'll come frantic, in coats opened wide,
Gregarious, in zits and blackheads,
In light jackets, in two-wheeled bouncy rides,
Lean and pale—like the sheets on their beds.
The expert in the ways snipes escape,
Shiny helmet and cartridge belts sporting,
Will not shoot wood grouse while it's courting,
But will whip the loudmouths in shape.
Fire chief—an individuum in years,
Whom asthma and blisters made sour,
In April, when the stars are so clear,
Will slowly ascend his watchtower.
The intern on guard tells the story,
Saluting the helmet, yet chary,
Of fires that burn in Izhory,
But cunningly meaning Stozhary.
The chief will salute back: But not here.
And he'll look toward the estuary,
Where he wasted so many years,
At the fire-watch gruel preparing.

He will look—and his calm will decline,
So at dawn, angry and bellicose,
At the firewall, all the interns in line
Fire chief drenches from fire hose.

NOTE XXI

OVERBROWEARS

(A GARLAND OF NOTES)

1

Unsettling moments. Period of disgrace.
Pranks set the brows and the ears on fire.
"Can there be Overbrowears?" they inquired.
I responded: "It's a farm, a tiny place."

2

Does it behoove to tease and make a face?
To mock all things like spoiled brats, spreading sorrow,
Show no respect for yesterdays, tomorrows,
Forgetting conscience, honor, even grace?

3

Just look at me—what a trusting fool!
I failed to figure, though I am quite clever,

That over brow ears can't happen, ever,
While Overbrowears farm can, as a rule.

4

My ears are red—I'm no longer cool.
Unpleasant rumors circulate all over
That I'm a creep, a binger, a pushover,
A cabbagehead with two ears to pull.

5

Unsettling moments, period of disgrace.
Does it behoove to tease and make a face?
Just look at me—what a trusting fool!
My ears are red—I'm no longer cool.

NOTE XXII

FAREWELL OF THE TINKER FROM GORODNISHCHE

Sludge ice is gone. And at the harbor
The cashier clicked his register's keys.
Look at your circumstances much harder;
Hang your felts on the mantelpiece.
Limping and as if by accident vernal
Spring has wandered to our Valday.
Say—farewell, our dear taverna,

Take a hike, beat it, goodbye!
They sent a she-goat nut-picking
And a he-goat in the garden they let—
To fix teapots broken or leaking
Beyond rivers the tinkers are set.
So forgive us, dear joint, that we're parting,
When it snows, we'll be back, right behind.
You are always so kind and inviting,
A shelter for the mute and the blind.
Beyond rivers, the tin is much brighter,
There the borscht is thicker, and reeds.
In the leas with that windbag too flighty
You will deal—and you'll patch in the leas.
Beyond rivers, life seems to be freer,
And yet, rather than praise Tula tin,
With the cripples and revelers here
This whole summer I should have stayed in.
Fare-thee-well, Gorodnishche, my brothers,
As they say, flap your wing for goodbye,
'Cause who knows when again with each other
We will sit at this table—you and I?
So don't fuss with my clothes' rips and holes,
Since my cane can't wait to go forth.
But, old woman, now pour me a whole
Hunderd-fifty grams of sweet port.
There's a schedule at our harbor,
And on the steamboat—a café.
There, Graf-like conceited and hardened,
Stands the barkeep in his *galife*.

NOTE XXIII

PORTRAIT OF THE FERRYMAN

Sing, ferry driver,
Chatty and wacky,
Carrot-top jack.
Crafty conniver,
Sing of craft's cracking
And caulk the cracks.

Sing of boat's gears,
Rowlocks' responses,
And anchor's roll.
And of the years'
Entire nonsense,
Eh, darn them all.

I so adore it,
When, like a pixie,
Lively and spry,
Seeking no glory,
You're deftly fixing
What's lying by.

Your hammer's knocking
And outside calling
In April light.
Instead of talking,
Let us go strolling

Before the night.

It smells of mastic,
Foot-bindings, candles,
All over, but
Having no practice,
Miss Spring resembles
A splendid slut.

When on the morrow
Afar you see me—
Telescope eyes—
Forget your sorrows
And, widely beaming,
Get some supplies.

Don't skimp, you gap-tooth,
But open wide
Your smorgasbord.
And I'll be apt to
Some food provide—
Five kopecks worth.

Waters are splashing,
Flow by themselves
To reach their goal;
The years are passing,
And we ourselves
Just live, that's all.

NOTE XXIV

BETWEEN THE DOG

Once, between the dog and wolf,
By willows that weep,
A warden let his needle drop—
Did not stitch the rip.
He searched in the grassy pall
Each spot he could see,
And he found some kind of ball
In this verdant lea.
And he calls: My brothers, hey,
Just look what I found!
They came by, began to play,
And had lots of fun.
They would kick the ball around
Or play toss and catch,
'Til the evening dew set down
Right on the green patch.
And the thick fogs would alight
Crawling out from swamps,
In their huts folks would ignite
The wicks of their lamps.
And the fogs from Volga's swamps
Licked the keels and poked,
There was little oil in lamps

So the wicks just smoked.
And the tugboats floated by
Heavy barges towing,
While the hoopoes in the sky
Wooed oxpeckers, cawing.
Tugboats floated by the bogs
Without or with barges
And who knows if wolves or dogs
Into woods were charging.
Unexpectedly the ball
Lit up bright, not far.
They looked closely—it was all
Stozhary's main star.
On this foggy star, forsooth,
With their eyes aglow,
Lots of plain, unvarnished truth
All the wardens know.
There, the wispy fogs alight,
Crawling out from swamps,
People in their huts ignite
The wicks of their lamps.
There, between the dog and wolf
By willows that weep,
A warden let his needle drop—
Did not stitch the rip.

NOTE XXV

PORTRAIT OF A COURIER

(THE SECOND RECOLLECTION OF THE CITY)

What does "a courier" mean? Consider
That to ensure success for strangers
And in this world to make some changes
One goofball pedals hither-thither.
It's like a calling, someone said.

He's single. With his clueless head
Snapping the branches of bird cherry,
Addressing to it many queries—
Like what's "a courier," why, and when?—
Forgetting he should darn his stockings,
And also constantly chain-smoking,
His bike completely overworking,
He flickers like a wound-up man.

He's poor and foolish, and high-strung.
Nanny, why can't I sleep tonight?
If old—he makes himself look young
And if he's young—he'll soon be old.
He's feverish and he has a cold
With inflammation. But chin up:
I'll shave! Oh, nanny, where's my brush?

How come? It's very late, don't rush!
Silence, slop-slinger, in my nap
I saw a firebird in flight—
It said we'll marry in a snap.

And though he fears he'll get cut up,
He hones his blade in lunar light.

Crossing the country left and right,
Its center and provincial places,
He's stunned by how the world is turning
And like a boiling cauldron churning,
Revealing both events and faces
Cooler than movies new or old:
Here's lion hunting, here—a ball,
There—a half-naked lass in laces,
And—for your pleasure—even more:
A centipede on cellar's floor.
And from the window mother screams:
For winter seal the window seams!

Now winter's gone—spring will grow twigs;
The courier is the mud decrying,
With which the messy street keeps trying
To splash his buttocks and is using
To this end spokes of quite amusing
And fashionable britskas, gigs,
Landaus, and other kinds of rigs.

And like a decoy mallard duck
In rifle sight condemned to quack
And with a line for drying clothes
Tied to the hunter, lest it's lost,
The courier cannot ever see
How very different he could be
If he were not worn out by riding
More than the decoy by its gliding,
If he were born beneath a star
Unlike the courier's, shining far,
And duck—beyond its decoy star.

(NB: A river, when the dusk has set,
When it's too late for bilboquet,
When samovars are finally ready
And on verandas chatter's steady,
When, having bid his knitting bye,
Grandpa *The Catcher in the Rye*
Reads out to Grandma; also when
She seemed to be in doubt,
But held cheese in her mouth;
When knocks of flint stones got quite loud
And let us add another *when*—
When wires disappeared—just then
We see the stars in waters deep:
But they're all decoys, there they sleep,
And to be with them, from the skies
Others fall down and please the eyes:
So make a wish, don't hesitate.)

But no such luck. It seems that fate
Sets all decisions right in stone.
From a department in some state
I brought this mail, for you alone.
Say, will this junk be never gone?
I'm sorry, ma'am, but I don't know,
Therefore, sign on the line below.

And so the courier rides once more,
He turns or goes straight as before.
Please tell me who you are, my dear?
Well, old man, I am not from here.
A dog will bark at him, and follow,
The boob will look around and swallow,
Swallow and look, and gulp some air,
And take a catnap, one could swear,
And then he'll spit, and with his shoe
Rub in the spittle,
And afterward, out of the blue,
He'll sob a little.

The time will come—all things will pass:
People are happy. The mead drips
Upon a dickey from the glass,
Not reaching the bissextile lips,
While Hoopoe begs outside the joint
For loose change to buy booze,
And inside someone yells, annoyed:
You want a swig?—You lose!

Now nightingale begins to mill,
Now windmill starts to trill!

Crossing the land both bright and dreary,
The land unquenched and mostly arid,
And with his head washed only rarely
Snapping the branches of bird cherry,
Addressing to it many queries,
The courier speeds and rushes, weary,
And toward morning, home, on board,
He moans and groans: Oh, my dear Lord,
That's what it means . . .

NOTE XXVI

POSTAL CHORES IN THE MONTH OF MAY

Why doesn't he write to me, my most esteemed *oncle*,
Is it possible he does not have time again whatsoever?
It's strange—because he promised: I will write to you
    unfailingly.
Well, look, he doesn't write and doesn't come back,
    absolutely.
5   Gazing beyond the river, I gazed-out my eyes
    completely,
He could have sent me at least a pictogram, my dear
    relative,

He could have said, it's so-and-so, such-and-such plans
    I consider,
'Cause otherwise, where to run—I couldn't even
    imagine,
With such an uncle topsy-turvy things constantly
    happen.
10   Washing my feet with the dew as I'm walking,
I will set out at dawn to welcome our mail carrier:
Are you bringing me at this time a package, as we
    usually call it?
No, he disappoints, apparently, he disappoints, they're
    still writing,
Apparently, your addressees are careful and thoughtful.
15   Fine, we will stand there, shoot the breeze for a few
    moments,
Afterward I will invite him to my humble dwelling:
Eh, drop in for a while, my dear friend Sila Silych,
You'll be my guest, you know, we'll converse a little,
Did I brew the nectar yesterday for no reason?
20   For no reason, my dear Nestor, nobody here brews
    nectars,
For no reason, in the world practically nothing can
    happen,
For no reason, even a curly hare won't appear in night
    ravings.
We will, of course, partake of your nectar without
    postponement.
So the dearest postman Sila Silych comes in, so he
    enters,

25   Such a shorty, extremely unimpressive to look at,
Although he could drink under the table even Krylobyl
    in person;
That means: Trust the appearances, but always keep
    double-checking.
Yep, so he dropped in to visit me, Sila Silych,
Uh, he dropped in, and, having taken his hat off, wiped
    his lips with it,

30   Well, right away I poured for the messenger and for
    myself also:
Let us drink, good folks, let us drink, fellow villagers,
Let us drink, since today we're alive, and who knows
    what will happen tomorrow.
Who knows, who knows, he nods, nothing here is clear,
Now you find it and now in an instant you lose it,

35   Not to mention that when you allow yourself to kick
    the bucket,
Then, whether you write or not—everything into dust
    is turning,
There your postscriptums are as useless as a dead
    horse's beating.
Saying this, Silych instantly emptied the glass entirely,
And my actions corresponded to Silych's exactly:

40   I gulped and afterward dispensed some more, with no
    ceremony,
In order not to procrastinate cunningly with the
    second.
And then I says to him, to my dear pal Sila Silych,
So here you and I live, so here we chew our daily,

But you know what the folks on the other shore are
    gabbing,
45   Many things, honest, on that shore they're gabbing,
"The wolves," they are gabbing, "ate you there,
    apparently,"
What do you think—are those facts or perhaps just
    fables?
I heard, I heard, they reported to me the news also,
The guest rejoined, caressing in unison my ocelot.
50   But I am slightly thrown off my kilt and befuddled,
Perhaps they ate but perhaps it's just an empty rumor,
It's anybody's guess, as Grandma used to say wisely.
Then Silych and I had another mouthful, roundly-
    soundly,
Or, as it is commonly called, we redoubled.
55   With my friend Silych having seen to the brew's
    termination,
I decided to incite my friend Silych to engage in
    something:
Why don't we read at random some of the messages?
Right, Yasha, your pate is reasoning properly,
Silych answers with dignity my proposition,
60   Are we supposed to be worser than the other mail
    carriers?
It's an unheard of thing not to read someone's epistles.
What other stuff would you expect us to be reading?
And then we've opened several scrolls together.
We look—what kind of stuff people compose to each
    other,

65   With what, it appears, don't they seem to be concerned:

Widely and mightily flows epistle-writing between the
    people,

Like some epidemic it is spreading all over.

For instance, Pavel from Gorodnishche writes to Pyotr
    in Bydogoshch,

Begs his uncle to purchase the yeast for hooch-brewing,

70   He implores him to find without fail some alphabet
    letter,

He keeps prying, a knife to his throat he is holding,

He doesn't let his uncle get sloshed in the crashbaret
    even a smidgen.

Pyotr from Gorodnishche sharply replies to Pavel in
    Bydogoshch:

My dear, keep up your incessant search for the letter,

75   But the money, given by you, I pissed away entirely,

Therefore, you should know that the yeast I will bring
    you unlikely,

And besides, Ilya the grinder, a total outsider,

In his old age suddenly also became attracted to a *stilo*,

A grievance to Sidor Fomich Pozhilykh he scribbled,

80   He complains—during a snowstorm someone lifted his
    crutches,

The wardens of Shallow Reach, he claims, absconded
    with them.

After a while, the whipper-in will also get a document:

Hunting-dog master, if there was no necessity to do it,

Would I really outline the following to you? Not really.

85   Halloo, your people a pair of my supports pilfered,
They'd better return them as soon as possible, drifters,
Or, tell them, all of you won't be safe even in heaven.
The wardens scratch the birch bark to the grinder
      collectively,
Apparently, the whipper-in passed to them Ilya's
      ultimatum:
90   Master-buster, a specter both stupid and foolish,
We couldn't care less even if we saw you in the box with
      your crutches,
You'd better hop, bloated, to your lonesome babe at the
      farmhouse,
And if you start snitching—you'll taste the real
      misfortune.
Having read the writs and with chewed crumbs having
      resealed them,
95   We finished drinking, emptied the spacious jug to the
      bottom,
The time to part arrived then for me and for Silych.
Eh, he put on his hat and proceeded to exit,
He hugged me, his soul mate, kissed me—and
      departed.
Silych, I said, why is my *oncle* to me endlessly writing?
100   For no reason, he responded, not even a hare to us, the
      curly.
In the meantime, in Bydogoshch, all the alders—
      florescence.

NOTE XXVII

NOT THE FIREBIRD'S . . .

Not the firebird's bright outfit
Hops and rumbles in the grass,
But Elijah, our prophet,
In his chariot rides to us.
God be with him! Ergo—thunder!
Ergo—lightning! Never mind!
So the wardens smoke and wonder
Why the rain still lags behind.
Lightning turns all things to sterling,
In the keeve the mash aboil,
And above it stands the twirling,
Serpentine condensing coil.
And this viper, self-constructed,
Source of profit and delight,
Was mysteriously abducted
From the grinders to this site.
We're not looking for excuses,
Well, we pilfered it, so what?
He who mocks the poor, abuses
His own Maker a whole lot.
The procedure is consistent:
Wardens wait, the drops still lag.
And in contrast—in an instant
Tomcat pounces on a bug.
Plus, quite often, now as ever,

Just to spite us—life's a flash,
And in contrast—lasts forever
The most common scraper brush.
I will pass. Who would believe this?
I was—I'll be just a ghoul,
And the dawn, blind and oblivious,
Will trip over my pulped soul.
To my lonesome babes' loud snivel
And weed-trampling underfoot,
My white body—a soap's sliver
Will be hauled on its last route.
But so far—on shore, delighted,
In my cap I sit with pals,
Please preserve, oh God Almighty,
Our rowboats from the squalls.
For auspicious outcome hoping,
Now, a hunter's suit I hem,
But my needles, darn, are dropping:
Ergo—pickled, hence—I am.

DISCORDS BEYOND THE ITIL

12

We've gathered closer to discuss what happened but the orchestrion resounded and we could not stop ourselves from a potpoorie. Eh, you gal with flair, you're my dancin pair, with an awkward air, and no longer fair. Woe is you, great Gorodnishche, the most mightiest town, briefly flashed through my mind durin the dance. And really. Precisely on that day started these discords Beyond the Itil, that is, these mishaps that are the reason I'm gettin broke payin the office fees. Have you heard the news? Burbots, in love with the moon, try to swim to it thru the air and slowly suck holes in ice. Similarly, the male species lost their cool and went crazy on account of that dame. They, our crucians, surface on the hillock at dusk, sit on whatever they can, and dream all out about her, suckin from the bottle. They're waitin, hopin she'll appear again, even though everyone knows she visits rarely, and when she does visit, she can be seen only by the chosen ones, for whom these randevoos, as a rule, turn into a disaster. So let's give what's due to the mentioned Gury, Fyodor, Kaluga, or to V. Karaban, who did not depart yet but dried up and barks: Keeps clearin his throat. Woe is you, Gorodnishche and your environs; everythin around you is both desolate and false. A lonely fellow assures his lonesome babe: I am goin to our backwater to round up some fish. But he'll circle around the islands, make a few drafts—and all folks suddenly see him among them in the crashbaret havin a glass of vino. The invalidual returns home, starts doin what he did before. We stir up trouble, clown around, mischief-makers, don't care about anythin, it's disgustin to look at us. Do You think we don't know the proper manners? Ain't we well bred, as we should? We know, we're well bred, even hands before eatin, like them Farisees, we strive to wash, but mainly it makes no difference—we misbehave, find ourselves outside of the norms of decency. And the greed overcame us too. We are lyin under the elms, begin to celebrate, and various folks appear out of the blue: Won't you give us some? And we ain't givin, we are pissed: Scram, the store's still open, manage your feast yourself, freakin alkies. And thievery, excuse me, thievery out of this world, and it turns out there's nothin to push off with.

■ □ ■

I was walkin, keep readin, from the other side of our common river, returnin on Christmas Eve from Gury, from his funeral. The refreshments were provided by that undertaker; he invited: Crawl in, all who want, let's have a gulp to keep the buzz goin; hearts are trumps. I crawled in. A young fellow was rottin, they say, in a Caucasian damp joint, and when the captivity got tiresome—he ran away. And I also got bored with this wake, I wanted to go back to my repairmen, I wanted to celebrate Christmas with them. The youngster got lost in the mountains—and I in the dusk. I was skatin homeward, and the strong wind was squeezin the tear out, and it—it was rollin merrily. So far we're not missin any screws, we know what it means to get our legs shod in blades. Nevertheless, it's sort of sad between the dog in the expanses of native rivers, it makes you feel an urge to whimper like that tramp at a quarter after three. Fog—who knows whether it's a place or a face, shadow or light, Gorodnishche or Bygodoshch: I revved up the tempo. A miner's storm lamp, given to me by the head dog master as payment for various minor services, was knockin about in the bast creel behind my spine, and there was gurglin in the container. But I did not hurry to light it; in the night blindness it'll get even blinder, so—we call it a bat. Contradiction, blunder. After all, it doesn't make itself blind—it makes us blind with its rays, therefore it appears we are bats, and bats ain't us, ever. Why, I hasten to ask, Aladdin Rakhmatullin ain't among us now, but stays lonely under water? And why did he, the rash racer, light his lantern in the grayish air? The homeless clouds stiffened, my clothes also stiffened, the ground draft crawled up my ankels. And as soon as the timber town, like in a water decal, started faintly showin through the murk, I, old shoe that I am, understood that all of its houses are sewn from the ash-colored corduroy with a wide wale, and their roofs from felt, or perhaps someone stole from the hat factory undyed matted wool. Psst . . . Evenin is bein evenin, folks walk from fact'ry, free, Marusya swallowed poison, hospital-bound she'll be. Who knows if from the factory or not, but various river folks kept walkin on hockey and figure skates over this dark blue worsted

wool; some with an idea of a promenaid, some from the woods
with Christmas trees, some to the store, but all of them far, far
away, not nearby. It turns dreary when one's alone; I got tense.
Believe it or not, but there is someone invisible among us. I
applied the skate's brake and extracted the lamp—burn, burn
brightly, with fire it's not as scary. And at that moment I spotted
a wolf behind the snow piles. Don't be surprised, in winter that
public keeps wandrin hither and thither—boatload of tracks.
They're lucky, the animals, that the freeze bridges the waters
and one can manage without any Doom. Ferry over, they tell
him, to the other side a goat, a cabbage, and even a jackaloo.
Only not together but in turns, so they don't finish each other
off after unloadin. And who will be paired with whom, and
who will ride alone—it's your decision. I don't wanna carry
either a goat or a cabbage, said Doom, and much less the other
one, even if in a muzzle; we have enough peripeties at the
crossin without that. And when I noticed beyond the snowdrifts the gray hide and the eyes resemblin the precious iridescent Christmas tree ball, I got discouraged, a fearful billy goat.
If I run, the predator will give chase, grab by the nape—and
it's all over, you've bit the dust. Yes, I got anxious, but more
precisely—got angry, rebellious. There's nothin out of the ordinary in dyin, and accordin to the earlier-mentioned reasons,
it's required. But to have the master suffer death on account of
the primeval beast is inappropriate, rude; one has to get some
respect, even if the most tiniest; after all, not all of us are harried
alive, we're not a complete ragtag rabble. I won't succumb to the
pangs of his fangs; I will fight, like that escaped youngster in the
Chuchmek mountains fought, breathin rapidly. I put the bat

down on the snow, took off the creel; my courage came back. The beast is sittin, observin, he turned his head sideways. Why are you sorrowful, Wolfie, attack, if you dare. He's stubborn, doesn't do it. I take from under my shirt a bread ration of peeled rye and beckon: Come, devour, you're probably starvin. The wolf stole up, ferocious, keeps waggin his tail—snap—and swallowed my piece. I was nimble, Citizen Pozhilykh, grabbed him by his collar—and started poundin. It's no picnic for an invalidual to keep his balance durin such fracases, especially on a single blade, but some experience had been accumulated; here, rarely a week passes without battles on ice. When we, the stumps, gather to twist and turn over the slick, one word leads to another; with the prosthesis across the temple—and with whatever is around we start mutilatin our fellow creatures. Such strategies make little sense, of course, but still: Friendship gets stronger and excessive foolishness gets knocked out and away. The adversary initially showed obstinacy, just kept spinnin around like on a stake, yelpin, but subsequently could not take it—and darted. He overturned Ilya, but as long as the collar held, I was thwartin the flight, and our twosome rolled, completely wild, dappled white, like devils in the mill. And suddenly my lamp went out, my hand weakened—and the jackaloo flew the coop. And the boozin daze overwhelmed me, I am lyin sauced, steamin—like a jellied pike perch on the crystal of the Itil. And though the blizzard crawls into the folds of my clothes and my hair is splittin—I am delighted. With hand on my heart, where and when else can one experience things like that? What a victory—I overcame the predator. But if you tell someone—they'll doubt it: Where's the hide? We are stalwart materialists, Pozhilykh, we believe in the hide, but about happiness—we're on our gard. And from the hill, from the highest hill, like the tsar's decree about clemencies, a huge huntin party was rollin down to the crashbaret, retirin from the watchful thickets. Krylobyl was carryin on his shoulder a small kill, and the shooters, up to twelve in number—the corpse of a razorback. It's intrestin that the mugs of those carriers, due to what they've been downin beforehand, became exactly like snouts, and they were walkin for some reason on half-bent legs. Congrats, congrats, I greeted the hunters. Rats, rats, they trumpet, gloomy as if they had died. Apparently the cold deprived their tongues of their rights. Happy approachin, I said. Roachin, garbled Krylobyl, poachin. Listen, what a pleasant twilight, I said, evenin's smokin. Right, agreed the old man, croakin.

■ □ ■

At last I've rolled up to my destination, and I tumble into the workshop. By these hours the entire grindin co-op gathered there—it gathered, started frolickin. Some got involved in the sacrilegious beetle, others in the break-them-up, and some, not afraid of hernia, allowed themselves to play juggle ball, firmin up a few rags together with twine. They behave outrageously, dissolutely, and to straighten them up, to slap them on the wrist, there's positively nobody; happy-go-lucky behaviors had spread all over—a million of them. And then, havin gulped some plunk, I flung at my colleagues the Christmas Eve confession-homily. About-goners and youngsters, I summoned, more than a thousand years ago, Mary the Southerner gave birth to the Son of Man. He grew up and, in particular, announced: If even one palm corrupts you—don't be shy, cut it off immediately. 'Cuz how much more wonderful it is to partially flourish in these here times than smolder whole in that Gehenna. We're all amputees, and our future is bright. Take, for example, me personally. An offspring of my mother and father, permanent fools in Christ from the stoop of Vagankovo and All Saints, respectively, I began the same way, but after the famed event, my cursed fate, fanned with carbolic acid and insence, changes to the core. I engage in various trades and learn them—inside out. As a result of my wandrin ordeals, in their conclusion, I arrive here and join this co-op. I am standin here in front of you, you all know me. Let the abomination of complete desolation, the flabby, decrepit, and slurrin dwarf with a woodpecker beak, descend on us tomorrow at lunch. But even in front of her mugognomy I will claim, sayin it with pride, that I know no name loftier than the modest soberquet of the Russian riverside grinder. And if I hear a thunderin voice—throw Your knives-scissors away, but sharpen, if You know what I mean, for the sake of the common good the right shore of the Itil until it's an awesome sting, similar to a scythe, then I will answer: You asked for it, You got it! But don't be envious that from the outside I am mighty and tough—inside I am simply a softy. And whether I grind my teeth or metal—I just grind them, while my longin after Orina is grindin me. What a woman, one won't forget her at any price. But don't cast dispersions, better repent. All of you did secure for yourself permanent honey pies, but the sweetness of the unknown ladies, of the temporary ones, attracts, and you desire them, committin a sin. I know, you pity your usual lonesome babes 'til death do you part, 'cuz, fortifyin themselves, they endure the unbearable burdens of your corrupt bodies and natures. But you also fell in love with the visitin dame, and you love her devotedly, even though she's nobody to you, and I will call this, like the scandals and thievery, Discords Beyond the Itil. In principle, one should bring down fire on you, but I will wait a bit 'cuz I am also no angel, no better than you—I'm registered with one, share a household with her, but I am burnin for another. That's why the tall tales of crickets behind the stove are bothering Ilya. The moment I hear them—our outins and rides to suburban little towns with grasshoppers come to the surface. So don't cast dispersions and that's the end of it. In those tipsy periods, different visitors like tinkers, buoy keepers, and loggers appeared here. They made excuses—we were drawn to the light—but in fact came to get treated for free. And they inquired: Won't you reveal who bangothumped all the mange out from the dog-master's bitch? Gentlemen, I have no clue; if the jackaloo, then yep, he did get beat up—tufts were flyin all over. And I gave them my account of the battle, receivin a shower of applause. When the holidays ended, I leave the co-op and, a braggart, ascend to Gorodnishche. Yearnin after homemade pancakes was drivin me under the warm roof; I also needed some tenderness. What did I understand, wandrin—how everythin is arranged? I did not understand nothin, wandrin, includin how everythin is arranged. I only see every lonesome babe is a trap net, Fomich, she's a trap net, and we—we're ordinary ruffs, and sooner or later we'll be hers. Do You remember that case: a drawin called *Unexpected Return*? I also lumbered back, filled with remorse, and she's beratin me: What, you lumbered back, you darned lame horse? I could not bear such slander, on Candlemas I gave my hands free rein, but my pal-gal did not fall far behind, took advantage of my condition. After that we made peace, she got generous and fried pancakes for me, and later even allowed me to get close. As soon as the mornin has broken, I jump out into the entrance hall—my indispensable accessories are missin, though I, bein of sound mind and memory, left them there, in a pickle barrel, and even covered them with a lid. I got used to keepin them there—my lonesome babe, Her Neatfreakness, does not permit me to bring crutches into the chambers: Even with your single sole there's plenty of trouble, I just walk behind you and keep wipin. And I: But you yourself husk the sunflower seeds on the floor. And she: I haven't asked you what I can husk; so far it's not me who's a squatter here but you. I looked at the porch—analogy. The witch was already warmin up the chow on the stovetop. My friend, quoth I to that woman, why did you dispatch my supports into the stove for the benefit of the ever-burnin fire? Eh, you don't know what you're babblin, she cuts me off. In that case—they got filched, I concluded. Serves you right, she scoffed, how many times I warned you not to be lazy to stick the bolt in the latch in the evenin—and you didn't even prick up your ears, so now sort it out. No, it serves you right, you pipette, it was you who forced me to leave them in the entrance hall, so from now on you'll have to drive Ilya everywhere on a sled, 'cuz personally I find no evidence of any savins to purchase a new pair, and whether you will have enough strength to meddle with the wretch or not—it's nobody's concern, and on which sled are you plannin to pull me on May Day, it doesn't worry me in the least. Yak-yak-yak, she utters, yak-yak-yak, the tattered chatterbox. The same day, I discovered by the gate a note delivered on the sly, secured with the indecent elastic from underwear and entitled: Affidavit. I'm quotatin: Given to Citizen I. P. Sindirela and attestin that his accessories went missin in connection with the fact that on such-and-such date of the river-freezin month he walloped with them the huntin bitch Mumu, therefore it's unlikely they'll be returned to him; the wardens of the Shallow Reach. So I scribble to their whipper-in—a wolf. The whipper-in responds—a Vizsla. And our chronicle started. It started and continues and I am sittin here without stirrin, stuck in place. My professional calluses slowly begin to shrink, and instead I am developin writin ones. What else am I involved in? I keep fightin with my scatterbrain, I recall for her zesty chastushkas: Girls once argued at the dacha which one had the shaggiest cha-cha; it turned out the shaggiest cha-cha had the owner of the dacha. She's gigglin—like a jingle bell. In addition, I am gazin at the past—my journeys, wandrins.

■ □ ■

So depict somethin for farewell, the courier kept grievin, start somethin ours, make it as heartrendin as possible, or play somethin general railroad-like. I yanked the bellows and the inspector's providin description. He's providin description and I am singin: To distant destination will soon depart the train, the cars will leave the station, the platform will remain. The station has a clock, the brick wall is all red, the kerchiefs a white flock, the eyes so deeply sad. Uh, that's a great one, grieved the bro. I am singin and he reports. About the hunt, about the time when, not so long ago, he went huntin for the firebird, and how, on the approach to Zhmerinka, someone shamelessly carried off from the car his huntin boots. Or how in his youth a certain person lost her head gazin at him; she served at the N-junction, with a motley *schlagbauman*, and the lieutenant, in those years a cornet, paid zero attention. The smokin car will ask about my now, my past, I'll tell a bunch of crap to shock and make them pout. What truly I gave up they don't need to find out. Durin the hunt, flabbergasted by the theft, he shot at the target but missed, and now, attired in regalia, but havin wasted the entire century, he's got the feelin that he blew off the most importantest bird of his fate, very likely not around Zhmerinka but on that motleyish switch, givin the gal the cold shoulder. And they found her, he says, at the foot of the embankment. A sailor in striped shirt will open his poor heart, he'll say that he is hurt and that his life is hard. He'll reach his destination, won't look back at the train, the cars will leave the station, the platform will remain. I sang and suffered: Oh, you swallow of mine, for whom did you leave me, havin taken the son and havin changed your and his last name, and where are you both right now—nobody knows. On the Don's shore, a branch of maple, and on your kerchief, soaked through with tears. You were called around the barracks Orina Neklina, and to whom do you belong now, to what kind of, let's suppose, Spacklin, ah? And the sailor—the sailor You met in the car—have You figured out who he was? Earlier I also didn't know who he was, from which fleet, lost or discharged? He seemed so unknown that one could erect a monument to him. Right now I believe he was the sailor Albatrosov, discharged for good. Be patient, we got acquainted as the train went on. And the deputy started weepin, can't enjoy the song enough. You see, a Russian tune moves even the big ranks, so what do You expect from me, a tiny worm—I completely lost it. And if one looks out of the window—there's also not much joy: shacks made of timber, December. And some vagabond Gypsy—exactly like us—with a sack on a stick and bunches of pretzels on his neck instead of necklaces, tramples the shroud of native expanses, and even if he acts like the devil-may-care, we read in his eyes that the situation sucks, that wandrins are distant and constant, even if not personally for us, and when we croak, it will be the others' turn, and no special indulgences are anticipated. My past and present fiascos I esplained in two words—and it was rockin on switches. You may get envious: Yes, Ilya, you are truly blessed, you suffered and knew much sorrow. Don't say that, I says, I'm so blessed that I could cry. We took a swig, swallowed. Hittin the sack?—the inspector hiccupped. I tell him: I'm not sleepy, I got enough sleep in hospitals. Gonna brush your teeth? Pardon? Your teeth, I am askin, he asks, are you gonna brush? I apologize, I—pas, I don't need to. Coincidence, he said, both jaws ain't mine. So whose?—I stared. Official issue, on suction cups, said the lieutenant, here. And he took them out. I looked. I did like them a great deal—white, sharp, as if a bonesetter prescribed; here's what your health services do. Go ahead, try them, try them, don't be shy, the lieutenant encouraged. I inserted. How are they, do they fit? Like in a pharmacy, lieutenant, as if they sculpted these details for Ilya. It's a gift, he yelled. Oh my, are you nuts, how's that possible, such presents. Ain't you my kin, he kept yellin, don't I have the right to offer my bro the teeth? Suck and remember. Well, what a benefactor, you helped me out, I yelled. Forget it, the deputy grinned to me, empty-mouthed, just play. I started singin, playin—swiftly, swiftly, as if escapin from the Siberian mines. The inspector doesn't give a spit about close quarters—he broke into a bop, keeps shakin his charms. In our blessed memory's early years we called such fellows blubberlubbers: No problem, they all responded without fail. I was performin "Carousel," probably in the rhythm of the squabble of the wheels. A filigree "Carousel": Shake your lure, I cheered him on, chevelure. And in the same rhythm a fortunate thought came to Ilya that, say, he unexpectedly put in the gratis teeth. Ah, I put in the new teeth, eh, the new teeth I put in fast, I put them in myself, and so forth. To the accompaniment of squeakin wheel flanges, a thoughtful invalidual will mill over all kinds of stuff durin a long trip from an infirmary to the Tower Junction; he will mill it over—and there will be flour. And it was rockin on switches. My bopper bopped 'til he dropped: He crashed on the berth and started sawin wood. So I took off his tall boots lined with fur, threw them for good memories into the knapsack, polished off what was left in the flask—for the road—and I greet the sailor in the car's gangway: On leave to *maman*? Durin our cabotage, he says, the followin emergency occurred. On the Mariupol dry-cargo ship served two chums, two stokers—the second and the first—and the sea spread in front of them quite widely. But when the second, out of the most sincerest considerations for his attachment to the first's gal from Anapa, secretly added to his antrasite some kind of bad substance and left, they were cruisin precisely to Balaklava, to the factory of bubbly water. The comrade left, so this one opens the door to the furnace with a habitual bump—and it's all over. That is, when he swooshed his shovel into the ash pit and shoved it in up to, as they say in them fleets, its turnip and started stirrin with the shovel, then everythin went kaboom—a total nightmare. And the flame illuminated him. At that time the other stoker runs into the boiler room, and this one says to him: Stand from under, we're havin a malfunction, our valves and all their flaps are gone—for that reason, gimme a cig, bro, stick it in my kisser, so the smoke comes out of me. I don't mind givin, his bro teases him, only with what, I would like to know, do you intend to hold it? I looked, he says, and it seems I have no palms, they got torn off—a tear glimmers in his eye—and it's a done deal. And I, he says, said then, a stoker to a stoker: Darn, you call yourself a pal, but stokerly speakin, you are a mop after that, not a sailor, and your mother's a bulkhead.

PICTURES FROM AN EXHIBITION

13

The hoarfrost—may pass. The chickens—may walk over the sand, looking surprised that they leave prints with their chicken feet. Not to like these birds, but to like watching how they leave prints on the wet sand, without suspecting it, without suspecting anything. The chatterboxes could be heard. They kept shouting to each other but did not halloo because they were walking together, in a tight flock. Moira, who was spending her overripe years on the bench in the front yard, also heard the voices. Then she put aside her knitting needles, with which she had been picking in her ears since morning, jumped up, looked carefully in that direction, and cawed: They are leading her. A ball of gray wool rolled off her knees, hopped on the flower bed, and, crushing the anemic anemones, rolled somewhere, having turned into a ball of courting vipers. The barracks—may wait. Stepping into the space of April delight, they kept saying: They are leading her; she has had enough swinging. The complex, mixed smell of roll-ups and state-rolled *papirosy* may soar above the gathering of the interested. Not to know anybody here. The delinquent tenant, living in the truncated room under the stairs, was outside; he may hang out at the water reservoir, near the boat-houses, begging shameless oarswomen for candy wrappers. Brawny trainers, people of middle age, humiliated the scrounger. She was walking with her hair loose, having thrown her head back to see only the azure. Her white *demi-saison* coat is unbuttoned. But tomorrow it will get warmer—and she is already in a sarafan. And the witches—in black. The highway is violet, covered with purple puddles, and if we continue with the colors, with impressions—then the tiny young leaves, on the background of which the walk is taking place, convey to us the impression of green smoke. Two ghastly skin-and-bones are holding her under her arms. The others are walking in a circle, guarding, and all are trying to touch. For a long time, for several moments, he has been observing what was happening there; he has been observing it from his window for several years. At first—just once; later—occasionally and then—constantly. Whenever, wherever: the black jubilant centipede, the hunch-backed semibasement wood louse. The time of year and day is changing, the long dresses of the flock are turning into long-skirted sacks. The decorations and lighting and the footwear of the extras are changing, but their gestures, grimaces, and gait do not show any variations. When it is October and the melted butter of the slush spreads on the stale zwieback of the black-top; whether there is fog, and mildew, God's false milky dew, oozes down the gutters of the old women's wrinkles; if it is late, dark, and the pieces of glass from broken bottles glimmer nei-ther in the harbor nor in the trash of garbage piles; or when January puts wind-and-snow gags in the thin-lipped mouths of the babblers; or February-crooked-paths, having outfitted itself with the pincers of snowstorms, tries to tear out the sinewy tongues of the prophetic tattlers; or when it is summer, but it is cloudy, and the stratocumuli, udder-shaped, grow, ripen above the site—when and whether, and if, and wherever, and while—then, therefore, and consequently, it follows that no one will notice the approach of the expedition, and even if one notices, one will not caw, and if one does caw, one will not be heard, and if one is heard, there will be no response: Cozying up in the warm daze of kerosene, fearing polyps and glands, the barracks will not meet her, will not look out. Only you, the apprentice-enchanter, pretending to be the admirer of the Celsius scale but actually evaluating the universe—more precisely, one of its paths—every time you will discover them again on their way to the plywood dwelling. If the light dimmed, went out, the ne'er-do-wells would light the candle ends. You will see them—poor, shaggy, and ugly; their features are revolting. However, when the procession came down from the railroad embankment, came closer to the gardens populated by stooping scarecrows, when it stepped on the solid ground of the yard flattened by children's games and printing chicken feet, then everything achieved by the blabbermouths in the case of overcoming distances turned into purest fiction. Not thinking about going back, not making even a step backward, the procession has already returned, transferred, moved to the starting position, toward the horizon, and clearly not noticing what happened, continues what had been started—walks, marches, goes forward, dragging and pushing, urging and scolding the one whose head is thrown back and crowned with a quite tainted—but from afar, through the cleansing crystal of empty space, astonishingly fresh ribbon. And when, many Aprils later, one of the disobedient pupils of the courier institute will become an accidental witness of the Sisyphean gliding next to the river-cesspool, it, despite all its particulars, will not seem to the inspired youngster like a frightening revelation. He will juxtapose, compare both marches, and note their similar and different features. Both of them—you will assure yourself, having turned with the help of the flannel into something resembling a cocoon and going to the official dormitory sleep—both of them are symptoms of terminal temporal disease that distorted the natural flow of events and years, the flow of being, the course of the flow. And winter did visit—all in cheviot coats and thaws. It came, feverishly breathing with the bowels of the bed table; it was a sum of smells—*asidol*, paste, wax, a dirt-cheap remedy, called without beating around the bushes a remedy against sores, soap, and, of course, Maria biscuits, sent by their namesake in a registered package. You would have preferred if winter wafted with Matthiola, you would have desired the aroma of Hawaiian amalia, but you did not wince, did not turn away in disgust, fearing that it would get offended and pass, while you wanted to remember it as well as possible—so the next day, in spring, having left the cocoon before the bugle of reveille, you would offer the meeting to pencil and gouache. It came and kept breathing. With an ashen mane, strange, and clinking with horseshoes made of ice. And to wake up in flowers and cicadas, under the camel-embroidered sheet that suddenly became too small. And to wake up in an Egyptian sarcophagus, in a hunting hideout made of tree branches, in the tower of Monsieur Flaubert, in the one in Pisa, in a hollow of a thousand-year-old baobab, having changed into a large long-eared koala, hanging with its ears down. And to wake up meaning nothing, as a handful of ash from Tushino, firmly jammed into a Tula mortar. Maria is leaving; it is dawn. To crack, to fry, and to eat three eggs. To feed the crumbs to two tweeting fugel. They will finish pecking, clean their feathers, and tweet again. And other birds, beyond the window, were flying in the direction of the sun, and some were sitting on whitish branches, and others still were trying to print on the roseate frozen sand, but unfortunately they were leaving no tracks. Looking askance at the factory, at the smokes from distant plants, and at the laborer who, straining himself, pushed along the planks the overtime wagtail with junk, the celestial body was coming up. *A Visit of the Ragpicker*. The genre-painter-wanderer is not needed and not known. The cook of an impoverished aristocrat is treating with some leftovers the suitor who dropped in for an hour. They are having tea in the kitchen at the sticky table. The door to the backyard is partially open; a cart loaded with noble junk can be seen there. Right beyond the backyard begins the backdrop. Behind it, a drinking joint, a *schlagbaum*, *verstas* of blurry road, a jail, Siberia, and a cemetery are lined up. The visitor is poorly groomed, unbuttoned, with a face like a trough; his visage bears traces of all kinds of excesses, while the cook is by and large untidy, and her master, the emaciated graying dotard, hiding for some reason in the larder and gingerly looking through his lorgnon at the laborer (the most faded corner of the painting), having slightly pushed aside the filthy curtain with his refined, long-fingered hand, her master—in a nightcap and some kind of cheap undergarment with frayed lace of jabot and cuffs—is a total slob. And should we not wake up at his ancestral estate? In the library? On the ornate settee? On the best days of its owner? As him in person? The works of the departed overachievers may start glimmering in the bookcases with the gold stamping of their spines, as soon as Selene, the brainless child of deaf and mute dusk, seemingly having swallowed itself and astonished and proud of it, Selene with the features of a dictatorial idiot, gulps with her sardonic mouth, with the pores of her highborn face the darkness of the study, and the light may dominate, and everything that is able to reflect, mirror, shine, and glimmer—all this may glimmer, shine, mirror, and reflect. But then the stirring of poplars, the rustling of their meaty leaves may forecast the sudden morning, and the moon may already start fading and falling back, tumbling backward, like during an attack of epilepsy, rolling off the roofs as a not-yet-eaten round bun, dropping behind them, dripping into the corrugated auricle, where big-cheeked pipers pipe on Saturdays, plunging into the park of cultural recreation, into clusters of planted plane trees and the stirring lindens—rolling off, plunging, and spinning among them like a Ferris wheel. The morning dawn dethroned, diminished the moon; this way its fame was ending. The heavenly light penetrated your closed eyelids, and your face was soaring. But even in those moments of your youth, filled with lofty visions, you, then a common apprentice courier, would not ever dare to assume that a time will come—and you will become a whipper-in. The early brooms and the scratching of bread trays being taken out of the crates of the bread carriage, and the squeal of the same trays, sliding diagonally into the underworld: the bread of someone's early years. And someone of advanced years was walking by. He was walking slowly. He was walking, afflicted by shortness of breath and by foul language. He was walking for a long time. But even he passed by. And a while later the first electric clunker escaped from the purple fingers of Aurora—it was gliding over the rails, hissing with bearings and trolleys, and: But, look, the morn, in russet mantle clad, walks o'er the dew of yon high eastward hill—was posted on the route-board in hieroglyphics corresponding to the occasion. But the transport-absence of people did not last long: The coffeepot has not had time to boil yet, when along the entire street the self-propelled and chock-full-filled equipages already started making noise. The passengers' appearance seemed disagreeable, like the smell of the open, but as ill luck would have it, jammed umbrellas, which from the frowning point of view so vividly resemble armpits of archaeopteryxes and which the provincials keep sticking in each other's noses, having burst in, enthusiastically wet, at the stop named Theater, and having burst out, enthusiastically dry, after the premiere that opened another Aesopian season. Inconspicuous cricket of the outskirts, in October you are particularly mysterious. Sad-eyed, you listlessly soar as a patchy mist, walking quietly in the evening from the swings, from the slipways, from the waves of motorboats, gray like the wet sailcloth. You appear, walk out, step on the young thistle before the highway, then—on the highway, then—on the young thistle beyond it, on the cozy gully of Neglect, on beloved, hated—cross out what is not needed—fences and roofs, in order to dreamily, and blindly, and coolly mask it all, shield it, cover it, hide it from strangers' beholding, swirling, wriggling, and writhing noiselessly, and as if you were squashed between five and six o'clock. You are shielding it, covering it, hiding it, and if one asks from what, you will not answer; perhaps you do not know the answer? No, you do know, but you will not answer—and that is all. You will only answer someday, after going through your youth, after grieving, after burning up, but, as before, being envious of strangers in that old place, you will answer to everything. Foolish girl, an orphan and a child of orphans of this land, I am calling you—look back. Do you know how bright and clean is your unwashed face and how many earthly sorrows of your sisters are combined in its unearthly features? Lonely and lone among all the lone and lonely who are countless, burn, burn brightly—there, at the cobblestone highway; here, at the crossroads of turnouts, and at the dead end, where the burdock grows. Burn with white light, sinless flower, burn, bitter, burn, timid, burn, enchanting. Burn for Yakov, burn for everyone who is rushing to your light in confusion. From Saint George to the Intercession, from the river's standing to the river's flowing and from the black fields to the white roads sheltering autumn—burn through the summer, burn through the winter, and as a white shepherd's star spread everywhere gentle light, your secret charity. Be merry—your image is perennial, not involved in anything, and out of this world. There, on the cobblestone highway, here, on the crossroads of turnouts, burn incessantly in the circle of the funereal old women's heads that resemble firebrands—gray and smoldering. On that cemetery or on that hill—show white from a distance, burn rising up, captured by the army of crosses similar to warriors mounting brownish mounds. Come merry—to proclaim on the entire firmament your frenetic balabala. And the dusks cometh and the dark flyers gather toward the night into black flocks—and only the boundless spaces up high pay heed to this answer.

14

ACCORDIN TO ILYA PETRIKEICH

Bell-bottoms, a fleet cap with a crab, a pea coat with anchors—what a picture. And he presents himself—sailor Albatrosov, discharged without hands from the dry-cargo carrier to the ball of landlocked destiny; and what year did You launch from Your mother's port? I also introduce myself. To our harbor, he says, ocean ships kept steerin, to drop anchor, I says, when their job was done, in the tavern, he says, merry sailors kept on cheerin, drinkin, I says, to the health of their valiant ataman. That's all true, nodded the Black-fleeter, but for me you better touch upon love, adjust the music a little bit. Sure, even a hundred times. And I offer to the attention of the listener the cherished and sorrowful song. Chrysanthemums stopped bloomin long ago in the park, but despair's still abloom in my own dear heart. My Albatros dipped his rudder, started clearin his throat, the dry cough is shakin the seaman. And just then comes a way station, and a Ukrainian dawdler is peddlin mill cakes—periphery, outskirts. I jerked the door open and screamed: Hey, partner, do you need teeth? 'Cuz I overspent durin my ride. Oh, I do, she says, I do, without them I'm at my wits' end. I'm lettin both jaws go for three rubles, just look how white—like a bone. I did let them go and became a lisper again. It's nothin, we'll manage, for the grateful chum we'd even give an eye for analysis. The express moved forward and we moved to its restaurant: Munch to stop the hunger's rage, take your meds from early age. We captured by abordage two reserved seats and ordered everythin delightful—even the fish sticks. And he reports: You have upset my livers with them chrysanthemums, I'm a son of a witch, when I was a novice sailor, I was based on the trainin pontoon, on a cracked barge, and I did not even have a chance to blink, when on the park's bald spots with all kinds of carousels began to loom, he says, a foolhardy mamuasel—a gal not too appealin but always willin. At first I used to hang out with her alone, but later I would bring those mates who did not have to stand watch, and it was exactly she who was tormented by this song. And when we were raisin the anchors, I got away for an hour from all hands on deck—and to the girl. For farewell she gives me a piece of paper: She wrote down all the stanzas and put the address on the back—the lane, the buildin, and the room. As if to say: Don't forget, send snapshots. But durin a campaign there ain't much to write about, and it's forbidden too, and later we all got placed into school's custody, and there we're even less into letters, a complete rat race: either the solitary confinement, or scrubbin, or crammin the Morse, and with cadets there are scrapes 'cuz of hussies—it's no joke. No, seafarin soul, mine did not leave any address, just left God only knows where, and now try to claim damages. We tasted misfortune with her, lived together in her pad quite a while, but did not stockpile nothin except Yakov—a smartie but, nevertheless, a dummy, and even then she hinted that not I am his happy father, from a switchman, supposedly, she got like that, 'cuz she was servin at the switch, and in the beginnin was on duty round the clock. Where and how, I tried to learn, at what hour? Well, she esplains, on a pile of discarded wood chips, next to the storeroom, where they used to eat suppers. Suppers or not suppers, who's gonna check, but I was troubled a lot. Orya was cuttin me without a knife, but altogether, I underline, it was bearable, and it only turned unbearable when she advanced to a dispecher there and started actin as tactlessly as can be. A hair pick like any other, and yours, made of tortoiseshell, I lost on the rails. Well, and this one here, how on earth?—I was askin, feelin completely cheated but not ready for a clash. She kept givin me runarounds, insolent to the max—I found it on the rails too. Your vale is like the railroad, came to my mind, but you yourself—you're a slutty broad, you ain't mine, your most strongest friendship ain't with me, not in this here hovel, not on this here reclinin device, but on those same rails; they even managed to make you Yashka on the ties. I started wondrin.

■ □ ■

And the dawn, I'll say frankly, is catchin fire stronger than any dawn on the other side of the Wolf, although You, most likely, can hardly understand what we, the inhabitants, call Beyond the Wolf. That's why I am rowin, a water strider, to the other shore. Briskly-briskly I row, sprightly-sprightly, and the masts are bendin and they creak, but the Itil outdid my brisk pace with its width, and the day midges are already at the heels of the swarms of mornin moskitos. I reach it before lunch, and my scull like a fish jumps out on the sand at full speed. I celebrated my achievement with Your second smoke and I'm hobblin along on my squeakers, observin the growth of lilies. I confirm: They toil not, they spin not, and yet they're dressed spic-and-span. But skimmin thru these here sketches of mine, You have the right to exclaim in protest. I am sensin Your puzzlement, I'm not a knucklehead, even if I'm disfigured, but let's agree once and forever: Crutches are crutches, but mushrooms— nuts. And I cannot, due to the first, whilst they ain't present, and havin abandoned the trips for the third and the second, sit like my namesake from Murom without stirrin for thirty years plus three more of travel restrictions. Thank goodness, Krylobyl visited me and, feelin sympathy, enlightened. Ilya Petrikeich, he declares cleverly, do you insist that the time fuctions everywhere in unison? I said: I do not insist. I have nothin to hide, Sidor Fatherovich; when I insist, then I do insist, but if I don't—then right away: I don't insist and that's it, why drag it on. And I told him squarely: You may be offended, complain, you have the right, but I am givin you my word: Yes, I do not insist. Look, Krylobyl, this know-it-all, instructs, let's take not time, but an ordinary river. Well, let's. And turn your imagination, he pesters, that it practically doesn't move in the backwater; duckweed and grasses are stranglin it, while at the channel line it rushes; and the time fuctions the same way, he esplained, in Gorodnishche it moves, approximately, like a stroke of a swift's wing, in Bydogoshch, not too fast and not too slow, and in the woods, a total peace and quiet. For that reason, mind my assurances that the theft, of which you are the victim, took place so far only in our beloved town and nowhere else, and on the other side nobody even heard about it. That means, if you move over there—everythin will be right again. I took all this under consideration and started goin on the future scow to bygone years. The main difficulty—how to get to the moorin posts. Regardless of graphs and paragraphs, around here there was and still is a severe shortage of volunteers to assist the defectives, that's why we are the chosen ones. And for that reason, in adventures of the given kind, I, a good chap, am aided only by the familiar to You thrice-removed relatives. I have rowed across and hobble aimlessly, havin trampled lameness with lameness, and You—here, in the present—are studyin this Volapuke. You've gone up on the porch to get some air and turned Your imagination to me; You shield your eyes: Our scamp has a finger in every pie—I see the grinder Beyond the Wolf. No, I see You there, 'cuz not I am there but You. In a word, we both are right. After all, since we are on different sides, we also have a different geography: You are Beyond the Wolf and I am too. Well, so she misplaced her attention to the tot, returns tanked up, and I—I'm a scandal-maker. And one day Orina tells me straight on: Say, let's divide our toys in half. Ilya has nothin to divide, all his toys from the belongins kind, of plates-foot-bindins type—are one or two and he's ready to go. I loaded the ammunition into my indestructible snatch-it-all, into a sack, bowed to the cheater, kissed sonny, probably not my own, rolled down the banisters to the basement, and opened under the stairs a kind of a fur-makin workshop, I became a sort of a chillin furrier. But actually I was makin a livin by paintin and sellin various inflatable balloons from a pharmacy and inventin squeak-squaks. There's no doubt that I slept there too, and slightly later, to avoid tiffs with the powers that be, obtained a patent. How the heck—it's on the bottom of the list now—but I gathered as many orders as cat's tears, so I was forced to beg on local trains and make repairs to this or that old thing; I also became a whiz on a few instruments. Or somethin else—one may wander now and then at dawn to the dump—one may look, but I'm just a spook, a fidgety bum. Widely and freely, I dare to mention, spread these malodorous fields; occasionally, you'll go far-far in search of joys—and you'll get lost. When you're workin hard, everythin drags by imperceptibly; it's already noon, and if not the frosty sparks, then skylarks. You'll ascend the garbage mound to get some rest—your spirit will flare up: A tip-top site! Look around: In the west, in the valley, the ragpicker scrapes the garbage with her rake; in the north, a three-pawed bitch scours for some grub; in the east, a sergeant-reservist rummages in the stream—raves about assemblin a motorcycle out of spare parts; and in the south, some riffraff scavenges for cigarette butts. Peace, calm, nobody's doin nothin to nobody, 'cuz here a man is a man to man, nothin more; and the smokes of the fatherland are everywhere, like durin that uprisin—garbage smolders softly, a real panorama wherever you'd turn your head. And such closeness to it pinches inside, that to return home—to hell with it! Our inhabitant is attracted to the expanses of his land and he needs nothin else. In those same quarters I put together a decent lidrary, so to speak, that is, a collection of multicolored tops from various mixtures: colognes, perfumes, You know what. In this sense, invaluable help by her advices and greetins used to gimme that western rag-picker, auntie with meat on her bones, well-bred and with experience, and she was sixty-plus years old—a delicacy, no more no less. It's an adventure from the past, and I will not hide what was: I had a fleetin crush on her, as also happened, incidently, with her grand-ward, or similar to it, for which, of course, in retrospect, I blame myself, if that's required. Ladies' flesh is a great temptation; that certain thing—we yearn for it but can't be held accountable. The same here: Everythin started almost like when you just fool around. She kept objectin, avoided me, frowned, but if you dig more deeply—there's no difference. In the barracks they used to say that she's nuts, she's like that from birth, but personally I wouldn't claim nothin exceptional. The only thing that her head was really rather absurdly small, but the ragpicker assured—it'll ripen to the weddin, it will heal; well, if it'll ripen, it'll ripen, the caretaker knows better. One day she sends her girlie with some hide for me to scrape—and I got excited in my declinin fate. Only don't look for faults, Fomich, in the beginnin I curbed my curiosity, what things are like with her, that is, at her age, You know, well, so accidently I put the bolt in the lock, in secret, that is, from myself. Later I reckon—devil has his ways—I'll take a gamble, not everythin is done by calculation, like with grandmas, it would be nice with their grandkids every now and then, spontaneously. And the incorrigible happened, I deployed myself with the adolescent in excitement and at the heat of the moment. We agreed to meet; sometimes we please each other under the stairs, other times under the bowroat. After several months, on the side, from a friendly guitarist, to whom I am eternally grateful for teachin me how to read music, I learn that some rivermen secretly cleave my teenager. I turned a blind eye—she's not made of soap, she won't foam away, and they're doin what the young do, that's their right—they'll cleave and leave. Orina worried me, her contacts led me off the rails, and feelin lonely without her, I grieved under the scow, crawlin on the rags that should be burned so they won't stink. And the ticklin trash like flies fed on the junk and made its habit to walk over the exposed places. At first they didn't bother me; on the contrary, I derived some pleasure from them, but closer to the Assumption they ate me alive, and my encouragement ended. And in the hole of the rowlock there lived a wolf spider. The entire bottom, like heavens above, he entwined with his web. I kept catchin the insects and throwin them into his nets. How neatly he, unscrupulous, kept takin out the souls of these creatures, yikes! Pasha, my comin, my Spider, wrote Pyotr to his nephew from the village, I haven't seen an event more borin than January without yeast, so bring it hook or crook. In my heart I believe, he continued, in my heart I know you won't lemme down, but the mind is weak, gets tempted: You will not bring it, after all; woe is us, tipplers, in that case. Precisely then, Pavel sends me the news by the Fenist. Ilyusha, sir, our prophet, I and Pyotr here got into our heads to stockpile some home brew, and 'cuz you wish us well even without that, and helped us with the letter *zhe*, won't you loan us, besides that, some money, as I will liken the yeast Beyond the Wolf to everythin marvles, and winter without it I will compare to spring without top boots, or to the same winter but without *valenki*; like a dreadful nightmare, he exploits, will be the flutterin above us, apostles, so please. I procured some paper, sand, dipped the pen into the inkwell and started gazin with admiration outside, where the lonesome snowbabe, sculpted by me, broke into a serious drip. On the calendar—the end of the side-warmer, but wait a bit with grinnin, March may still force you to sell your last shirt. Stop sendin the Fenist in vain, I answered Pavel, you and your uncle won't get money from Ilya, so far I'm not dispensin money but healins, and these only to those that show respect, and even more not to be guzzled away: 'Nuf of gettin pickled; but before I, maybe, send you money, before that, you'll deliver to me by a courier my accessories. Which? Well, those that you and the saints like you filched in December, havin chosen for this the confusion of darkness and the hubbub of the blizzie. And I passed on to the whipper-in the ultimat to take care of and solve our discord in secrecy, without proclaimin it from the housetops, by agreein that neither the wolf nor the hound, but somehow neither this nor that, somethin like the mornin evenin, and that I, bein amenable, would hope for the return of one instead of two. And the reply: Wipe clean, he offends, your bodily beacons and watch out so you won't get tossed accidentally into the outside darkness. And then I decided to undertake this here supplication to You, and to forget the Spider and his request, havin punished him with a chill rebuff. What's been said—we will do, but let's not forget—or else the night will remind us—how with his trunk he kept takin out the souls of the flies under the boat.

■ □ ■

And I started wondrin. Orya, my Orya, they also kept chafin you all over the hollows in the same manner. On weekdays of the paycheck or on Fridays of the advance, in the famed alders beyond the tracks, unknown to me trainees, your darin buddies from railroad vocational schools, were audaciously carousin with you. You are quite weak, Orina Ignatyevna, as it became clear, between Your legs, You ain't indifferent to sweets, and not a hair pick You've lost on the rails but honor. For a faceted tumbler of the poison from Kashin you caressed them every which way, you wanton shrew. Why, I would quietly wanna find out, you never fondled Ilya like that? And a certain bush grew over there, inconspicuous, but thick and close by, and durin lengthy twilights I observed indecencies from there; You were a Sodomite, little mother. Afterward I would go to the nutty one, tryin to recoup my losses, but with her—like with a doll—she would look at me as if she was made of lead, not indulgin me in any whim. On the weekday of railroad paycheck or on Friday of the advance, I knocked back a few on account of someone's generosity, picked up a piece of iron by the depot, and I'm waitin in the famous alders beyond the tracks. And these rascals, shorties sixteen boyish years old, appear and lead my workin girl on the execution meadow of love. I decided to wait—let them begin; then, filled with more courage, I will attack from behind the kurgan like a perfidious infidel. Quickly, five of them got pickled and started doin what each was good at. Eh, I think, ready or not, here I come. But then I reckon: If you rush the stuff you will make them laugh, you'll scare them inadvertently; I better hold my fire. And from nothin to do I keep rereadin a ticket that I also picked up, with a number, truly, 8,420 to be exact, suitable for travel last year to such an unforgettable land as the Meadow Saturday. This cardboard piece affected Ilya, affected him a great deal. Just imagine, Fomich, the Meadow Saturday. That is, not only Saturday but in addition framed by meadows, perhaps even water ones. And streams of concertina are splashin over them. And the weekenders, in ironed clothes, and even with canes, keep strollin, beamin about somethin appropriate. Everythin is calm, no mug-thrashin, only the coachmen swear at water carriers, but even that with yawns. And if they decide to sit for a while in the shadow with company—retire, gentlemen, into the bushes, to special stands, and relax to your health. I pictured for myself this bliss, so unlike our places, and I make a commitment: Whatever happens, regardless of any scrapes or anythin else—to pay Meadow Saturday a visit in the future existence. And I tied a knot. On my necktie. And when together with the sailor Albatrosov we whistled ourselves all hands on deck, havin abruptly abandoned the buffet car 'cuz our funds ran out, and we moved to the foksel, our steamboat was dockin at the proper embarcadero. We disembarked, looked around, and lingered in that hole a couple of weeks—what boonies and wastes! With no money and desperate, we hanged around there like jerboas, and havin conversations with the locals, we were talkin to them, sayin: And you dare to call yourself Meadow Saturday. We scrounged half a ruble for smokes and followin the dictates of our hearts plodded down to Gorodnishche to have some fun and, after arrivin, we inquire: How's that young life of yours? So-so, they answer, we're gettin by little by little. And how are you managin with chasers? Well, we almost always manage to fill our stomachs with some innards. So after our arrival, we got to be there, and havin a surplus of ailments, started hangin about. On the day of railroad paycheck or the day of the advance, I've had a gulp in the joint near the station with rail workers-tipplers—and I stand jealous in the bush with the danglin iron. How I jumped out, how I leaped out with the hatchet: Aha, I threaten them, aha! And they: Grab him, grab him! Brace yourself, they yell, such-and-such jerk! Four of them caught up with me and knocked me down as I fled. And they kept stompin on me, askin: How about that, did we catch you fair and square, you mother-sucker? You did catch me, I cry, cap-bands, you banged me up, hammers in button loops, as fair and square as can be. I try to break free—but they hold fast. They pounded me like Sidor's goat, got me filthy all over and—I see—they are draggin me, the poor wretch, along the gray slag with my mug down. And they've pulled me up the embankment, spiders, and, relentless, are clampin me to the rail with barbed wire. Why do it, kiddos, I agonized, am I some kind of a fox cub to you? Tenacious, with their crafty mitts they completely squash me on the stinky ties, deviously don't lemme breathe. They had fastened me like a *valenok* to the speed skate—crosswise and leavin no slack, with linesman's pliers, and then they split, chickens. I'm also scared—I'm waitin for the express. And—as it is customary—I started refreshin my past: How did I live this time, decently or not? I reckoned this and that, and the characteristic turned out mostly not bad. I had the reputation of a serious, respectable gentleman, had not committed, as they say, highway robbery. And when the embers of the heavenly matters were already pourin down from above, then, in spite of everythin, this strange Orya appeared to help. She kept callin the obnoxious Ilya a poor fox, started to unwind the wires—and was shakin like a leaf. And I felt with my whole shoulder blades that my express is comin close, and the wires are many and thick. It had but a few meters left, it was humiliatin with its lanterns, made noise. I said: Orya, sweetie, so long, step aside. And she: And maybe together? Not with me, I negate, you stick with the cap-bands. And she: Don't be cross about that, with them urchins I just so—to have a little fun, to visit for a while—but my joy was bein with you, I felt with you like earth with grass, she says, and forget my excesses—everythin passed, healed, sharp teeth, long tail. You have mixed it up, little mother, you're confusin somethin, seriously, do I take after a fox? The magpie is sick, she claims, the crow is sick too, she says, and Ilya is healthy and glad, she casts the spell. I jerked, jerked, pulled, but partially did not succeed. It swooped, mangled, hot, and my hands-legs scattered all over. The battalion of about-goners grew larger; commander, receive the reinforcements. And the infirmary. Havin not found this and that in the makeup of my body, I came to a boil and demanded consolation. A hulk of a doc in a cap floats in. To my question, Where is my friend?—he says the miserly: She's done for. To the bonesetter: Go, heal Thyself, I permit myself not to believe You—just look what You've thought up; I made a row. And my treatment went on. There were newspapers, slippers, shavin was provided.

■ □ ■

And I recalled how, braggin about his sharpened blades, Gury kept tootin his horn among the masters in the co-op that so far he missed the sad chore of racin races against the whipper-in; I'll blow by, he claimed, as if he was standin in place. As a result, they started arguin, put wine in the kitty. Havin received the notification-declaration, the whipper-in approves. They agreed to run as usual, in the dark, and, possessin the mental hypervision, I see them like now—one in clothes patched, the other in mismatched. At the takeoff, they clawed nose by nose, and they aspired to run almost exactly from the pant-washin deck to the Sloboda tributary, to the Tavern Island number two—and back. And they rushed along, cuttin the ice with their skates. The whirlin snow dusted the tracks of their heroic deed, and the fishes not as much saw the athletes as heard them, but in the near future perhaps they'll have a chance to taste one of the participants; come and pray, large and small fishie. A few *verstas* before the turn, Gury began gainin and the whipper-in fallin behind, but Gury aimed slightly more to the right than he should and fell into a polynya, an ice hole in the area of the fairway. It does not freeze there under any conditions, and quite a number of sleepyhead coachmen and lunatic speed skaters fell in over there. They failed to account for Gury too; he plopped in and right away got sucked under the ice, so the dog master on his part just started sobbin. They decided to hold the wake for the wolf-slayer without his factual presence; nobody was in the mood to wait until he floats up somewhere or until the kiddos pull him out with a dragnet: In most of their cases our folks embrace the lack of time. And so they gathered at the gravedigger's. You know Beyond the Itil, here it's impossible to put an end, even if relative, to quarrels and disputes: They started arguin about love—say, who she is, that thoroughly beautiful madame. Everyone stuck to his guns; one, like Vasily Karaban, that Everlastin Existens dropped in to visit, the other—on the contrary: discords, bad harvest, events. And I, stayin pas, don't butt in, keep neutral. But to You—to You I admit, obviously not to tell the others, since even without that they consider Ilya a chucklehead. Why, what on earth for did she persuade the medical four-eyes to powder my brains—I can't make sense of it. And now she's remorseful, searches along the entire river, ain't there among you the one, you know, who. They are lyin that no, as they themselves are head over heels in love: We don't know who you are concerned about, but all of us wouldn't mind bein with you. And Gury's also like them, even though he's a Chud. Oh my precious, he pleaded, our reach ain't narrow—it's wide, and where this youngster is nestin, I have no clue, I only realize that if you popped in to my place for a short while, then the road of my life, narrow as a sharpened blade, would become as wide as this reach. She stayed, they say, with him for a while on the eve of his decisive heat with the head dog master, but even that was more than the supplicant could handle. I am worried: She is my intended demise, and she, Orya, is lookin for me, Fomich, pinin. And I don't know what measures to undertake—to get lost without a trace or to hobble to her with a confession. But neither this nor that is possible right now. Krylobyl—that's whom I trust, whom I praise—Krylobyl admonished the wardens: You, light of your own eyes, return to the cripple what's the cripple's. They started scurryin, but the sought for completely vanished.

Perhaps it was drunk away, perhaps thrown behind a bush of brittle willow, perhaps it simply floated down the stream. But for Ilya it makes no difference, put it back where you took it, Ilya needs it here and now. He got stuck, he got stuck for good without them. Some have Sloboda, some Overbrowears, some Gorodnishche, but he—he is sittin here like a dog on vomit. Just look, as long as we're talkin about it, how many of them hold a watch in a circle around our establishment. Do You think they are waitin for alms? No way, there's nothin they could hope for, so far they didn't earn it. No, not for alms— they're waitin for those who celebrate their promotions. And as soon as you promptly get outta there, these doggish mutts begin to swallow their frozen turds and show their tongues. Their calculations are simple: Probably, lookin at these revoltin things, or simply due to the fresh air, you'll serve them ten-ko-peck macaroni à la fleet. And if you get stingy—a more noble regular will split his sides. And the droolers will run up and snarf everythin. And they get drunk right away, and at once engage in marriages-weddins, right in public, and as a result, they give birth to such mongrels that better don't let anybody see them. They get born, get stronger, and, like their grand-dads and moms—along the beaten track, with their famous side-amble—march, march to the sickler. Halloo, the chain of these generations ain't breakin here, it rings, clanks, and the snack bar, standin in full view, doesn't disappear from our eyes. We're all mankind's brood, my dear, and we're no strangers to knockin down a shot. Now consider truthfully my position, how can Ilya get his body goin, not to mention the more se-cret things. My companion escorts me to the bench near the gate—and I'm sittin, enfeebled, under the pines, temptin my female neybors. Hark! A snowcap fell on my forhead; stop it, woodpecker, watch out, hoopoe, you'll get what you've been askin for. They pulled, they pulled the wool over Ilya's eyes, he found himself cast aside, and the public makes fun of his Saturdays. Here they are, Discords Beyond the Itil as such, Fomich, and we cannot wait to taste the nonexistence. But do me a favor, don't worry: We'll get milled over—and back. Everythin had already happened on the Itil, all the folks had already been there before. Let's say, somebody appears, and they call him: Hey, feller wanderer, will you have some? But the comer cuts them short: You took me for someone else, I'm yours, homegrown, you simply forgot about me, so just pour. I also claim— Dzhinzherela kicked his heels about, settled here and there, happened to visit the Wolf River, drank the vino, sharpened the unsharpened, caressed lonesome babes, and went, whenever he needed, for seasonal work into the wild blue yonder. Hence, I am smart like, approximately, Krylobyl. He remarks with insistence: Everythin around is drunkenness, everyone comes drunk and leaves drunk, and the river just flows and flows, and she don't give a hoot about nothin. I agree, but lemme be more precise: They come drunk and sit, never leavin the crashbaret, and she flows, but the shores remain. And on the shores we're nestin—and our life is eternal. But I chatted with You too long, I've got to hit the sack. If You need anythin, wander in to have some tea; don't be shy—we'll do some tea-drinkin, tea-sippin. At the same time I dare to bother You about the followin: Do You have any spare candy wrappers? I'm a fan, I possess a passion for collectin. Bring them as they are, along with the candy.

And salt, matches, and other necessities are constantly with us. And for the bad writin You will, undoubtedly, excuse me, I was composin in a considerable haste, and I also took a little bit of medicine thanks to my merciful hostess. And the signature, if I may. And those who are illiterate—a cross. Listen, where in the world did I find such a last name, where did I snag it? Maybe I'm a Gypsy baron or maybe the wind simply blew it in. Whatever's the case, somehow I have to set on paper the abovementioned. And pour some sand on it. All the most exceptional to You.

THE BINGER'S JOURNAL

NOTE XXVIII

SPARROW NIGHT

Sparrow Night. I will not pound
Pillows, sheets, and even the cover.
Take a look, again in my hovel
Spooky bats are flying around.

Go away! Enough being mean!
Why'd you bother the poor hunter now?
Anyhow, on his sickly pale brow
The stamp of great torments is seen.

They flew off. Ah, what great sadness.
And alarm. And all that you'd wish.

A washstand. A shovel. A boat.
A stile. Dandelion. A saddle.
A curtain. A needle in a haystack.

And myself, in the eye of my cat.
White jasmine. A frog and a moth.

A completely dry paddle.

The result of events is unknown.
Will the flashes turn into blunder,
Or the word of the prophet will thunder,
Or will it just trickle a bit?

Ocarina. A cart. And a glass.
Wooden ducks. Swallowwort. And a roach.
A seine. A nose-warmer. A jug.
A tench or a bream for some air
Will leap up from the mirrorlike stream,
It will leap and an instant hang there.
As a mark of a scream
Or a question?

A snail and a moth. And a nail.
And on this nail an old gun.
And a harrow. And eaves. Scraper brush.
Empty bottles. A mallet. A bun.
Jar with grease. Two Ostashkov-made boots.
And the swifts sitting under
The eaves.

A completely different paddle.

So, who'll bellow in panic? The cutter
Who his thimble lost in the clutter?
Or the king who promised a meager
Half a kingdom for a decrepit horse?
Or the jaeger who, being too eager,
Hit his pate with his saber full force?

Islands. Or a dragonfly's shadow.
River's bend—like Death's shiny scythe.
Freezing twigs on a distant meadow.
Piece of fatback. And a boar's hide.

And a flint stone. And a rusty skate.

A hair pick. A mortar. A broom.
And a note: "Went to get 'shrooms"
From October two years before.

A discarded horseshoe:
Like the cast of her lip.
Or the strummer who strings of steel
In the garden plucked with great zeal?

Or a smile of Mama-Maria.

Repetition: White jasmine. A toad.
A washstand. And a puddle beneath.

Psst . . . on that shore, alone like a peg,
Chuckled the angler with one leg.

Smell of ozone. Illuminations.

NOTE XXIX

TALES OF THE FACTORY HUNTER

Entre perro y lobo
Or between wolf and hound,
Hung like sticking-out earlobe
Weightless crescent, skybound.
At that time nothing mattered,
But the drink on the ridge,
And the trains softly muttered
Somewhere far on the bridge.
And the forest abutting
The mill droned with its cogs,
From the wood it was cutting
They made boards, beams, and logs.
And the mug we've been sharing
Smelled of fish just a bit,
While the river flowed, bearing
Scents of sawdust and peat.
And the factory hunter
Was there telling us that
He's a factory hunter,
He was telling us that.

This is always the process:
As the wine disappears,
Eyes turn watchful and glossy,
And the bottom appears.
But an evil smirk throttled
Smiles on lips, as a clue
That right now the third bottle
Came to be empty too.
Yet a certain green mare,
Somewhat skinny and bent,
Not for naught lived out there
Just beyond river's bend.
And this lonesome babe-mare
For the drinkers who asked
Always kept as a spare
A big jug or a flask.
Like the crescent, my brothers,
Our boat was air-light.
So we, teasing each other,
Splashed with oars in the night.

NOTE XXX

CHASING THE FIREBIRD

By the green saplings of heather, of heather,
Express is not going, but rapidly pacing
And inside in tall boots, in tall boots of leather

A hunter paces, the firebird chasing.
Strict with passengers is the train's conductor:
Foresee no tea! It ran out long ago.
The barkeep's strict too: Like a silent actor,
He ran out somewhere, and as long ago.
Yeah, thinks the owner of the boots and loosens
These boots of his, these boots, very tall,
While he is reading: "You should drink fruit juices!"
Command from heaven that hangs on the wall.
Dusk. Here's the border. Now sleep goes to pieces.
And through the cars, comparing the rolls
Of mountain, river, even swamp polices,
Wander the guards, and check the boots' soles.
Your boots! They're here, but I have a comment:
The right is too narrow and the left too big.
You're under arrest! But no, wait a moment,
Misunderstanding—it's not you we seek.
Station. Some couplers. The air is quite misty.
A carpenter carries a plank or a tool,
One greaser jests with another, twisting
His own large schnozzle and playing the fool.
From his cigarette case, a train-platform turd,
With snotty nose and eyes out of kilter,
Articulating like one speech-impaired,
Gives an old hag five smokes without filters.
The train speeds on. And you're still not sleeping.
Night shines and smells like the tar's black stains.
Anxiously, hotly, like the mentioned bird leaping,
Alcohol rushes and shoots through your veins.

NOTE XXXI

EPITAPHS OF THE BYDOGOSHCHI CEMETERY

A little church, abandoned,
Tall weeds grow all around,
And the cuckoo at sundown
Flies to the burial ground.
Is she counting the living?
Is she cursing the dead?
Is she mourning and grieving,
Or just singing like that?
At this time or another—
To make the story short—
Among these hillocks gather
The wardens for a snort.
Immediately—two glasses
And quickly the same blend,
You wonder how time passes,
When you're with them, my friend.
You never find it boring
To listen to their lore,
'Cause such amazing stories
You had not heard before.
And leaning, famished fellow,
Against the nameless mound,
Say, Bydogoshchi, hello,
Thanks for the alms we found.

Since drinks are so exquisite
We won't mind what we've lost,
And each time, when we visit,
We'll honor our hosts.

*

Here's Pyotr—now worms' fodder.
His nickname was Pike Pole.
All people called him Fyodor,
He called himself Yegor.
He was a fine gamekeeper,
A boor, though, and a thief,
So on the beam he pilfered,
He bet he could hang stiff.
You, who bet him—don't fear,
Live and thank God, too:
Don't wait when he'll appear,
He'll be waiting for you.

*

There's Pavel—ferryman brave.
His life was in a slump;
He hoped that his own grave
Would save him from his hump.
He drowned and then was gone,
They looked for him—no use.
But he'd float up anon,
Bloated and without shoes.
The seventeenth of May,
They buried the poor chump.
His grave mound, by the way,
Is not a nicer hump.

*

Ivan, a glass man seasoned,
Thought that crystal stank,
And only for this reason,
From the bottle drank.
Shards of glass he'd ever
Chew as snacks—no pain,
But choked and he will never
Be the same again.
Love is happiness,
And happiness—glass.
But glassy happiness
Breaks with ease, alas.
✵

He lived alone—a reclusive rake,
But no loose screws or peccadilloes.
They say that he could perfectly make
Flutes from twigs of young pussy willows.

You may blow flutes or blow your nose,
Bend horseshoes or the truth,
It's not important, not even close,
If company's right, forsooth.

The bitter lips of black poplar sway,
And hum a wind motif each morrow.
When Gury the hunter drank his gun away
He went out and died of great sorrow.
✵

One would find no poacher greater:
Bought fish all day long,
But he used to sell it later
For a song.

Hapless poachers grudged the giver
His tenches and chubs.
They met Kolya by the river
With their clubs.

Sleep, Nikolka, Volga's splashing,
Fires gently gleam.
Dream about a tench that's thrashing
And a bream.

NOTE XXXII

ECLOGUE

After lunch that was just a trifle,
I made sure my duster fit right
And took down my old faithful rifle
To inspect its barrel and sight.
I stepped out. It seemed that a clever
Dog decided to stick there with me.
'Twas considered homeless, however,
Rather fat it appeared to be.
But I was not in the least troubled.

'Cause what counts? That the dog doesn't bite.
While "appeared," "considered" are babble.
Yes—stepped out. Ah, what a sight!
I walked, while the sun's rays were warming
The road's dust, and crickets' chimes
Grew louder. The eclogue was forming
By itself. Mumbling its rhymes,
I reached Polenov's house, inviting,
Followed Savrasov's winding tracks,
And soon, like in Turgenev's writing
I spooked some of Aksakov's ducks.
I raised my gun and shot, atremble,
But just the echo was my loot.
And the smoke's color much resembled
The fur of leshy in the woods.
In the meantime, a gold leaf descended
From a branch of the cherished oak tree.
Why? I attempted to understand it,
But in vain. And what did I see?
In a village, when I was returning,
I saw happy peasants around,
In the tree shade dancing and whirling
To the old bayan's whizzing sound.
And the moon seemed to be hanging
Like a fang of a wolf, bright and young.
Good to see you, my native hangouts,
I salute you, my native tongue.

NOTE XXXIII

RETURN

The hunter pulled the trigger—but the gun misfired.
A crow emitted an untimely caw.
Somewhere, a gramophone screamed, inspired,
And turnips smelled just like a life ago.

Why do we rush, waste effort, as deranged,
And hasten through the plowed field and the glen?
When we come home—nothing's really changed,
And in the mirror—the same good *citoyen*.

NOTE XXXIV

SAGITTARIAN

On the eve I was drinking alone in the light of the day,
And then until dark I was drinking with the fugleman
    bruiser.
I cried about something, and braving the thorns on the
    way,
I walked to the village, where I was known as a loser.
I dreamed that I died. And from above, someone filled
    with great might,
Whose face, though I was trying, I could not recognize,
Advised me: Listen, you Binger, get up and do your job
    right:
To serve as the Archer high to the heavens you'll rise.

In forests of pine, where the razorbacks like to ramble,
And near the meadows that deer use as their feeding
ground,
At night, as the moon gently shone on gray bushes of
bramble,
The start of the way from here to there I had found.
'Twas milky. The green buckhorn did not grow over
there,
In clover could be heard no sweet moderate whine,
The acorns were not falling from maples as they do
everywhere,
And millers of time at the dikes did not thirst for the
wine.
I was ordered to follow the Scorpio—and soon I
encountered
Winged boys who supplied me with a bow and a quiver;
They gave me a gold hunting bag and a box of colorful
lanterns,
And a bucket-size jug of deluxe Hunter's Vodka
delivered.
I'm shooting and drinking. But much more I would relish
A gulp of the Volga home brew, and a pickle chaser I'd
use.
These are just hunters' tales that I live, I am happy, and
flourish,
'Cause drinking and hunting bring joy nowhere else but
in Rus.
So stop being envious, while butting the stars with your
eyes,

Of my way of walking—as soft as the eider duck's
down.
Here no one can ever outshine lonesome babes from
the Valday,
And no one will give you a sleigh ride the way they had
done.
I'm dead, not alive. And like the Brahmaputra are pure
My rags and my thoughts—now they rarely make me
upset.
But tell me, is it true that, as earlier, in the morning
azure
On pumpkins, like on the beaters' foreheads, gleams
sweat?

NOTE XXXV

SPACKLE

Make a cork to plug the drink
From the local paper,
Look out at Valday and think:
Where are you, my helper?
Apple. But in essence—crab.
Crab. But look closer—apple.
The slope it's trying to grab,
Lethargic and slow, but supple.
Push your cap on brow, and free,
Feeling hunky-dory,

Make up, walking to the tree,
Stuff 'bout Wolf. A story?
Crabapple. And still—apple.
Apple. But really—crabapple.
Obsessed by its inner glow
And in its movements slow.
Wolf lived on one Volga shore,
Hound—the other roamed.
Couldn't reach it as before
So he drank and groaned.
Crab. But in general—apple.
Apple. And slow, but supple.
In autumn its leaves are aflame
As brass and copper the same.
Daily, he drank a whole *shtof*,
Drank rotgut and groaned,
That one day he went off
And upset the Hound.
Crabapple. Look closer—apple.
Apple. Look again—crab.
Is it you or that chap,
The trash nicknamed Spackle?
Sharply pricks the naked foot
Stubble of mown grain,
Sit beneath crabapple, dude,
You will feel less pain.
Crabapple. Nickname—apple.
Apple. Occupation—crabapple.
Inebriated pretty well,

By the way, all go to hell.
With your teeth pull out the cork,
Made of paper crumpled.
What kind of a crazy dork
Scribbles all these pamphlets?
Crab. You got smashed—apple.
Apple. You'll sober up—crab.
By the dusk blinded and grappled,
And by the wood louse enwrapped.

NOTE XXXVI

SUPPLEMENTAL

Settling down in a land far away
With a lonesome babe, fairly nifty,
I composed the Notes that today
To you in this bottle came drifting.
I did compose them on the go
Avoiding stress and strain—
In gardens, when the leaves were gone,
On boats or on the plain.
Or on the rafts, when it was light
'Til midnight dimmed the skies,
Or in a sleigh, when snow gusts tried
To blind my wolfish eyes.
Composed them, and on hunting binged,
Drank with the wardens rotgut,

Or binge drank, 'til I got unhinged,
With fishermen their vodka.
When you have finished reading this,
To the post office make a dash,
And, gulping air like a beached fish,
Send these Notes out. But rush
The sending; folks can wait no more.
That's how, for the best hoping,
In times of troubles, my pals wait for
Free bars to open.

16

THE TRAPPER'S TALE

T hat is how, trying to collect his thoughts, the hunting guard Yakov Ilyich Palamakhterov, a man of middling height, ordinary age, and easily forgettable face, philosophized. Yakov Ilyich lived beyond the Volga, in a small but uncomfortable ranger's cabin at the edge of the forest, on the muddy shore, keeping the old warden Krylobylov company. Palamakhterov lived, sewed slippers and hi-tops, looked at the water, drank, went hunting, snacked on potatoes in skins, and, wishing to reflect on who he was, tried to gather his thoughts. On the kitchen table, among the objects of trapping and household equipment, he frequently noticed a kerosene lamp. Now and then, the fuel in the container would end and the wick would mercilessly smoke. At the same time it would become clear that in the copper teakettle, patched once by a certain grinder that became a total drunk and ended badly, in the teakettle with a handmade wire handle, now used to store kerosene, not even a few drops of the latter could be found. I had a teakettle with me—Palamakhterov mumbled, looking at sparks detaching from the smoldering wick and flying up the transparent contraption—a teakettle, my only joy during my travels in the Caucasus. Thinking occasionally about this mountainous region, Yakov Ilyich smiled, recalling that as a boy, having read a lot of nonsense, he passionately dreamed about it; later the Caucasus, like all the other places he never had a chance to visit, became completely indifferent to him. Whenever he realized that he is thinking aloud, Palamakhterov would get surprised. And he would speak, apparently addressing only himself, because, as a rule, he was at home alone: Krylobyl almost never dropped in here. After spending a while beyond the river, Yakov would come back to the guard post without yeast and before leaving again to get it, he would passionately bang for hours on the iron plate that hung on the birch tree behind the kennel; at that point, its dwellers would get extremely excited. And the gloomy and spiteful beggar woman, whom Yakov Ilyich and Fedot Fyodorovich used to pick up in the spring at the fish market and adapt to their bachelor needs—she, having left in the morning to pick mushrooms, not infrequently would be slow coming back, and before the first frosts she would disappear for good. And Palamakhterov would reassure himself: One should not think this way but the other. At the same time, he even tried to gesticulate, but the result was unnatural and silly, like in theater, and afterward he would admonish himself, standing motionlessly and having dropped his hands, listless from confusion. One needs to think with more energy, he would emphasize, one has to inculcate some kind of certainty in the mind, one has to constantly—here he would decide to stop, planning to find for sure a replacement for the awkward word that was getting ready to finish his phrase, but he would not stop soon enough and the word would break loose, jump out—every day, Yakov Ilyich would say, keep inculcating. Strange, smacking of ventriloquism, the word would hang in the semidarkness as a row of letters of different size, sickly shining with a hazy photogen radiation and, after being written, would turn out even less welcome than the uttered one. Agitated, Yakov Ilyich would look at it and completely unexpectedly—after all, it had not snowed yet—would find himself lying in a wide sleigh with his legs in front and with his head hanging or even dragging behind, and every time, when the sleigh passed a bump or a snow-covered stump, letting it pass between the runners, his head—regardless of how much Yakov tried to raise it up soon enough to prevent the blow—would knock on the fly with its occiput against the obstruction and bounce with some kind of a nutlike crack or crunch, and right away, having rattled with its teeth as if it were dead, would fall back again. The situation was even more serious because there was no hat; the latter, as Palamakhterov was compelled to conclude, most likely fell off; otherwise, feeling pity for himself—feeling pity, although, as a result of everything befalling him, he experienced neither pain, nor the obvious inconvenience, nor humiliation, as if everything were happening not to him, as if he were looking at it from the side—otherwise, the whipper-in considered, otherwise the blows wouldn't have been so severe. However, having fallen off, the hat—as he would notice later—was not getting lost but, tied by the strap to the hanger of his sheepskin jacket, was dragging behind the sleigh, like the head, even though the latter bounced more than dragged. On flat spots, when it was not shaking, his consciousness would come to life. Smiling at the small multicolored balls recklessly scurrying in the heights over the felts of otherworldly billiards—it is the freeze, that is the reason it is like that—he would think about the head: It stiffened in the cold, and now it is hard, and now it bounces and cracks. And even if he suspected in the given explanation a certain falsehood and cunning, especially because he could not detect a particularly strong freeze, it satisfied him completely and he did not require any other. They are moving at a brisk pace. But the kneeling coachman who installed himself at the very front of the sleigh keeps urging on, flinging into the darkness of the thicket the squawks and whizzes of the prodding. Worried about his hat with earflaps, Yakov Ilyich keeps looking back—inasmuch as he is able to look back at all—to make sure it did not get lost. But no, as before, it bounces and drags, keeping up with those riding in the mobile wagon train, and Yakov Ilyich, with an intention to thank for the performed service, for the fact that someone with a foresight took care of his headgear—tied it like that—but not knowing whom to thank, addresses the coachman, in an inscrutable way having guessed that precisely he, the coachman, had tied it, and that now his, Palamakhterov's, fate depends on him, and it is advisable to flatter the fellow traveler, tell him something nice, somehow win his favor; and so, Yakov Ilyich addresses the stranger, speaking for some reason in a completely uncharacteristic-for-him voice of somebody unknown: Thank You, I'm so grateful, You've secured my hat, else I am ridin and simply have no clue, where my hat can be, and it is, as it turns out, right here, attached to the hanger; much obliged, I wish You great health, and don't be angry that Krylobylchik and I treated the sharpener like that—anythin can happen in the daily grind. What's done is done, we've lost our temper, made mischief, it happens to everyone, but, after all, as far as he's concerned, he's no saint either; we have forgiven him the stolen storm lamp as a deductible loss, and yet, who has ever heard of exterminatin the hounds. Does he think that 'cuz he is an invalidual, everythin is permitted? No, we have certain limits set for the disabled too, even if they're wider, but in addition he, the petty slanderer, started scribblin them denunciations that, supposedly, we pilfered his crutches, as if there were no other wardens. The voice, the words, and the manner—everything in his speech smacks of artificiality and affectation, everything in his monologue seems strange to him. However, aware of this, he does not feel any awkwardness; on the contrary, he derives pleasure from ingratiating himself with the coachman, and he would like the trip to last and last, and he, Yakov Ilyich, a pitiful, hapless, and grateful person, with this head of his, would like to be carried and carried somewhere, and keep saying quietly and deferentially: Thanks for my hattie, with earflappies, tied to the hangerkin—and would sweetly pity himself, and perhaps, if he were able to cry, he would shed a few tears. Because, he tries to philosophize, what is suffering, what is it as such, indeed, in its essence, if it is analyzed thoroughly? How can it be labeled, defined, at long last? But not being able to elucidate the essence of suffering and analyze it thoroughly, as well as define and label it, the hunter makes peace with the circumstances and no longer wants to worry about anything at all, but wishes that everything would end, be finished, pass, and never repeat itself again. To cross over, cross over, he fantasizes, to turn into a chilling rain of Brumaire and to hover above the bazaar junk of the suburbs, above some utterly remote *versta*, why not the thirty-fourth, counting from the point where it is convenient or desirable; but not counting, because it is not convenient and not desirable. Counting nothing, to linger incessantly above the muck of gutters and retention ponds, above the loam of gardens and wiesenboden of meadows, above the bunch of plywood barracks, warehouses, and shacks; to hang for a long time, disgracing the winged ones—black and large, and despising their migrations, and chasing the sentries and neighborhood dogs under the awnings and into their booths; to remain, piercing from side to side the eruptions of the factory pipes, made of sheet metal or brick, and forcing the smokes of the fire-breathing switchers to spread over their paths; and to walk across the roofs of depots, imitating the railroad roofer of the corresponding section of the track, mumbling and monotonously babbling the same thing, and like a drunken glass installer from the same section, carrying on nonsense and a basket of shards to glaze the yawning gaps of vistas; and to last, increasing the bedlam of crossroads and telegraph wires, and messing up the look of the old-fashioned—once ballroom, but now workday—tailcoats and top hats of garden hay-men, scarecrows, and all the other characters.

THE LAST REMARKS

17

Citizen Pozhilykh. After the end of days, at azure hour, we're relaxin with some folks on the pant-washin deck; we're dusk-baskin. And, as usual, thru the fogs, from the other side of the river, emerge the notorious never-to-be-forgotten. Either Aladdin Rakhmatullin accidently flashes his teeth, or Kolya Helperov winks softly-softly, or that tall one, with a stolen baluster of the same length, appears—leads the weepin old woman with a creel: Permit me to introduce my widow; for almost a century she's been roamin without a fella, thank you—she finally met the Wintry Man. And Krylobyl surfaces from beyond the river, walkin like on dry land: Why are you sittin here? Well, just so. We're waitin for the Heavenly Kingdom—and what the heck brings you here? Courage, I am in possession of good news. Well, out with it, if you ain't lazy! He begins: Do you remember how we were buryin Gury? Who knows whether Gury or not Gury, I says, 'cuz personally I did not happen to grace this empty burial with my presence, considerin it incorrect, but accordin to the grievin bereavers, the empty package was buried with honors. Precisely, says the ranger, and just before we carried him out, for the sake of greater respectability we agreed to stick inside somethin similar, thinkin that if he appears in person, we'll make the exchange. Unfortunately, nothin either similar or dissimilar was found and nobody had nothin—all of them, devils, wagered and lost everythin, brother to brother, all of them made each other poor as church mice. But on the cot in the dayroom there happened to recline a certain unassumin guest from among the drifters who, as a result of havin too many, kept slurrin his words and feelin shabby and faint. In order for his face not to disturb anyone, they turned him toward the wall, to the east, covered him with a mat, and to answer who he is would be difficult from the side; and nobody particularly tried; after all, here everythin is simple: You got smashed, you're snorin thru both holes—so you're welcome to rest, whoever you are, only don't make a ruckus. And the inventory—whether his or not his, who can tell?—was blatantly standin in the icon corner under Our Lady of Sorrows. So we put these sticks in and carried them out—both for edification and for the sake of their not too great, but still, durin a fishin lull, resemblance. And now, in my involuntary repasts, I am rackin my brains: Wasn't it 'cuz of these supports that the wardens bumped Ilya off, and he the hounds, and wasn't it he who, accordingly, was restin at that moment on the stove bench? I'm rackin my brains back and forth and everythin seems to fit: Nothin else, but the grinder's sticks were buried then; I should probably go and tell. Well, everythin is turnin out perfect, I says to Krylobyl, and so we need to dig them up tomorrow. And so tomorrow we'll dig them up. Only how did I manage to get without them after the wake to Gorodnishche, with what,

I'd like to ask, did I overcome the wolf and ascended to my own haunts? It's your concern, Petrikeich, don't drag us into your seductive scandals. And he fades in the smoke, gets lost in the haze, but the next day disturbs again. Hail to you, my kind soul, Fedot Fyodorov, may your good deed be recorded where it should, and may all your trespasses be forgotten, especially my drownin. Courage, sayeth he, I'm in possession of good news. Right, old man, we'll set out at dawn, though we should sharpen our spades first; with unsharpened ones we'll be pokin until the Last Judgment: It's covered with sod, I reckon. These are our latest, Fomich. Excuse me, it turns out, for unfounded worries, so long, be who You are, and have Yourself a happy resurrection, so to speak. And the last remarks. What they are babblin about Ilya—don't believe it, rein in the evil tongues. Just look at them—they got too eager, wanna pin all the dogs on me, while I only had enough time to gun down in revenge a couple of Vizsla bitches, and even those worth nothin. One, I heard, always pretended to be deaf, the other mute, intentionally did not bay at all durin the hunt. Well, miserable pooch, come here, lick my scabs without holdin the grudge, gimme some healin, whenever you want. And how come your rump got so thin? When you were alive you weren't such a skin and bones. Say—I believe, say—at dawn, and we'll set out, we'll rescue our accessories. Well, let's shoot the breeze for a while, no need to keep the mouth shut and pout without reason. Or maybe mysterious for you are these words of mine?

THE NOTE, SENT IN A SEPARATE BOTTLE

NOTE XXXVII

POST SCRIPTUM

Woe is us; this clime's bad for health and the mood,
Every day chains of clouds just get denser,
The one who later will find these Notes should
Burn and scatter on the Wind Rose my verses.
Like the Mongol Horde's treasure, its crown in old tales,
Amztarakhan once vanished, passed on,
And like roaches that fed in the Khan's ponytails
With time passing, would also be gone;
Like during the thaw, tracks of sleighs and of elks
Melt and leave no marks to observe;
Like—without a trace also—did vanish the works
Of nations and the nations themselves;
Like after a bottle, despair may be banished
Though at first our souls wrings and smotes,
The same way—seeking no glory—may vanish,
Together with the bottle, these Notes.

But who needs this stuff? Therein lies the rub.
Why did I, the hunter-ragpicker,
On the face of existence a blemish, a scab,
A lecher, and a pimp who loves liquor,
Compose all these Notes at this river's spring
And floated them down in a hurry?
Such a meaningless loss of candles and ink
And a waste of the force of the current.
How annoying: All these years irretrievably lost,
Playing, singing, and having much fun;
You gaze in the tumbler—and you're just a ghost.
Alas, things look bad, you are done.
Now I darn my old sack during pre-winter's spell,
Fix the fishnets, and sharpen tools' tines,
But I know—pushy buds will stealthily swell
And burst out from their narrow confines.

So I dare you to burn, you dumb-as-a-bell,
My amazing, ingenious lines!

ANNOTATIONS

EPIGRAPHS

entre chien et loup: Between dog and wolf (French).

1. DISCORDS BEYOND THE ITIL

Discords Beyond the Itil: The Russian title of the chapter, *Zaitil'shchina*, is a paraphrase of and a pun on *Zadonshchina*, the title of the sixteenth-century description of the battle of the Russians with the Mongols on Kulikovo Field in 1380. No standard accurate translation of this word exists, but its meaning alludes to an epic tale of the events that took place beyond the Don River. Our narrator's paraphrase implies an epic tale of discords beyond the Itil River (a Khazar name for the Volga).

moonth: The Russian expression "*mesiats iasen*" has two meanings: the moon is bright, and the month is clear. To signal this duality, and the importance of wordplays throughout the novel, "moon" and "month" are combined into one word here. Such a combination resembles similar constructions created by the narrator and, at the same time, indicates the derivation of the word "month" in many languages (including Russian and English) from the word "moon."

Ilya Petrikeich Zynzyrela: The name of the narrator provides links to a number of themes or motifs in the novel: Ilya (Elijah) compares himself to the biblical prophet who controls the weather; in Russian folklore the prophet Ilya was associated with wolves because in some regions his feast day (July 20 / August 2) was the first day of wolf hunting; his patronymic resembles the popular name used in folklore for a female fox (Petrikeyevna), echoing the fox motif in the novel; his strange last name (and the name of his distant relative), spelled in ten different ways (Zynzyrela, Zynzyrella, Zhizhirella, Dzyndzyrela, Dzynzyrela, Dzynzyrella, Dzyndzyrella, Dzhynzhirela, Dzhinzherela, and Sindirela), may be derived from the onomatopoeic *dzyn'-dzyn'* (ding-ding), appropriate for a grinder dealing with metal objects, but its last variant, Sindirela, should remind the readers about the Cinderella story, strangely transformed and distorted in the text.

Your: Throughout, the capitalization of the pronouns "You" and "Your" indicates the narrator's use of the formal form, *vy*, instead of the familiar form, *ty*.

invalidual: Combination of individual and invalid.

A. Sharpenhauer: In the original it was D. Zatochnik (Daniel the Prisoner). His Russian name is also related to the verb *zatochit'* (to sharpen), providing the double meaning relevant to the story of the grinder who is writing a complaint to the criminal investigator, almost like his medieval predecessor who wrote a supplication to his prince about his unjust imprisonment. Since it was impossible to preserve both of these meanings of the name, the novel's author suggested the replacement of "Zatochnik" with "Sharpenhauer" not only because so few English readers would know anything about Daniel but because the substitution is funny (the narrator distorts the name of Schopenhauer, making it relevant to his profession) and because various institutions and enterprises in Russia bore completely unexpected, obscure, and even ridiculous names.

sickler: A drinking hole, where customers get sick after drinking too much.

crashbaret: In the original, *kubare*, a combination of *kubarem* (to fall head over heels) and *cabaret* (using the French pronunciation).

Thou shall not find: The narrator uses an archaic biblical expression.

sharps: Skates.

beneficially social: Instead of the expected socially beneficial, the narrator says beneficially social.

Valday: Valdai or Valdaiskaia vozvyshennost (Valday Hills), a region in northwest Russia, encompassing the Tver, Novgorod, Smolensk, and parts of Pskov and Leningrad Oblast; a source of the Volga.

prolong: Rather than use the word *"prodolzhit'"* (continue), the narrator uses *"prodlit'"* (prolong, lengthen).

skated to his maker: In the original, *"otbrosil kon'ki."* *"Otbrosit' kon'ki"* (to throw the skates away) is a phraseological expression meaning to die, to meet one's maker, to kick the bucket, or to give up the ghost.

fraughtful: Fraught with consequences.

Gorodnishche: Also Gorodnishchi, a name of the fictional city, resembling the word *"gorodishche"* (a fortified settlement), but here joining the words *"gorod"* (town) and *"nishchii"* (beggar); thus, the town of beggars.

embarcadero: A word of Spanish origin, used here for the Russian *debarkader* (a landing stage, a jetty, a floating wharf) because it has the same energy as the original.

musick: The narrator uses the archaic word "*musikiia*" (derived from the Greek *musiké*) as a synonym for a musical instrument.

pachoolies: Patchoulis.

Wintry: In Russian, *Zimar'*, a word coined from *zima* (winter) and the ending of *ianvar'* (January) to indicate any winter month, was used in Andrei Voznesenskii's 1963 poem "Pesenka travesti iz spektaklia 'Antimiry'" (Song-travesty from the spectacle "Antiworlds").

strument: Instrument, tool.

Sloboda: A popular name of a village, settlement, or suburb of a city; its name is derived from the word "*svoboda*" (freedom); originally, the inhabitants of a *sloboda* were freed from some kind of state obligation. Today it is a name of literally dozens of villages and settlements in Russia and Ukraine.

versta: An old Russian unit of length, approximately 0.66 miles.

crasp: Crappy rasp.

glasswear: Glassware.

in the dales and in the hills: A reference to "Marsh dal'nevostochnykh partizan" (March of the Far-East Partisans), written in 1922 at the end of the Civil War; music by Il'ia Aturov, lyrics by Petr Parfenov.

slantily: The narrator makes up the word "*naiskosiak*" instead of using the correct *naiskos'* or *naiskosok* (slantwise, diagonally).

passes: The narrator creates an incorrect plural form of the word "*pas*" used in card games; the translation creates a similar incorrect form.

more younger: The narrator frequently creates incorrect comparative and superlative forms of adjectives. They are rendered by equally incorrect forms in English.

Ploski: village on the Volga, in Konakov District, Tver Oblast.

valenki, singular *valenok*: Felt boots.

outscrape: Outrun on skates.

accounter: Instead of *schetovod* (accountant), the narrator says *schetoved* (rendered here by a neologism: accounter).

gatecharmer: The narrator says "*privorotnitse*," creating the word from the expressions "*privorotnoe zel'e*" (witch's brew) and "*privratnitsa*" (a female gatekeeper). The word "gatecharmer" renders the narrator's neologism.

mere future: Instead of saying "*v skorom budushchem*" (in the near future), the narrator says "*v skromnom budushchem*" (in the modest future). A similar effect is achieved in English by using *mere* instead of *near*.

krambambuli: Originally a strong cordial made from cloves and cherry pits, produced in Danzig. In Russia the name became synonymous with a strong sweet punch after 1827, when Nikolai Iazykov translated the German student drinking song composed in 1745 by Christoph Friedrich Wedekind, "Krambambuli." The punch combined champagne, rum, desert white wine, sugar, and pineapple.

Orina: The name of the narrator's beloved can be found in Nikolai Nekrasov's 1863 poem "Orina, mat' soldatskaia" (Orina, Soldier's Mother).

"Joy": A reference to the popular nineteenth-century folk song "Otrada" (lyrics by Sergei Ryskin, music by Mikhail Shishkin) and its first line: "*Zhivet moia otrada v vysokom teremu*" (My joy lives in a tall tower).

ramjunctious: In the original, the narrator uses the word "*uzlovatoi*" (knotty) instead of "*uzlovoi*" (junction).

unmown ditches: A reference to a line from Aleksandr Blok's 1910 poem "Na zheleznoi doroge" (At the Railroad).

hurry nowhere no more: A slight paraphrase of a line from the early twentieth-century song "Iamshchik ne goni loshadei" (Coachman, Don't Race Your Horses), lyrics by Nikolai von Ritter and music by Iakov Fel'dman.

leaf-slayer: In Russian, *listoboi*, a strong wind that tears the leaves off trees; commonly associated with the month of October.

supplethal: Another mix-up in the vocabulary of the narrator—rather than saying "*gibkaia*" (supple, flexible), he says "*gibuchaia*" (an adjective related to "*gibnut'*"—to perish, to die). The English translation is a combination of supple and lethal.

fell in enrapture: Fell in rapture.

you look best: A quote from the song "Luchshee plat'e—tvoia nagota" (Your Best Dress Is Your Nakedness), composer unknown.

semafors: Semaphores.

the nights there are full of fire: A reference to "Taganka," the famous song about the Taganka prison in Moscow. The first line of the chorus, "Taganka, all the nights are full of fire," reflects the custom in Russian prisons to not turn off the light at night.

unfatomable: Unfathomable.

lonely acordeon: A reference to the 1945 song "Odinokaia garmon'" (Lonely Accordion), lyrics by Mikhail Isakovskii and music by Boris Mokrousov.

filharmonic: Philharmonic.

Bydogoshch: A fictional city with a cemetery, lying across the river from Gorodnishche; it is also called Bydogoshchi, Bydogozhd, Vygodoshchi, and Gybodoshchi.

Crystal Goose: Gus'-Khrustal'nyi, a town in Vladimir Oblast, located on the Gus' River sixty-three kilometers (thirty-nine miles) south of Vladimir and known for its glass and crystal factory.

sarafan: A traditional Russian long peasant dress with thin shoulder straps.

2. THE TRAPPER'S TALE

southerizon: Southern horizon.

how my head is spinning: A line from the 1960s song "Starye slova" (Old Words), lyrics by Robert Rozhdestvenskii and music by Oskar Fel'tsman.

chansonnette: Little song (French); here it is used as a synonym for a female singer.

gramophone figs: The record-holding pin is likened to the international hand gesture, in which the thumb is placed between two fingers.

rail and road gloom: "*Toska zheleznaia, dorozhnaia*"—a reference to Blok's "Na zheleznoi doroge" (At the Railroad).

Orekhovo to Zuevo: To underscore the meaninglessness and repetitive nature of the engineer's speech, Orekhovo-Zuevo, a town in Moscow Oblast, located eighty-five kilometers (fifty-three miles) east of Moscow, is changed into two separate towns.

I love you, my old park: The first line of the chorus from the song "Moi staryi park" (My Old Park), lyrics by Vladlen Bazhnov and Iakov Kostiukovich, music by Arkadii Ostrovskii, popularized by Klavdiia Shul'zhenko (1954).

rattler: In the original, *pogremok*, a neologism created from *pogremushka* (rattle) and *korobok* (matchbox).

Kazbek or Kazbich: Kazbek is the name of a mountain peak in the Caucasus Mountains (Georgia) and of the brand of Russian cigarettes with cardboard mouthpieces and low-grade rough tobacco; Kazbich is a character in Mikhail Lermontov's 1841 novel, *A Hero of Our Time*.

Azamat: Another character from *A Hero of Our Time*. In Lermontov's novel, Azamat exchanges his sister, Bela, for a horse named Karagyoz.

merry girlfriends: A reference to a line from Nekrasov's 1846 poem "Troika": "*v storone ot veselykh podrug*" (at a distance from merry girlfriends).

from the early youthful years: In Russian, "*s molodykh iunykh let*," a quote from the traditional song "Sirota" (Orphan).

balalaika: a three-stringed folk instrument.

return of the hunters: The following description, as well as Note XVII in chapter 7, are based on Pieter Bruegel the Elder's famous painting *Hunters in the Snow* (1565), also known as *Return of the Hunters*.

abortzois: Aborted borzois.

Filippov pretzels: Ivan Maksimovich Filippov (1824–1878) was a famous Russian merchant and baker. Baked goods with his name were considered of the highest quality.

vernissage: A preview of an art exhibition before its formal opening.

Amztarakhan: Also Khozitarakhan and Khadzhi-Tarkhan, old Tatar names of today's Astrakhan.

Fedot and Yakov: To stop the hiccups, Russians use a rhymed spell: "*Ikota, ikota, pereidi na Fedota, s Fedota na Iakova, a s Iakova na vsiakogo*" (Hiccup, hiccup, move over to Fedot, from Fedot to Yakov, and from Yakov to everyone else). The spell is related to the belief that people named Fedot and Yakov suffer from hiccups more often than others.

Vita sine libertate nihil: Life without freedom is nothing; Latin, author unknown.

vivere est militare: To live is to fight; Latin, attributed to Seneca (Ep. 96.5).

3. NOTES OF A BINGING HUNTER

Notes of a Binging Hunter: Here, and in other cycles of Notes, the title is a reference to the celebrated 1852 book *Zapiski okhotnika* (known as *Notes of a Hunter, Sketches from a Hunter's Album* or *A Sportsman's Sketches*) by Ivan Turgenev.

grandpa's tobacco: "*Dedushkin tabak*"—the Russian name for puffballs.

Cracow: Kraków, a large city in southern Poland, which gave the name to a popular dance, Krakowiak.

Cahors: A type of French red wine from the region around the town of Cahors; throughout the novel, it means a cheap fortified wine like Thunderbird or Mad Dog.

Monsieur Gévelot: Joseph Marin Gévelot (1786–1843), a French inventor and manufacturer of arms.

Sir French: French coat.

Jomini: Antoine-Henri Jomini (1779–1869), a Swiss officer who served as a general in both the French and the Russian armies; the author of *The Art of War* (1838).

kissel: A popular Russian soupy dessert made of currants or cranberries boiled in sweetened water and thickened with flour or starch.

Do I love such weather: A paraphrased quote from Vladimir Sokolov's untitled 1967 poem "Na vlazhnye planki ogrady" (On the wet planks of the fence); in the original, "*Ty liubish' takuiu pogodu*" (Do you love such weather).

When the clouds are suddenly gone: A reference to Boris Pasternak's 1956–1959 poem cycle *Kogda razguliaetsia* (When the weather clears).

hakeem: A sage, a prophet (Arabic).

akyn: A poet and singer (Kazakh).

What a dank, clammy autumn: A paraphrase of the first line of the untitled 1854 poem by Afanasii Fet, "*Kakaia kholodnaia osen'*" (What a cold autumn).

put on my scarf and my coat: A slight paraphrase of the second line from the poem by Fet: "*Naden' svoiu shal' i kapot*" (Put on your scarf and your coat).

Sings something about motherland: "*O rodine chto-to poet*"—a quote from the celebrated traditional song "Brodiaga" (Wanderer).

scorching sun: In the original, "*solncem palimy*" (scorched by the sun), a quote from Nekrasov's 1858 poem "Razmyshleniia u paradnogo pod' 'ezda" (Thoughts at the Vestibule).

verb-herd: A herd of verbs.

farnowheres: A neologism corresponding to *nikudali* in the original.

Spindlewort . . . solanum: Various names for the plants *Euonymus europaens* and *Solanum dulcamara*.

freeshooters: A reference to Carl Maria von Weber's 1821 opera *The Freeshooter* (*Der Freischütz*).

Pas d'Espaigne: The title and four lines in the middle of the poem are quotes from the popular dance song "Padespanets."

restaurant: The French form of the word has the stress on the last syllable.

Saint Vitus's dance: A traditional name of chorea, a disease manifesting in uncontrollable muscle spasms and movements of various parts of the body; here it is a metaphor for the time of day when the air flickers and shivers, making things blurry and difficult to identify.

stilo: A pen (French).

Bin ich?: Am I? (German).

vespertilio: A long-eared bat (Latin).

canotier: A hat often made of straw with a ribbon around its base (French).

Pushchin: Ivan Ivanovich Pushchin (1798–1859), Aleksandr Pushkin's best friend and the author of *Zapiski o Pushkine* (Notes on Pushkin; 1858).

chibouk: A long-stemmed Turkish tobacco pipe.

pour l'appetite: For appetite (French).

cerseau: The game of hoop and stick (French), in which one person launches a small hoop with a stick and the other has to catch the flying hoop on a stick.

à petit: A little bit (French).

charabanc: From the French, a carriage with benches often used for sightseeing.

Oh, nanny: A reference to chapter 3 of Pushkin's 1830 novel in verse, *Eugene Onegin*, where the heroine, Tatiana, talks to her nanny.

4. DZYNDZYRELA'S DISCORDS BEYOND THE ITIL

purrcolate: To purr and percolate.

drink your fill, but understand the drill: A reference to Ivan Krylov's 1808 fable "Muzykanty" (Musicians).

zhe: Pyotr discusses the shapes of Russian letters G, D, B, V, and Zh, written in Cyrillic as Г, Д, Б, В, and Ж. The significance of the letter Zh depends less on its being a part of the word *drozzhi* (yeast; pronounced drozhzhi), but more on being the initial letter of the words *zhizn'* (life) and *zhenshchina* (woman), two mysteries the narrators try to clarify and explain throughout the novel.

who stole . . . two hours of light: According to folklore, the prophet Elijah shortens the daylight by two hours (*Il'ia prorok dva chasa uvolok*).

blind man: A reference to Matthew 15:7–14 and Luke 6:39 and, perhaps, to its visual rendering, Pieter Bruegel the Elder's 1568 painting *The Parable of the Blind*.

Hay-rot season: According to the folk calendar, on June 27 / July 10 (feast day of Saint Sampson the Hospitable) the rains begin, which often continue for a week, causing the cut but not gathered hay to rot. For this reason, the saint is often called Sampson the Hay-rot.

lined with fish fur: The expression derives from the Russian proverb "*U bedniaka shuba na ryb'em mekhu*" (A poor man wears a fur coat lined with fish fur), which means a thin, poor-quality coat or, in modern usage, a fake fur. The term was also used to describe the uniforms of the Soviet army, which were made from cheap wool pile.

teaches the one bein taught: A paraphrase of and a pun on the saying "*Ne uchi uchenogo*" (Don't teach the one who's wise, or Don't teach the teacher). A similar expression (*Quia doctum doces*) was first used by Plautus in *Poenulus* (*The Little Carthaginian*).

fysik: Physique.

light bay: The narrator applies equine terminology to describe the woman working in the bar.

anaconda purses: The narrator compares money purses to anacondas, indicating that they swallow the money.

exetera: Et cetera.

upstreamer: Someone from upriver.

pantofle: Slipper, shoe (from the Italian *pantofola*).

unsofiscated: Unsophisticated.

scares-nightmares: A reference to the folk song "Strasti-Mordasti"; also the title of a 1912 Maksim Gorkii short story.

mantilla: A short cloak or cape (from the Spanish); here it refers to a jacket or a coat.

ironwares: Pieces of metal.

vobla: A popular dried-fish snack.

unto the sky: A paraphrase of the first line of Psalm 121.

Mumbo-jumbo: In the original, *tutorki-matutorki*, the nonsensical title of a Russian folk song popular in the 1950s and 1960s.

clapsnaps: Mousetraps.

Gutenacht: In German, *Gute Nacht* (Good night).

Fenist: *Fenist* or *Finist iasnyi sokol* (Fenist the bright falcon), the name of a miraculous bridegroom in Russian folklore who at night, after his feather is dropped on the ground, turns into a prince. The name is probably a distortion of the mythical phoenix.

instigators: In the original the narrator mixes up *sledovateli* (investigators, detectives) and *issledovateli* (researchers, scholars). In English, he mixes up investigators and instigators.

undoubtfully: Doubtlessly, undoubtedly.

impersonator: Rather than saying *figura* (person, figure), the narrator says *figurant* (a person involved in something, a member of a troupe, a faker, a pretender). In translation he confuses person with impersonator.

Intercession: *Pokrov*, an Eastern Orthodox feast celebrated on October 1/October 14.

figurelatively: Figuratively or relatively.

defective: Instead of saying *deficit* (deficit, shortage), the narrator makes a noun *defektiv* (defect) from the adjective *defektivnyi* (defective). In English, a substantivized adjective reflects this confusion.

left claw: The narrator plays with the Russian proverb "*Kuda kon' s kopytom, tuda i rak s kleshnei*" (Where the horse puts its hoof, there the crayfish puts its claw), derived from a fable where the crayfish imitates what the horse is doing and, seeing the horse being shod, puts out its claw to have the same done to it. The meaning of the proverb is to know your place and not to follow others blindly.

for the last time: A reference to the anonymous camp song "Idut na sever—sroka ogromnye" (They're Going North—All with Huge Sentences), known in many variants.

Botfortovo: Most likely, a misnomer for Lefortovo, a region of Moscow named after one of Peter the Great's friends, the Swiss mercenary François Lefort.

thru the pane . . . shakes his fist in vain: A paraphrase, based on Walter Arndt's translation, of "*Emu i bol'no i smeshno, a mat' grozit emu v okno*" (He's both hurting and laughing, and mother in the window shakes her fist at him), from Pushkin's *Eugene Onegin*, chapter 5.

bathhouse twigs: In the Russian bath, twigs are used to improve circulation and open the pores of the bathers to the steam.

Anatomical Theater: A dissecting room; a morgue.

a girl saw the soldier off: Part of the first line of the song "Ogonek" (A Little Fire); music by Mikhail Isakovskii, lyrics traditional.

Okeydokey . . . to the war: A reference to the lyrics of a popular song: "*Aty— baty—shli—soldaty, aty—baty—na voinu*" (Aty—baty—soldiers were walking, aty—baty—to the war).

were figures: Rather than saying *figurirovali* (figured), the narrator says the incorrect *figurovali*.

from what kind of a highway . . . had come about: A combined reference to the famous highway Shosse Entuziastov (Enthusiasts' Highway) in Moscow and to "*otkuda est' poshla russkaia zemlia*" (from whence had the Russian land come), a part of the opening sentence of the twelfth-century Russian chronicle *Povest' vremennykh let* (*The Tale of Bygone Years*).

speckled one: A reference to the fairy tale "Kurochka riaba" (The Speckled Hen).

frog princesses: A reference to the fairy tale "Tsarevna liagushka" (The Frog Princess).

broken trough: A reference to "*razbitoe koryto*," from Pushkin's 1835 fairy tale "Skazka o rybake i rybke" ("The Tale of the Fisherman and the Little Fish").

situcraption: Crappy situation.

side-warmer: In Russian, *bokogrei*, a traditional folk name for February.

chlamyses: Plural of chlamys, a type of an ancient Greek mantle.

galife: A style of breeches developed primarily for horseback riding. The Russian word derives from the name of the French general Gaston Alexandre Auguste, Marquis de Galliffet, who was supposedly the first to have ordered such breeches to be worn by his soldiers.

lapserdak: A long jacket (Yiddish).

zhorzhet: Georgette.

Hop, don't stop . . . granny sowed the peas for crop: Two slightly altered lines from the Russian children's song "Baba seiala gorokh" (A woman sowed peas), often sung after a swim and accompanied by jumping up and down to warm the swimmers.

5. THE TRAPPER'S TALE OR PICTURES FROM AN EXHIBITION

Pictures from an Exhibition: Throughout, this is a reference to the celebrated *Kartinki s vystavki* by Modest Mussorgskii (1874). The title implies that the composer has carried in his mind the pictures from the exhibition and later turned them into musical compositions. Unexpectedly, the commonly accepted English translation is *Pictures at an Exhibition*, which in Russian would have been *Kartinki na vystavke*.

Carus Sterne: The pen name of Ernest Krause (1839–1903), a German supporter of Darwinism. Between 1876 and 1903, his book *Werden und Vergehen* went through eleven editions.

***Werden und Vergehen*:** Growth and Decay (German).

From the carriage: This chapter is, to a great extent, a parody on Gogol's exuberant style and his predilection for creating colorful portraits of characters with amusing names and patronymics, describing elaborate culinary feasts, and indulging in insignificant details. It should be noted that Gogol's famous novel, *Dead Souls*, begins with an arrival of a carriage at an inn.

***mein Hertz*:** My dear—literally, my heart (German).

Entre-Deux-Mers: Between Two Seas, a white dry Bordeaux.

***ambré*:** Aroma (French).

Asmolov smokes: In 1871, Vasilii Ivanovich Asmolov founded a tobacco and cigarette factory in Rostov-on-Don. It received many international awards, dominated the Russian market, and was the official supplier of the Imperial Court.

***jour fixes*:** Regularly scheduled days for visiting, meetings, or parties (French).

Buhre clock: In Russian, Bure, the name of a famous clock and watch maker. At the end of the nineteenth-century the Pavel Bure firm was the largest watch company in Russia. All of its watches were manufactured in Switzerland, which enabled the firm to survive after the October Revolution.

do not judge, so you will not be judged: Paraphrase of Matthew 7:1 and Luke 6:37.

bashi-bazouks: Irregular and often undisciplined soldiers in the Ottoman army who received no fixed pay.

Ehrlich: Probably the name of a men's clothing or a shoe store in Moscow.

***bellevue*:** Beautiful view (French).

montecristo: In prerevolutionary Russia the name for a light, small-caliber shotgun.

Yar: The name of a restaurant in Moscow, founded by the Frenchman Tranquille Yard in 1826 and later renowned for its decadent atmosphere and superior Gypsy music.

tzimmes: A traditional sweet Jewish dish; the word is often used to denote something first-class, excellent, a delicacy.

6. ACCORDIN TO ILYA PETRIKEICH

huge, playful, and she barks: A paraphrase of an expression from Vasilii Trediak-ovskii's 1766 *Telemakhida*: "*Chudishche oblo, ozorno, ogromno, stozevno, i laiai*" (A heavy, horrid, huge, hundred-jawed, and barking monster); it was popularized by Aleksandr Radishchev, who used it as an epigraph to his 1790 *Puteshestvie iz Peterburga v Moskvu* (A Journey from Petersburg to Moscow) as a description of autocratic Russia.

prodigerant: The narrator combines two words—*bludnyi* (lecherous, sinful, prodigal) and *bluzhdaiushchii* (wandering) into one—*bludushchii*. In English a combination of prodigal and itinerant has been used.

fowls of the air: A reference to Matthew 6:26.

to my dearest friend: A paraphrase of a popular song or chastushka, a folk rhyme consisting of four-line stanzas.

have you sold some manure: When a poor person buys an expensive thing, he may be asked, jokingly, "Have you sold some manure?" The question indicates that the only expected possession of such a poor person is manure.

gold tooth: A partial quote from the popular anonymous song "Paren' v kepke da zub zolotoi" (A guy in a cap and with a gold tooth).

kirza: A leather substitute, used to manufacture Russian army boots.

bandura: Ukrainian stringed instrument. In popular use, the word could denote any kind of a musical instrument; here the narrator uses the word as a synonym for accordion.

chastushkas: Singular chastushka, a short poem with four-line stanzas, often irreverent or funny, sung to a familiar chastushka melody.

hurdy-gurdy: Used as another synonym for accordion.

bayan: A small accordion-like instrument with buttons rather than keys on both sides.

Armenian delight: Armenian brandy, one of the most famous Soviet-made "cognacs."

my own brother is a drunk: A paraphrase of the saying "*Ne govori kuma, u samoi muzh p'ianitsa*" (You don't say, friend, my own husband is a drunk), used to express understanding of someone's problems, knowing what's being discussed.

clinkin with his irons: A quote from the popular song "Brodiaga" (Wanderer).

Kandalaksha: A port town on the White Sea in Murmansk Oblast. The town's name resembles the word *kandaly* (fetters, irons).

Kazan and Ryazan, nor in Syzran: Names of three cities, used here because of their euphonic similarity. Kazan is the capital of the Republic of Tatarstan, Ryazan is a city in the Ryazan Oblast on the Oka River, and Syzran is a city on the right bank of the Saratov Reservoir on the Volga in Samara Oblast.

manul's eyes: *Felis manul*, Pallas's cat, a species of wild cat of Central Asia.

Millerovo: A town in Rostov Oblast.

assorti: Assortment (French).

***Bruderschaft*:** A German (now international) expression used when two people join in drinking a toast to switch from the formal *Sie* (You) to informal *du* (you).

onewomber: A neologism rendering the Russian neologism *odnoutrob* and indicating that both men came from the same womb.

Dimka: A diminutive form of Dimitrii.

Uglich: A reference to the story of Prince Dimitrii, the young son of Ivan the Terrible, who died under mysterious circumstances in Uglich.

memory broke the loop: A reference to the memory loop in palmistry.

departee: Departing passenger.

bare footsie: *"Nozhen'ka golaia"*—a reference to Nekrasov's 1862–1863 poem "V polnom razgare strada derevenskaia" (The village harvest is in full swing).

yatagan: A short Turkish saber.

7. NOTES OF A HUNTER

deux côtes: Two Shores or Two Coasts, the name of a French wine.

châteaux: The Castle, a part of the name of many French wines from the Bordeaux region—for instance, Châteaux Lafitte, Châteaux Margaux, or Châteaux Latour.

Negru de Purcari: The name of a popular Moldavian dry red wine.

Where do pheasants get fat around here: *"Gde zhiruet fazan"* in Russian, a paraphrase of *"Kazhdyi okhotnik zhelaet znat', gde sidit fazan"* (Every hunter wants to know where the pheasant is sitting), a mnemonic device for remembering the order of the color spectrum: *krasnyi* (red), *oranzhevyi* (orange), *zheltyi* (yellow), *zelenyi* (green), *goluboi* (blue), *sinii* (dark blue or navy), and *fioletovyi* (purple).

Mage: Magician, healer, shaman.

river Crow . . . river Nerl: The Crow (Vorona) is a river in the Penza, Tambov, and Voronezh Oblasts. The Nerl is a right tributary of the Volga in the Yaroslavl and Tver Oblasts.

Brumaire: The second month of the French Revolution.

a thing per se: A reference to Immanuel Kant's *"Das Ding an sich"* (the thing in itself) from *The Critique of Pure Reason* (1781).

wolf's tail—be cold, be cold: In Russian, *"merzni, merzni, volchii khvost"* (freeze, freeze, wolf's tail), a quote from the folktale "Lisichka sestrichka i volk" (The sister fox and the wolf).

Chauliodus: A viperfish, a saltwater predatory fish with long, protruding teeth and a light-emitting organ called a photophore.

anglerfish: Also known as football fish, goosefish, double angler, or sea toad, a predatory bony fish named for the characteristic growth from its head, which acts as a lure.

wasisdas: From German *"was is das"* (literally, "what is this"), a little window built into a large window to allow fresh air to come in without lowering the temperature drastically. The sentence is a paraphrase of the expression "to open a window into Europe," commemorating the actions of Peter the Great, who built St. Petersburg and introduced a set of wide-reaching Westernizing reforms.

Binger: A notorious drinker, guzzler.

tears of grain: In Russian, *"Khlebnaia sleza,"* the name of a popular brand of vodka.

Yakshi: How are things, what's up (Tatar).

Hunchbacked pony: A reference to Petr Yershov's famous 1834 fairy tale in verse, "Konek-gorbunok" (A little hunchbacked pony).

yok: Is not, are not, is absent (Tatar).

whack the goat: In Russian, *"zabit' kozla,"* to play a game of dominoes.

chimaera: Cartilaginous deep-water fish in the order Chimaeriformes, known informally as ghost shark or ratfish.

Kunstkammer: Kunstkamera, a famous museum in St. Petersburg, was established by Peter the Great to house and preserve "natural and human curiosities and rarities." Such cabinets of curiosities were popular in Europe from the time of the Renaissance and were the predecessors of modern museums.

Erzia: One of the ethnic groups of the Mordvins who today inhabit the Autonomous Republic of Mordovia in the middle region of the Volga River.

quasimodic: Quasimodo-like, ugly.

chisma: A boot (Serbo-Croatian).

imbibamus: We are drinking (Latin).

8. DISCORDS BEYOND THE ITIL

Foma Doom: One of the ferrymen on the Itil.

Stozhary: In folklore, the name for the Pleiades.

Kimry model sluices: The narrator refers to the celebrated sluices on the canal linking the Volga and the Moskva. The 128-kilometer-long canal, built by prisoners and officially opened in 1937, features eleven sluices and ten dams.

old barrel: A reference to Matthew 9:17, Mark 2:22, and Luke 5:37.

A sower . . . sowin: A paraphrase of the Parable of the Sower (Luke 8:4–15, Matthew 13:3–23, and Mark 4:2–20).

Kondraty caught her: A euphemism for a sudden death. The meaning of the expression relates to the uprising of the Cossack ataman Kondratii (Kondrashka) Bulavin in 1707, during which the rebels unexpectedly attacked and killed Prince Dolgorukov, his officers, and many soldiers.

two elbows: An elbow is an old measurement of approximately fifty-five centimeters.

Carl stole . . . a coral tiara: An English paraphrase of a popular Russian tongue twister: "*Karl u Klary ukral korally*" (Carl stole Clara's necklace).

a certain day . . . will come: A paraphrase of the title of Nikolai Dobroliubov's famous 1862 essay "Kogda zhe pridet nastoiashchii den'" (When will the real day finally come), a response to Ivan Turgenev's 1860 novel *Nakanune* (On the eve). Here the narrator refers to the Judgment Day.

beevaks: Bivouacs.

pretend to snuggle with manure: I only pretend to be poor; I make myself look poor.

bequeeted: Bequeathed.

kulelemed: Nonsensical verb related by sound to the name of the settlement Malokulelemovo.

forcast: Forecast.

uke: Is not, is absent (Mari).

e-e: Is present (Mari).

setteth a net for his brother: A Russian rendition of the line from the Book of Micah 7:2. In English translation the expression appears as "every one hunteth his brother to death."

nunset years: Instead of saying "*na starosti let*" (in our old age, in our sunset years), the narrator says "*na staritse let*" (in our old nun's years, in our nunset years).

teasin geese: The expression comes from Ivan Krylov's 1811 fable "Gusi" (The geese), but the narrator gives it a sexual meaning.

Gorynych: Zmei (Dragon) Gorynych is a character in Russian heroic epic and folk tales.

unhappiness leads to happiness: A paraphrase of the proverb "*Ne bylo by schast'ia da neschast'e pomoglo*" (There would be no good luck / happiness, but bad luck / unhappiness helped), comparable to the English "Every cloud has a silver lining."

papirosy: Russian-style cigarettes with poor-quality tobacco and a carton mouthpiece.

Bugbear: A variant of a nursery rhyme used to make children aware of their body (spine); as used here, it may indicate intimate contact between Orina and Ilya.

9. PICTURES FROM AN EXHIBITION

tarantassi: The narrator makes tarantas (a large Russian carriage without springs) sound Italian.

Konotop: A city in northern Ukraine in the Sumy Oblast.

shines by its absence: The expression "to shine by its absence" goes back to the Tacitus's *Annals* but became popular in Russia through Marie-Joseph Blaise de Chénier's 1819 drama *Tibre* (Tiber).

Yanko is not afraid of the wind or waves: A quote from Lermontov's *A Hero of Our Time*.

defectological: An adjective derived from *defectology*. In Russia, it was a branch of science concerned with the study of the development of children with physical and mental defects and the problems of their training and upbringing.

Rain, dear rain . . . to Arestan: *"Dozhdik, dozhdik perestan', ia poedu v Arestan'"*— one of many variants of children's rhyme, used to "stop" the rain. Arestan is a fictitious name of a town, based on the word *arest* (arrest) and created to rhyme with the imperative *perestan'* (stop).

Razin: Stenka (Stepan) Timofeevich Razin was a leader of an uprising of 1667–1671 against the Russian government.

poorly cut, yet solidly sewn: In the original, *"neladno skroennyi da krepko poshityi,"* a slight paraphrase of the saying *"neladno skroen, da krepko sshit,"* denoting an awkward-looking but strong man.

Nobody is able . . . one's tortoise: One of the most famous paradoxes of Zeno of Elea.

lonely accordions: A reference to the song "Odinokaia garmon'" (Lonely accordion).

Ahasuerus: One of the names for Wandering Jew.

arshin: A unit of measure formerly used in Russia, equal to about seventy-one centimeters (twenty-eight inches).

dogs' heads were being cut off: An expression popular in China during the Boxer Rebellion and Cultural Revolution.

Kastrioti: George Kastrioti Skanderbeg (1405–1468), the leader of the Albanian rebellion against the Ottoman Turks and the national hero of Albania.

Rymnikskoe wine: Romanian wine sold in Russia. Its name commemorates the Russian victory over the Turks in 1789 near Ramnicu (Rimnicu) Sarat. The commanding officer of the Russian army, General Alexander Suvorov, was awarded the title of the Graf of Rymnik.

rode . . . on stolen velocycles: References to two renowned Italian films, *No Peace Under the Olive Tree* (1950) and *Bicycle Thieves* (1948).

All is calm on Shipka: During the Russo-Turkish war of 1877–1878, General Joseph Radetskii kept sending official reports from Shipka that everything was calm there, while his soldiers were attacked from three sides by the Turks and, in addition, were freezing to death. The events were immortalized by Vasilii Vereshchagin in a cycle of paintings with the same name.

Go out . . . and jumps like a ball: The last stanza of an untitled 1854 poem by Afanasii Fet, beginning with "*Lastochki propali*" (The swallows had vanished).

Parcae and Moirae: In Roman and Greek mythologies, the personifications of destiny, the Fates.

Chartreuse: French liqueur.

Fräuleins: Court ladies (German).

mon Dieu: My God (French).

monarque: Monarch (French).

Pierrot: A stock character of pantomime and Commedia dell' Arte.

mon cher: My dear (French).

laberdan: A salted codfish fillet.

As I Drove Up to Izhory: The first line of an 1829 poem by Aleksandr Pushkin.

dormeuse: A traveling carriage with a seat that can be expanded into a bed.

curly sideburns: The appearance of the passenger is based on the existing portraits of Pushkin.

I remembered . . . dark blue eyes: The third and fourth lines of Pushkin's poem.

eyes resembling the rabbit's: A reference to "*i p'ianitsy s glazami krolikov*" (and the drunks with the eyes of rabbits), a line from Blok's 1906 poem "Neznakomka" (Unknown lady).

pood: An old Russian measure of weight; approximately thirty-six pounds.

10. DZYNZYRELLA'S

Chistopol: A town in the Republic of Tatarstan. During the Great Patriotic War, Chistopol became a place of evacuation for many Soviet citizens, including the members of the Union of the Soviet Writers.

mersi: Merci, thank you (French).

mors: A popular nonalcoholic Russian drink made from cranberries.

three axes: A popular nickname of Portvein 777, a cheap fortified sweet red wine.

weep like a wolverine: A paraphrase of a line from the book of Micah 1:8: "*vyt',
kak shakaly, i plakat', kak strausy*" (howl like the jackals and cry like the
ostriches).

Yegor: The abbreviated variant of Georgii or Yegorii [Yegory], used in Russian with
the adjective Khrabryi (George the Brave).

asfyxiation: Asphyxiation.

fussbustle: Fuss and bustle.

It turns out too mechanical: A reference to a line in Nekrasov's 1864 poem
"Zheleznaia doroga" (The railroad).

the Bygodoshch folks: Since Bydogoshch/Bygodoshch is the city of the dead, this
is a funny synonym for undertakers.

fortold: Foretold.

belladonna: The poisonous plant deadly nightshade; in Russian, it is called *volch'ia
iagoda* (wolf berry). The word "belladonna" is used here to avoid confusing the
plant with the beneficial wolfberry (goji).

Be on gard: Julius Fučík (1903–1943), a Czech journalist arrested by the Nazis in
1942, wrote in prison his celebrated *Notes from the Gallows*, with the famous last
two sentences: "People, I loved you. Be on guard!"

dream about eggs: According to many dream-interpretation books, to see eggs in
a dream means an unexpected visit.

splashhouse: Bathhouse.

pristipoma: A Pacific Ocean edible fish, sometimes called boarfish.

11. AGAIN THE NOTES

fixter: Solution (key) to problems.

Sterlitamak: The second-largest city in the Republic of Bashkortostan, located on
the left bank of the Belaya River, 121 kilometers (75 miles) from Ufa.

shtof: A large, square-edged bottle (Russian).

snuff covers your nose: The Russian expression "*syt, p'ian, i nos v tabake*" (full,
drunk, and nose in snuff) denotes a state of complete satisfaction, bliss, and
happiness.

individuum: An individual being as distinguished from a group of similar beings.

They sent a she-goat nut-picking: A reference to the cumulative folktale "Koza"
(She-goat), in which a he-goat sends a she-goat to pick nuts. When she does not
return, he solicits the help of various animals (wolf, bear) and elements (fire,
water, wind) to help him bring her back.

And a he-goat in the garden they let: Derived from *"pustit' kozla v ogorod"* (to let a he-goat into the garden), an idiomatic expression indicating that someone is given permission or an opportunity to act in a situation or place where his or her actions are particularly harmful.

Tula tin: Tula is a city located 311 km (193 miles) south of Moscow. In the eighteenth century, it became the greatest iron-working center in Eastern Europe.

hunderd: Hundred.

Nanny, why can't I sleep: A reference to Pushkin's *Eugene Onegin*, chapter 3.

britska: A horse-drawn carriage or buggy with a foldable top.

NB: Nota bene, mark well.

bilboquet: A game of cup and ball (from the French).

She seemed . . . in her mouth: A quote from the 1812 fable "The Crow and the Fox" by Ivan Krylov.

bissextile lips: In the original, *"visokosnyi rot"* (a bissextile mouth)—a pun on the Russian name of a leap year, *"visokosnyi god"*; hence, the expression indicates that the drink does not reach every fourth mouth.

Now nightingale . . . Now windmill: A reference to the line *"To mel'nitsa, to solovei"* (now windmill, now nightingale) from Afanasii Fet's 1842 untitled poem beginning *"Sosna tak temna, khot' i mesiats"* (The pine is so dark, despite the moon).

***oncle*:** Uncle (French), a hidden reference to the beginning of Pushkin's *Eugene Onegin*.

postscriptums: A Russianized plural form of the Latin word for postscript.

He who mocks the poor: Proverbs 17:5.

12. DISCORDS BEYOND THE ITIL

potpoorie: Potpourri.

randevoos: Rendezvous.

Farisees: Pharisees.

he ran away: A reference to Lermontov's 1840 poem "Mtsyri" (The Novice), in which the hero fights a fierce leopard.

Psst . . . hospital-bound she'll be: A quote from the early twentieth-century urban romance "Marusia otravilas'" (Marusya poisoned herself), with many variants and alternative lyrics.

burn, burn brightly: A quote from a song accompanying the game of *gorelki* (catch).

jackaloo: Wolf.

And who will be paired: A famous logic puzzle dating back to the ninth century and popular in many countries: How many crossings will a ferryman have to make to take across the river a wolf, a goat, and a head of cabbage if he can only ferry one or none of them at a time and has to make sure the wolf doesn't eat the goat and the goat doesn't eat the cabbage in his absence? The answer is seven: (1) he takes the goat; (2) he goes back empty; (3) he takes the wolf; (4) he takes the goat back; (5) he takes the cabbage; (6) he goes back empty; (7) he takes the goat.

harried alive: In Russian "*zazhivo ugnetennye*," a paraphrase of "*zazhivo pogrebennye*" (buried alive).

Chuchmek: A derogatory term for the inhabitants of the Caucasus; here, it is a continuation of the motif from Lermontov's "Mtsyri."

battles on ice: A reference to "*ledovoe poboishche*" (battle on ice), the 1242 victory of Prince Aleksandr Nevskii over the Teutonic Knights on the ice of Lake Peipus.

my hair is splittin: A reference to the folk saying "*Ot radosti kudri v'iutsia, a ot pechali sekutsia*" (From joy the hair is weaving and from sadness it is splitting).

Happy approachin: The narrator is referring to the approaching New Year.

sacrilegious beetle: In the popular card game of beetle (*zhuchok*), the loser is slapped on the ear and is supposed to guess who hit him. Since this reminds the narrator of a story in Matthew 26:67–68—in which Jesus is slapped and His abusers challenge Him to show His powers by telling them who exactly did it—he calls the game sacrilegious.

insence: Incense.

abomination of complete desolation: Matthew 24:15.

mugognomy: A distorted form of physiognomy.

soberquet: Sobriquet. The narrator uses this spelling because he connects it to the cyclical getting drunk and sobering up.

cast dispersions: The narrator's erroneous form of cast aspersions.

bangothumped: Banged and thumped.

Unexpected Return: The title of a famous 1884 painting by Il'ia Repin (*Ne zhdali*), also known as *They Did Not Expect Him*.

Mumu: The name of the dog in Ivan Turgenev's 1854 short story of the same title.

To distant destination: In the original, "Na Tikhoretskuiu" (To Tikhoretskaia), a popular song from the 1975 movie *Ironiia sud'by* (Irony of fate), music by Mikael Tariverdiev and lyrics by Mikhail L'vovskii. Written in 1962, the song was popularized by Alla Pugacheva.

Zhmerinka: A city in Vinnytsia Oblast in central Ukraine.

lost her head gazin at him: A reference to Nekrasov's poem "Troika," in which a traveling cornet gazes at a beautiful girl, but after she falls in love with him, he drives away to see another.

schlagbauman: The narrator makes a pun from *Schlagbaum* (in German and Russian, a crossing barrier) and Bauman, referring to Nikolai Ernestovich Bauman, 1873–1905, a relatively insignificant Bolshevik revolutionary, later turned by the Soviet propaganda into a cult figure.

at the foot of the embankment: A reference to *"Pod nasyp'iu, vo rvu nekoshennom, lezhit i smotrit kak zhivaia"* (At the foot of the embankment, in the unmown ditch, she lies and looks as if she were alive) from Blok's "Na zheleznoi doroge" (At the railroad).

Suck and remember: A paraphrase of the name of a popular game *beri i pomni* (take and remember), played with a wishbone. The name was also paraphrased in Valentin Rasputin's 1974 novella "Zhivi i pomni" (Live and remember).

escapin from the Siberian mines: A reference to the first line from Pushkin's 1827 poem "V Sibir'" (To Siberia): *"Vo glubine sibirskikh rud"* (In the depths of Siberian mines).

"Carousel": A virtuoso accordion piece by Alfred Fossen.

chevelure: A head of hair (from the French).

the sea spread . . . quite widely: A reference to the popular late nineteenth-century song about the death of a ship stoker "Raskinulos' more shiroko" (The sea spread widely) that has many variants.

antrasite: Anthracite.

opens the door . . . with a habitual bump: *"Privychnym tolchkom otvoril"*—a slightly altered quote from "Raskinulos' more shiroko."

And the flame illuminated him: *"I plamia ego ozarilo"*—another quote from "Raskinulos' more shiroko."

a tear glimmers in his eye: A paraphrase of *"i slezy u mnogikh blesnuli"* (and tears glimmered in many eyes) from "Raskinulos' more shiroko."

13. PICTURES FROM AN EXHIBITION

demi-saison: Spring or autumn, the seasons between the more extreme seasons (French).

asidol: A popular Russian strong-smelling cleaner.

Hawaiian amalia: A species of orchid.

ash from Tushino . . . into a Tula mortar: Combined references to the story of the first False Dimitrii, whose body, chopped into pieces, was burned, loaded into a cannon, and shot toward Poland, and to the story of the second False Dimitrii, nicknamed the Thief of Tushino.

fugel: An archaic English word for birds, rendering the archaic Russian *ptakh*.

the bread of someone's early years: A reference to Heinrich Böll's 1955 novel, *Das Brot der frühen Jahre* (The bread of those early years).

But, look, the morn . . . yon high eastward hill: *Hamlet* I:1.

14. ACCORDIN TO ILYA PETRIKEICH

from a dry-cargo carrier . . . landlocked destiny: A paraphrase of the expression "*s korablia na bal*" from Pushkin's *Eugene Onegin*, chapter 8, which indicates a sudden change in someone's fortune.

To our harbor . . . valiant ataman: The opening four lines from the song "V nashu gavan' zakhodili korabli" (Ships used to visit our harbor), composer unknown.

Chrysanthemums stopped bloomin: A paraphrase of the chorus from the popular 1910 romance "Ottsveli khrizantemy" (Chrysanthemums finished blooming), music by Nikolai Kharito, lyrics by Vasilii Shumskii.

dipped his rudder: Became sad, hung his head or nose down.

like a bone: In the original, the conversation between Ilya and the woman peddler is in Ukrainian.

Munch to stop . . . from early age: A jocular paraphrase of a proverb "*Beregi plat'e snovu, a chest' smolodu*" (Protect your clothes when they're new, and your honor from early age) into "*Kushai s golodu, lechis' smolodu*" (Have some chow when you're hungry, take medicines from early age), alluding to the medicinal benefits of starting to drink early in life.

mamuasel: Mademoiselle.

the masts . . . they creak: A slightly changed line from Lermontov's 1832 poem "Parus" (The sail).

moskitos: Mosquitoes.

growth of lilies . . . dressed spic-and-span: A paraphrase of Luke 12:27.

my namesake from Murom: A reference to the hero of Russian folk epics, Ilya of Murom (Muromets), who spent thirty-three years sitting on the stove bench unable to walk but was healed by the wandering pilgrims and became the mighty defender of Kiev.

fuctions: Functions.

Volapuke: Volapük, a language invented in 1879 by a German priest, Johann M. Schleyer. The narrator distorts the spelling of the word because its sound reminds him about the consequences of drinking too much.

squeak-squaks: In Russian, "*uidi-uidi*," a popular toy, a balloon with an attached squeaker, which, when released, made a sound similar to the words "*uidi-uidi*" (go away, go away).

in search of joys: A slight paraphrase of the title of Viktor Rozov's 1957 play, *V poiskakh radosti* (In search of joy).

smokes of the fatherland: A slight paraphrase of "*dym otechestva*" (the smoke of the fatherland), popularized in the works of many Russian writers but derived from Ovid's *Ex Ponto* (From Pontus), where the poet mentions Ulysses's wish to see the smoke of his ancestral hearth again.

lidrary: Library of lids.

bowroat: A spoonerism for rowboat.

Spider: In Russia people called Paul are sometimes called *pauk* (spider) because of the similarity of the words.

marvles: Marvelous.

blizzie: The narrator shows his emotional involvement by creating the endearing diminutive form of the word "blizzard."

ultimat: Ultimatum.

proclaimin it from the housetops: A paraphrase of Luke 12:3.

chill rebuff: A slight paraphrase of a line from Tatiana's letter to Onegin, in Pushkin's *Eugene Onegin*, chapter 3, in Walter Arndt's translation.

poison from Kashin: The distillery in Kashin, in Tver Oblast, was known for producing large quantities of poor-quality vodka. According to a popular belief, even the greatest drunk wouldn't drink that vodka without saying "God save us."

sixteen boyish years old: A quote from the 1936 song "Orlenok" (The Eaglet), lyrics by Iakov Shvedov and music by Viktor Belyi.

kurgan: Kurgan is an ancient burial mound; here the narrator exaggerates the image into some epic battle, even though he is hiding behind a bush.

foksel: Forecastle.

How I jumped out: A quote from the folktale *A Fox, a Hare, and a Rooster*, also known as *The Hare's Hut*.

cap-bands: The narrator addresses his assailants by naming parts of their uniforms; here, the bands encircling their caps.

Sidor's goat: Some scholars derive the origin of this phraseological expression from the Arabic "*sadar kaza*" (perhaps brought to Russia by the Mongols), a sentence that often involved punishment by beating with clubs.

The battalion . . . grew larger: A paraphrase of *"nashego polku pribylo,"* from the folk song "A my proso seiali" (We were sowing millet).

Go, heal Thyself: A paraphrase of Luke 4:23.

cuttin the ice with their skates: A reference to *Eugene Onegin*, chapter 4: *"kon'kami zvuchno rezhet led"* (and cuts the ice with ringing skates).

come and pray . . . fishie: A paraphrase of *"Lovis', rybka bol'shaia i malen'kaia"* (Come and get caught, big and small fish), from the folktale "Lisa i volk" (A fox and a wolf).

pull him out with a dragnet: A reference to *"tiatia, tiatia, nashi seti pritashchili mertvetsa"* (daddy, daddy, our nets dragged in a corpse) from Pushkin's 1826 poem "Utoplennik" (A drowned man).

Existens: Existence.

wouldn't mind bein with you: A paraphrase of a line from Nekrasov's "Troika": *"Poliubit' tebia vsiakii ne proch'"* (no one would mind falling in love with you).

even though he's a Chud: A slightly condescending remark reflecting Russians' attitude toward the Finno-Ugric ethnic minorities.

light of your own eyes: A paraphrase of a saying popular in many languages to indicate somebody precious and cared for, derived from the biblical expression "apple of your eye."

brittle willow: In a Russian folk epic, Mikula Selianinovich throws his plow behind a bush of brittle willow.

forhead: Forehead.

15. THE BINGER'S JOURNAL

The Binger's Journal: A reference to and a paraphrase of Pechorin's Journal in Lermontov's *A Hero of Our Time*.

Sparrow Night: In folklore, the name of a summer night with frequent lightning, which frightens the sparrows.

nose-warmer: A short pipe.

Ostashkov: A town and the administrative center of Ostashkovskii District of Tver Oblast, located 199 kilometers (124 miles) west of Tver, known for its tannery and shoe factory.

'shrooms: Mushrooms.

Illuminations: A reference to Arthur Rimbaud's unfinished collection of prose poems *Les Illuminations*, written between 1873 and 1875 and published first in 1886.

Entre perro y lobo: Between dog and wolf (Spanish).

green mare: In Russian, "*zelenaia kobylka*," the name of a large green cricket.

Polenov . . . Savrasov . . . Turgenev . . . Aksakov: References to two nineteenth-century painters, Vasilii Polenov (1844–1927) and Aleksei Savrasov (1830–1897), representatives of the realist school of painting, and to two nineteenth-century writers, Ivan Turgenev (1818–1883) and Sergei Aksakov (1791–1859), recognized for their descriptions of nature and hunting.

leshy: In Russian folklore, a spirit of the forest.

a gold leaf descended . . . cherished oak tree: A reference to Lermontov's 1841 poem "Listok" (Leaf).

The hunter pulled . . . gun misfired: A paraphrase of *On spustil kurok—ruzh'e dalo osechku*" (He pulled the trigger—but the gun misfired), from Anton Chekhov's 1895 story "Whitebrow."

citoyen: Citizen (French).

Rus: Pronounced *roos*; an archaic name for Russia. The entire sentence is a paraphrase of Prince Vladimir's famed apocryphal response to the Muslim Volga Bulgars trying to convince him to adopt Islam as the national religion: "Drinking is the joy of the Rus; we can't go without it."

Brahmaputra: One of the major rivers in Asia, flowing through China, India, and Bangladesh. Its name in Sanskrit means "Son of Brahma," and its lower reaches are sacred to the Hindus.

16. THE TRAPPER'S TALE

teakettle, my only joy . . . in the Caucasus: A slightly altered quotation from the first chapter of Lermontov's *A Hero of Our Time*.

hattie: Endearment for hat.

earflappies: Endearment for earflaps.

hangerkin: Endearment for hanger.

17. THE LAST REMARKS

accidently: Accidentally.

durin a fishin lull: A truncated saying "*Na bezryb'e i rak ryba*" (During a fishing lull, even a crayfish is a fish), similar to but not exactly like the English "In the land of the blind, the one-eyed man is a king" or simply "Something is better than nothing."